America's Soul

by

Roger Johnson

The characters in this novel are fictional except for the political leaders
and historical figures of the period. They are listed at the end of the book.
The teachers and students are creatures who jumped from my head as I
constructed this story, and I put them into situations that occurred when
I taught in a real school 65 miles to the north. Any similarities to real
persons are coincidental and not intended by the author

ISBN   978-8-9872510-0-3

Email: rogerj47@gmail.com
Website: Roger_Johnson.com

This book is dedicated to my colleagues at Greeley West High School from 1982-2008, especially to my Social Studies crew, the best ever. I stood with you and on your shoulders. . .

Marla, Con, Jeff (Gumby), Don, Bill, Ed, Edie, Doug, Dave, John, Mek, Karen (Heath)

Acknowledgements

My continued heartfelt appreciation to my small group of readers for their insightful comments and sincere encouragement for my writing.

Special thanks to my formatter Joe DesGeorges.
Cover adaptation: Joe DesGeorges

Books in Print by Roger Johnson

Laments for the Dead
Layers of Darkness
America's Soul

The Cheetah Basketball Series
On Point
Gifts: The Return
Coach Izzy

Other manuscripts in the queue include

The Hill, '67: A Love Affair
Lines
Jegos
Seeds and Hoops (working title)

America's Soul

Roger Johnson

IngramSpark

2022/2023

America's Soul

The Revolution arrived on September 5, 1974, in yellow chariots carrying warriors disguised as anxious students.

"Teaching is not a lost art, but the regard
for it is a lost tradition."

- Jacques Barzun

Jonas Cullen

Jonas studies his hands: two crooked fingers and a three-inch scar across the back of his right hand. Men in the Cullen clan work with their hands at seasonal jobs. A Cullen learns what he needs on the job and "don't need no books," at least that's what Grampa Cullen always told Jonas. They own neither cows nor horses—or property. Local ranchers derisively call the Cullens "truck cowboys." Now in a cell at the federal prison in Denver, Jonas paces and considers his bloodline. He is the Cullen who broke away, who left Montana, to get his college degree, to become—of all things—a teacher. Pacing may be the wrong word; more like wandering, if indeed one can wander in an eight-by-twelve cell. He gets to the back wall and stares vacantly. Suddenly, he slaps his hands against the concrete and swears. He pivots and glares through the bars on the cell door. He knows what they want. He won't give it to them.

A guard appears at the cell door. "It's that time again, Teacher-boy." Jonas slips an orange shirt on over his tee, stands at attention in front of the door, and waits for the guard to say something stupid. He usually does. Jekyll is about six-four and overweight, but Jonas would take a swing at him if they were on the outside. In here he simply stares straight ahead. The guard unlocks the door and flips his finger to release Jonas from his rigid position. He walks the corridor down to an interrogation room, just as he has twice a week for the past three months.

A routine has been established. The FBI interrogator will offer Jonas a cigarette, which he always refuses, then will set a can of generic cola on the table. He will accept this, sipping it slowly during the interview, one of the few treats he gets in prison. The interrogator will ask Jonas if he wants his lawyer present. He shakes his head. Small talk comes first, and then the interrogation begins anew.

"Mr. Cullen, we've kept a secret from you over the past few days." Jonas' jaw tightens with this small change in the procedure. "Your girlfriend was bused back to California over Thanksgiving. Extradited." He pauses. "We had hoped that the long bus ride would clear her mind. It only seems to have made her more bitter. Miss Archer will be starting her trial in March." Jonas' mind races: he assumed Abby has been in the same building as he all along. The two men look at each other attempting to anticipate what's next. "You have maintained your claim of innocence consistently, and I want to believe you, but for the record give it to me one last time." Jonas catches something in the "one last time" phrase. He takes a deep breath and tells his story again.

"I wasn't in California when the robbery took place; I didn't help plan it; I knew nothing about it until I ended up here. When Abby showed up at my apartment, she didn't tell me anything about it or why she had returned. Abby's that way. When she left, when we broke up for good, I thought I'd never see her again. Her last visit was unannounced." He has given this account over three dozen times before. He has kept count. He enjoys saying "Abby's that way" to see if the interrogator will flinch. He often does, but today, he doesn't and asks a follow-up question.

"In one of your letters, you referred to Miss Archer as explosive. Did she have a violent temper?"

Jonas refuses the bait. "Not that I know of. She was just moody like all girls." In his mind, a dozen examples of her violent behavior flash quickly. He runs a finger over the bump on the bone over his left eye and wonders if the interrogator senses his lie.

"You were Miss Archer's boyfriend for nearly two years, and she never told you of her plans to rob banks?"

Jonas shakes his head. "I don't think she had any plans to rob banks when we were together. We were going to be teachers and work the system from within."

"So that's why the two of you taught at the Emma Goldman Experimental School in black Denver, so you could learn the ways of the violent, revolutionary movement?"

"Abby didn't teach there. She found me the job. Part time. She *came down a lot to volunteer." He knows the interrogator has this information.*

"And the teachers there, were they radicals too?"

"Hardly. They were enthusiastic about trying different methods, about helping poor kids. We never sat around after school and planned the overthrow of the United States."

"Do you still keep in touch with these teachers?"

"No, they're older than me. You know the school closed for lack of funding. I don't know what happened to them. I took a job back in Boulder substitute teaching."

The interrogator smirks. "Ah, yes, Emma Goldman failed again in her attempts to bring socialism to America. And you avoided the draft."

"High draft number. 272. I'm missing out on all the fun."

"Would you agree to enlist if we dropped the charges?"

"No."

The interrogator reaches down to his briefcase and pulls out a small stack of papers. He pretends to read them, stalling for effect. "Mr. Cullen, you've been in here for over three months. While the FBI has a solid case against Miss Archer, they don't have much on you, except she was in your apartment when they arrested her." He pauses, and the hair on Jonas' neck stands up. "I know you'll be disappointed you can't stay any longer, but we're going to release you soon. You'll be free before Christmas. Still, we're going to keep a close eye on you. The charges will be dropped unless we find further evidence . . . and we'll keep looking." The interrogator nods and smiles, mostly to himself, reshuffles the papers, and slides them over to Jonas for his signature. Then he says, "Guard, take Mr. Cullen back."

Jonas stands at attention in front of his cell, waiting for the guard to release him to enter. There is no finger movement this time. Instead, Hyde suddenly shoves Jonas in his back, sending him sprawling into his cell. "Don't think you're home free, Teacher-boy. Don't think that for one minute! You can kiss off teaching ever again!" Jonas does not get up quickly; instead, he narrows his eyes and slides his hands under his shoulders. He waits for Hyde to leave before standing. He will not vent his anger on the guard; it will do no good.

In his cell Jonas writes two letters, one to his father and one to Paul Garrity, a close friend from the University of Colorado, telling them the news. He is not relieved. He paces now and plans. He will go back to Montana to live with his family and work on straightening out his life, beginning with a new job on an isolated ranch. He tries to write Abby, but he has no words just now. Shit, Abby! What were you thinking?

Two days later, Jonas' green Ford pickup is stolen from outside his Boulder apartment. It is December 1970.

I

LATE SUMMER, 1972

CHAPTER 1

Jonas Cullen tugged at his tie while he waited to meet his principal at south Denver's Andrew Jackson High School. *An affluent city school*, he thought, shaking his head. His eyes took in the pictures and plaques hanging on the walls in the main office. A light oak board labeled "Teacher of the Year" held forty brass plates, only seven of which were inscribed. One name, Ben Lucas, was etched for 1966 and 1971. The 1972 honoree was Jane Walburg. Thirty-three plates waited for names. The last plate, Jonas calculated, would have to wait until the 21st Century, about the time he could retire. He wondered if the building would be standing that long, and whether education would still be recognizable in its current form. Strange thought, Abby's influence maybe.

Next to the teacher plaque was a dark oak board holding eleven brass plates with student names. "Always in Our Hearts." Somewhere in his past, he remembered someone saying that losing a student too early was a teacher's greatest nightmare. The promise tragically cut short. Light oak in celebration; dark oak in grief.

President Richard Nixon smiled confidently at all visitors. *If only he knew*, thought Jonas. Nixon's portrait revealed a more presidential smile than Hubert Humphrey's would have, but that expression exposed a lesser man, nevertheless. What might have been, except for 1968. An unidentified black and white portrait hung on the wall directly across from the principal's door, the kind visage of a middle-aged woman.

The most intriguing feature in the office to Jonas was Miss Lane, the secretary. She had been his first contact, a voice on the phone twelve days ago, telling him, not asking him, that he was to meet with Archie King to discuss filling a late social studies opening. A face to the voice on the phone. Miss Lane had saucer-sized eyes and seemed all business. So far, she always referred to him as Mr. Cullen. Those eyes indicated alertness and her posture a certain amount of confidence. Jonas wondered if she had been born a decade too late to take full advantage of the feminist movement.

"Stop staring, Mr. Cullen. Mr. Cirillo will be right with you." As if on cue, the door to the principal's office opened and a tall woman stepped out followed by Mr. Cirillo. Jonas stopped wandering, his face still a little red.

The woman's head was turned away from Jonas as she and the principal wrapped up their conversation. "Miss Lane will take care of you from here. She's the one who really runs this place."

"Annette, I'll see Jonas now. Elyse will need keys and a plan book and see if our new AP is around to give her a quick tour." Cirillo shook Elyse Cottage's hand and nodded in Jonas' direction. "Introduce yourself to Jonas Cullen on your way out. He's a rookie too."

Jonas stood motionless, waiting for an opening to the principal's office. Miss Lane put her hand in the small of Elyse's back, easing her toward Jonas, and Mr. Cirillo returned to his office. The secretary whispered instructions to a student aide to find the new assistant principal.

"Hi, I'm Elyse," said the young woman, emphasizing a hard *E*.

Jonas leaned forward at the waist and offered his hand. "I'm Jonas. Social Studies. Congratulations."

"Thank you. Where are you from?"

"Montana. You?"

"West Texas originally, but mostly from here, the Denver area. Are you excited?"

Jonas didn't know how to answer Elyse's question. "Yeah, I guess. Mostly nervous." He smiled. "I still have to see the principal. I've never met him."

Elyse cocked her head. "Didn't you have to go through an

interview with him?"

"Apparently not. I've already signed a contract."

They were interrupted by Miss Lane, directing each new teacher in a different direction. "Jonas, go on in, hon. Ellie, here's a packet for you, and the AP will be here shortly to give you a tour."

Then Elyse did an unexpected thing. She stepped back to Jonas, gave him a kiss on his right cheek and said, "Good luck," before turning back to the secretary.

A little flustered, Jonas walked past Annette Long into Pete Cirillo's office. At the same moment, Charles Chartwell entered the main office with the secretary's student aide following. "Is that one of the new teachers?" Chartwell asked the secretary.

"Yes. Jonas Cullen," she responded.

"Hair's pretty long for a teacher. Don't we have a teacher dress code here?"

Annette didn't respond directly to the assistant principal's question. "Mr. Chartwell, this is Elyse Cottage. She needs a tour. Have you got a half-hour to show her around?"

Chartwell smiled at Elyse. "For this pretty lady? Of course."

§

"Have a seat, Jonas." Cirillo was powerfully built but just a tad shorter than Jonas. Even on this summer day without students in attendance, he wore a black, narrow tie over his white, short-sleeved shirt. On his desk, a copy of Jonathan Kozol's *Death at an Early Age* laid face up; a bronze football sat on a shelf to his right. Jonas sized him up as a former football coach, but probably more.

"Archie King got you this job, Jonas. Let me tell you a little about Archie. Originally, he's from South Carolina, but you wouldn't know it from his accent. Worked hard to get rid of it. He's a Vietnam vet. Volunteered. Started teaching here five years ago, a year before I became the principal." Cirillo paused. "Archie is the most unorthodox teacher I have. He yells at his students daily, and they yell back. He rubs people the wrong way a lot, comes in here every other week or so to tell me what a spineless son-of-a-bitch I am, wonders why anyone would want to be a principal in this day and age. He's prepared each day to the last detail, is impatient with laziness, arrives here before seven each morning, and stays past five. He maintains he has to make up for the years when he wasted his life. The social studies department loves him, even though the rest of the staff wonders about him." The principal leaned across the table and looked Jonas dead in the eye. "And if he says you're the guy we want, then I'm going to believe him, and he says you're the guy." Again, Cirillo paused to let it sink into the young man sitting across from him.

Without breaking eye contact, Jonas challenged, "How did he find out about me?"

"How he finds out about most of the stuff he brings to me is a mystery, but when I released Taylor, Archie came in and said he wanted to interview you. Warned me not to hire one of the candidates I interviewed last spring just because time was short. He asked me to give him a week." Cirillo laughed aloud. "Hell, I have to laugh at Archie, or he'd drive me out of my mind. Anyway, he walked in here after talking with you and said you'd be his first hiree. He'd already gotten Miss Lane to send you a contract." Cirillo scratched the back of his neck and clasped his hands behind his head. "Have you talked to him since you've been here?"

"No, I don't have a phone yet. Just found a place two days ago. I'm kind of living in a haze just now."

"Have you heard from Abby since you've been back?" There was a sly smile, and the tough mask eased a bit. "You don't have to answer that. It's just when I read your papers and you said you'd been in jail for several months, I had to find out why. The guards said she was a tough one, always yelling at them, demanding special attention."

"She was that way with me too, at least some of the time. You know I didn't know about the bank robbery then?"

"Yeah, we checked you out. I know that all charges against you were dropped; you couldn't get your license if they weren't. Archie said you wanted to teach in the inner city. That right?"

"I thought I did. This past year, I haven't thought about it much, you know, with all that went on. I'm just happy to get a job anywhere that's fulltime. You know my license is just provisional, don't you?"

"Yep. I'm working on getting that taken care of. You're sure you still want to teach though?"

"Yes, sir. My one semester stint in Montana has stirred the fire again."

"Well, Jonas, we're not inner city, but we may be in two or three years. The shit's gonna hit the fan for all of Denver because of our segregated schools. We'll lose our privileged status here, either by having our boundaries redrawn or court-ordered busing or something. You know, Jonas, we have hundreds of black and brown students living within a few miles of here. It's hard justifying them not being here with us."

"If they come, things will change fast," said Jonas.

Cirillo smiled at that, but Jonas' mind raced ahead to those two years. "Look, Jonas, I might have passed on you because of your record, but Archie sees something in you, and I trust him implicitly. Don't let him down." There was firmness to Cirillo's last statement. "Got any questions before I send you back out to the boss to get started?"

"Yeah, how many new teachers did you hire?"

"Four. You and Elyse, a new math teacher, and a Spanish teacher that I had to fill just last week. I'm going to get all of you together on September third for a meeting. About the only thing you have in common seems to be your youth. None of the other three have any experience in the classroom. Anything else?"

"Ah, who's the woman on the wall behind the secretary's desk?"

"Jonas, I believe one good parent is more valuable than a dozen good teachers. The photo reminds me of that every day. What we do here is so much easier, and we are so much more successful, if our parents do their job. Ruth, the lady on the wall, came in one afternoon with her kid in tow, obviously at the end of her rope. Annette sensed she needed me immediately. Ruth said, very simply, 'I need your help with this one. Your people did a marvelous job with my older two. Angie here is on the wrong road. I'll back you in whatever you do.'" Pete refocused on Jonas. "Last year, she endowed our silent reading program, and I hung her picture in the office. Ruth reminds me every day this is a joint effort. She's sort of the unofficial conscience of the building and a good listener."

§

Archie King showed up on Jonas' porch on the morning after Jonas had first spoken with Mr. Cirillo. He rang the bell five times before Jonas decided whoever it was wasn't going away. Archie walked in without being asked, picked up Jonas' cat in the hallway, and tucked her under his arm. When Archie came to Montana to interview him weeks earlier, Jonas was amazed at how closely Archie resembled Robert Redford without the Sundance Kid mustache, but his bass voice dispelled that image.

"Morning, kid. Get dressed. I'm taking you for a decent breakfast. What's your kitty's name?"

Jonas rubbed his head trying to straighten out his bed hair and figure out what was going on so early. "Digit . . . at the moment. She's a stray who wandered in the day I did. She's got an extra claw on her two front paws. Give me a minute."

Archie nodded and took Digit into the kitchen. There, he turned the faucet on slowly and put the cat down in the sink for a drink. "Pretty barren place you've got here," he yelled out. "We'll go down to the thrift shops after breakfast and get you a few things." While he talked, Archie moved around the kitchen opening drawers and cabinets, shaking his head, and mumbling. "I thought your stepmom said she was going to send you off with some stuff."

"Patty did," said Jonas entering the kitchen. "We don't have that much to spare."

"We've got about a week to get everything set up for you, but since we have to be at school for those damn teacher prep days on Thursday and Friday, we'll have to get most of it done today and tomorrow. That'll give you the weekend to prepare your lesson plans for the first week. I'll look at them on Monday. You do know that Monday's Labor Day, don't you?"

"Yeah."

"I assigned you to three U.S. history classes and two government classes. I just want you to have two preps first semester. You won't know squat about the material at first--no rookie ever does--but you'll be teaching history to sophomores, and they'll know even less. Stay a week ahead of them, okay?" Jonas nodded. "The boss said you'll need to do some extra-curricular stuff. Got any preferences?"

"Which boss? Mr. Cirillo or Miss Lane?"

"Pete. Don't let him fool you. He's the boss. He's definitely the boss. Anyway, what's your choice? Coaching? It's either that or a study hall during your planning period, and I don't recommend that. In fact, I sort of vetoed that for you to Pete. Told him you'd do something after school."

"Could I partner up with you in something?"

"No, as of this year I'm the department chair. That's my extra assignment. How about coaching in the winter or spring? That would give you a few months to get your feet wet."

"I could help with the basketball or baseball teams."

"The baseball team's pretty set, I think. Ever play any roundball?"

"Yeah, a little. I could do that."

"Good. I'll see Coach Ragni and tell him you'll be his C-team coach."

At breakfast Archie flirted with the waitress, teasing her about warming his coffee too often which messed with his precise sugar additions.

"I think you just want to come over to this table to be around us, sweetheart. Got to be honest with you, though, I'm taken already, and Jonas here isn't going to have any time for a lady this year. Besides, I think he's too young for you." Sweetheart thought Archie was hilarious.

For the rest of the morning, Archie found thrift shops on the streets just to the east and west of Broadway and south of the downtown area. He assured Jonas that color patterns didn't matter for a bachelor pad; furniture just needed to be in good shape. Jonas balked at a television, having given up the habit during college, but Archie put on his department chairman cloak and told him he would need one to watch the news. "You can't be a government teacher if you don't know current events." Along the same line, Archie set up delivery of the *Rocky Mountain News* beginning on Sunday. "It's a morning paper and will keep you ahead of the students. By my calculations, you owe me seventy-four dollars and change, Jonas. Divided by nine, you can pay me nine dollars each month, and that will include interest."

§

Elyse's supervisor was not at all like Archie. Ben Lucas was her department chair, but he believed she was prepared and ready to step into her job. Ben was also more inclined to allow new teachers to develop without daily supervision. Making mistakes to learn was a science axiom. Where Jonas scrambled the week before classes started to get his apartment in order, Elyse was on cruise control. For the three weeks before the first teachers meeting, she and her mother shopped the upscale women's boutiques in Cherry Creek to find just the right outfits for the opening week of school. Refined, dignified, stylish.

On Tuesday evening Elyse fixed a dinner for Warden, her UCLA boyfriend who was in Denver to repair their relationship. Elyse was having none of it. "When dinner's over, Ward, I have some studying to do to prep for my classes. It was nice of you to come, but we've run our course."

Ward Stapleton was Elyse's father's choice, but she held no feelings for him any longer. It was Ward who had been unfaithful in the relationship, and Elyse saw it becoming a lifetime habit. No thanks. She rebuked his kiss when he left, closed the door, and did exactly as she said. She cleared the table, got out her biology textbooks, and began preparing lesson plans for the first week of school. Teaching would not be her lifetime occupation, but as long as she did it, she would do her best.

§

Ben Lucas seldom sat still. Housed in a strong, compact, Nordic body, he moved constantly. When he first interviewed Elyse, he was leaning toward an experienced candidate from his alma mater, Ohio State. Elyse made him reconsider. When he asked his questions, he was pacing behind the others on the committee.

"Mr. Lucas, your openings are in biology and earth science, and my major is biology," said Elyse. "My minor is geology. Strange combination, but they both interested me."

"Miss Cottage, what specific thing would you bring to our department?" asked Ben.

Elyse looked over the interview panel and smiled. "Well, . . . you're all men. It might tell some of our female students that science is not just for boys, that girls can succeed in something other than English and home ec." Elyse paused for a reaction, and then continued. "It's not just image. Like many of my college classmates, we weren't sure what we wanted to do, but unlike some of my friends, I had options because I was a science major. It's important to tell our girls they're capable in many areas."

Elyse's use of the possessive in describing the Andrew Jackson female students did not go unnoticed.

Chapter 2

The first order of business on Thursday morning was the introduction of the four new teachers to the Andrew Jackson staff and for them to stand before the rest of the faculty and sing the school's song. The band director stood in front of the newbies in mock leadership as they sang the school's fight song. On the first rendition, no one clapped, and there was a scattering of boos and hisses, indicating to Pete Cirillo that the "kids" needed to try it again. The second time, after Elyse huddled them up and gave instructions, they put their arms around each other's shoulders and belted out the lyrics. At the same time at thousands of high schools around the country, first year teachers made fools of themselves in a similar manner.

Later in the morning amid Cirillo's presentations, a school board member welcomed everyone back and warned of upcoming changes in the manner students would be assigned to schools in Denver but without giving details. The head custodian, Carlos Herrera, asked if the teachers would avoid cleaning their erasers on the outside bricks. Before Carlos was able to leave the library, Cirillo shook his hand and gave him a certificate authenticating his completion of the electrician's course sponsored by the district. One of the shop teachers asked if Carlos would be getting a raise commensurate with his skills, to which Cirillo answered, "We can't pay him enough to do that." The last speaker before lunch was Greta Nelson, the chief cook. She announced there would be a separate teachers' line for lunch this year, and then she invited the faculty to the cafeteria to enjoy one last lunch without students. Charles Chartwell returned from the administration building and was introduced by Pete as the new assistant principal, a temporary assignment while Mrs. Burton battled cancer. Standing near the door opposite Pete, he waived and said, "I've heard a lot of good things about Jackson, and I'm excited to be working with y'all."

The afternoon was set aside for teachers to work in their own classrooms. The exceptions were the rookies. Joining Jonas and Elyse were Dave Fallon and Laura Sanders. Jonas was the old man at twenty-five; Dave and Elyse were two years younger, and Laura was the youngest at just twenty-two. Pete Cirillo liked his new kids, seeing great promise in them for the future. He had purposely selected young applicants to balance out his older, experienced staff. Cirillo and his four new teachers met in his office to go over rules and expectations.

"Once again, I want to tell you how excited I am to have you on board. Have all of you settled into housing?" All the young teachers nodded that they had. "Don't be afraid to ask for help if it doesn't work out. You'll have enough on your plate this first year, so you shouldn't be worrying about your apartment. I have a few rules that apply to all my teachers, but especially to first-year teachers. First is what your fellow teachers so sarcastically call 'Cirillo's Rule.' In a nutshell, you will be in your classroom a minimum of thirty minutes before the first bell and stay for at least forty-five minutes after school. You will honor my rule for as long as you work here. I won't explain it, but over time you'll understand it, and it'll become second nature to you. Never challenge this rule, not even by a minute or two." Mr. Cirillo allowed for this to sink in, and as he promised, he did no further explaining. "Things change for you today. You move out of the desks and to the front of the classroom. You're in charge now, and I expect you to concentrate on discipline. You will find classroom discipline is a core belief of mine. All student progress is based upon it. Lots of quality school reform is out there right now, but for any of it to work, there has to be discipline. All good teaching is based on getting students to behave and work. If you work hard and demand that they do too, then you'll earn their trust. You can't ask for their trust; you've got to earn it. You have mostly sophomore schedules, so it won't be easy, but try. I'll help with some exceptional cases." Cirillo looked each rookie in the eye. "Work hard. Everyone thinks this is an easy job. They went to high school once, and it looked easy then, but I'm here to tell you it isn't. If you fall behind, it becomes unbearable. I'll understand if you to go out for a beer on Friday afternoons, but this first year, your Sundays are mine and Andy Jackson's. When you show up on Monday mornings, the first person you see is me, and you'll have a copy of your week's lessons plans. Jonas, you're going to be expected to have yours to Archie on Friday afternoon. I'll still want a copy on Monday morning. Archie will demand corrections by Sunday morning." Cirillo took a step to the right and sat on his desk. "Keep your distance from your students. Each of you will have students who get a crush on you. If I find out you're seeing one of our students outside of school, I'll fire your ass on the spot and make sure you don't work in education again." Each new teacher understood this directive from the force of the delivery.

Miss Lane interrupted the meeting with the leftover doughnuts. "Would anyone like more coffee or juice?" All the teachers took a doughnut, and Dave held out his cup for a refill. Elyse took the last carton of orange juice. "By the way, which one of you is driving the dirty white truck? It's blocking a narrow delivery path."

Jonas flinched. "That would be me." He looked to Principal Cirillo. "Should I go move it now?"

"Yes, we'll wait. Let's take a bathroom break."

When Jonas returned, Cirillo continued. "Next topic: grading. We're in a period of grade inflation. None of you will be teaching an upper-level course this first semester, and I think only you, Dave, have one second semester, so think in terms of a bell curve. Make an A a real accomplishment for your students. They'll respect you for it. With those students who fail or get Ds on an assignment, make them revise their work until they get it right and then give them a higher grade. It's nearly impossible for students to excel if they start out behind. They lose motivation.

"Okay, let's see what's next. Ah, homework. Each of you is

teaching in a content area, so demand they read, and don't allow too much class time for it. It tends to be down time and leads to discipline problems. A half-hour to an hour a night at least three times a week. Dave, you can give math problems every night. That means you need to grade them too. Again, Sundays are mine. This first year is your foundation. It'll be hard." He looked down at his notes for a second. "I've been talking for quite a while, what questions do you have?"

"Mr. Cirillo, do Elyse and I have to wear dresses every day?"

"No, but I do expect that you dress conservatively. No jeans either. You're both attractive women. Don't give your boys any more ammunition. Guys, I'll expect you in ties most of the time. And iron your shirts."

"Mr. Cirillo, can I charge my students a fee for a weekly news magazine in my government classes?" asked Jonas. "Probably *Time.*"

"Ask Archie when you meet with your department later this afternoon for his guidelines. Seems like a good idea to me."

"Mr. Cirillo, I have a part-time job stocking groceries at Safeway two nights a week. Is there a problem with that?" asked Dave.

"If you were in your second or third year, it would be okay, but I think you'll find your teaching will suffer this first year because of it. I know the extra money would come in handy, but if it pulls your performance down, I won't allow it. Go ahead for a month, but let's talk about it again then."

"Is there someplace I can eat lunch other than the teachers' lounge? It's so smoky in there. I know I won't like it."

"Your room, maybe, but don't turn into a hermit, Elyse. All of you will need the support of your peers. Besides, some really funny things are said at lunch and right after school in the lounge. Any of you smoke?" Both Dave and Laura raised their hand. "Only in the lounge, and I would caution against lighting up in your car while it's in the parking lot."

"Seating charts?"

"Yes."

"I've been contacted to join the union."

"Obviously, I can't belong, but I did when I was a classroom teacher, and I recommend you give it serious consideration. It costs a little, probably more than you think you can afford this first year, but it's a good investment." Cirillo smiled. "You're going to find everything costs more than you think you can afford this first year. Your monthly check will be pretty small."

"What are we going to be evaluated on? I mean, everyone tells me I won't be very good this first year. Even you."

"Laura, show up each day prepared and do your best, and I'll want you back next year. I mean that. This is a tough-ass profession, even though most of the public doesn't see it. You can't help but be nervous when I show up, especially when it's unexpected, but it's part of what I do." Cirillo stood up. "You'll have lots more questions, but they'll get answered in time. I want you to have some time this afternoon in your classrooms, so I'll let you go for now. Last thing. Don't let problems build up. Come see me, and if you aren't comfortable with me, talk to someone in your department. But get over your fear of me. Share your stories, both good and bad, with each other. You're all in the same boat. Oh, and around 3:00, I want you all to meet out front for a picture."

When the four teachers left, Cirillo walked out to talk with Miss Lane. "I think we hired some good ones this year, Annette. Laura may have some problems with all this, but the other three seem ready. If you hear anything about Laura, let me know."

"Pete, I have one of my gut feelings about Jonas. Archie's right, that young man has an energy most rookies don't possess. There's a presence about him, and I don't mean just physically. He's been in his room before Carlos shows up all week."

"I've noticed. He also has a background, both positive and negative. He has this level of confidence, but it's wrapped around a layer of unsurity. He also has two semesters of experience the others don't have, and that will be to his advantage. Spending time in jail may also have focused him a bit more too, but he is edgy, like he's always looking over his shoulder. His background is rural and disadvantaged." Pete scratched his chin. "Maybe get him into an upper-level class or two next year."

Annette shook her head. "Northern Colorado offers a graduate major in gifted and talented. I'll look into it. Maybe summer school."

"Did you look at his financial situation, Annette?"

"Yeah, but you always find scholarship money for kids. Why not see if you can round some up for Jonas?"

§

Ben Lucas took a half-dozen shots of the four rookies standing in front of Andrew Jackson. The photo that showed up in the year-book had Dave and Jonas standing behind Laura and Elyse. The diminutive Laura was in front of Dave while Elyse stood slightly to Jonas' left and a half-body in front. They were smiling broadly, optimistically. Dave's hands were on Laura's shoulders, and Jonas had his left arm around Elyse's waist. Behind them stood a magnificent building.

Andrew Jackson was constructed in the early 1930s, and despite the Great Depression's desperate economic conditions, Denver did not scrimp. The Greek-style architecture featured four square columns supporting a temple front similar to early 19th-century American churches in the New England area. Designed to house twelve hundred students on three floors, Jackson included a two-story tower on top of the entryway atrium. The tower originally held the music rooms but was closed to students in 1963 as a fire hazard. Only a single, narrow circular staircase led up to the tower. Students were challenged by tradition to sneak into the tower and leave their mark or hang a political statement from its windows. The tree-lined walkway leading up to the entrance was referred to as "the lane," and all seniors wanted their graduation photos taken on benches that lined this path. Most of these were taken in the fall when the numerous maples were on display. The building faced to the west, and from the upper stories, the majestic Front Range of the Rockies was visible.

Chapter 3

Archie King did not see Jonas at the final pre-semester faculty meeting on Friday morning. Pete Cirillo noticed too, and it showed in his jaw. He assumed Jonas overslept, and that was inexcusable. When the meeting broke for a ten-minute bathroom break at 9:15, Pete pulled Archie aside and told him to call Jonas and get him to school. The meeting resumed, and the social committee was giving its schedule for the first semester when Archie told Pete there was no answer at Jonas' apartment.

"Go find him, Archie. Let him know he's in deep shit with me."

Archie returned to school with Jonas about 90 minutes later and led him directly to the front of the library where the meeting was being held. "I hate to interrupt something so important as our yearly refresher course on using the Gestetner and other types of media, but I thought you might enjoy this." He stepped back, indicating to Jonas he should speak.

Jonas looked back at Archie for some sign or guidance, but his department chair merely shrugged his shoulders and indicated he should address the faculty. When Jonas turned back, he didn't notice Archie stifling his laughter. "My truck caught on fire." Jonas waited and then continued. "It just started on fire in front of Don's Creamery . . . in the parking lot while I was getting a coffee. The whole thing burned up." For a moment, nobody spoke.

From the side of the room Pete Cirillo said, "I see you saved your notebook." Jonas looked down to the satchel he was carrying and nodded. Pete continued. "I think I told you short of death, you weren't to be late to any of my meetings." For a moment the room was silent, and then it exploded in laughter. Archie stepped forward and put his hand on Jonas' shoulder and whispered a word of support.

Pete Cirillo led his young charge out of the room into the hallway. "Archie called me when he found you. I knew you were okay, so I thought we'd have a little fun at your expense. Some of the faculty were in on it. You handled it very well. I like that."

"On the outside. Archie settled me down some on the way back. I was going to be on time for this morning's meeting. This isn't something I can afford just now. It wasn't much of a truck anymore, but at least it got me to school."

"I've got an old Chevy station wagon you can borrow for the next few weeks. I trust you had insurance?" asked Pete.

"Not enough."

"Jonas, does shit like this happen to you all the time?"

§

Jonas ate lunch with Elyse, Dave, and Laura in Elyse's room. Despite the brief time they had known one another, they seemed comfortable.

"I wish I had a different department chair," said Laura. "Bentert's so old and out of touch, and so negative. She's a Latin teacher, for criminy sake. She was probably an original language learner."

"The band teacher says she was a *Playboy* model when she was young."

"Gawd, Dave, they didn't have *Playboy* during the Depression."

Jonas shivered. "Bentert nude; that's an ugly thought."

"The science department's going out for a few beers this afternoon. Why don't all of you guys come too?" Elyse turned her head to Jonas. "There's a rumor going around you've got a prison record." She raised her eyebrows.

Jonas smiled. "You guys buy the beer, and I might come clean. Besides, I'm going to need to save every penny to buy another used car."

"I'm hearing the same thing, Jonas. Sounds like there are a few subplots too," said Dave.

"What would a math teacher know about subplots?"

"All I'm hearing, Jonas, is there's a beautiful woman still in jail somewhere just waiting for you to rescue her," said Laura.

"That settles it," said Elyse. "I'm buying."

"Jeez, this year is starting out well. I'm already the focus of the faculty."

§

The afternoon meeting was short, as Cirillo wanted to give his teachers a last few minutes to get their classrooms in order. He focused mostly on the state of Denver's desegregation plans.

"As most of you are aware, there's a lawsuit moving through the courts that might force the district to integrate all the schools. My guess is, if it wins, we'll get new boundaries or forced busing. Last year, we were at ninety-five percent white, maybe a little higher. This year, I doubt if we'll get to eighty-five percent. Our traditional population is starting to move out. 'White flight.' It may even be closer to four-fifths with the increasing Chicano enrollment." Cirillo pointed to his new AP who had raised his hand.

"The school board already tried busing, and the voters turned them out. Aren't the courts listening? This school is turning out a good product; why mess with that?"

"Charles, I don't think the courts give a damn. If they perceive Denver's intentionally drawing school boundaries to keep black kids in black schools, they'll make the whole city change. Our neighborhoods are all white, but up north in the Park Hill sections, there's been some manipulation. There won't be a decision this year, and probably not next, but white families are already beginning to move to the suburbs. We need to prepare for a different student body. In two years, we'll be down to around sixty-five percent, even if they don't order mandatory busing."

Archie King spoke out. "You mean Denver's going to have to live up to *Brown v. Board of Education?*"

"Your sarcasm is noted, Arch, but what will have the biggest impact on us will be revenues. If the white middle class and upper class reject our schools for the suburbs, they'll take their money with them. Hell, I really don't care what color our kids are; I just want the money to teach them."

Jonas leaned toward Dave. "Did you think you were signing up to teach in the inner city?"

Dave let out a quiet laugh. "I've never even had a real conversation with a black person. At my college, the only blacks were football and basketball players, and I wasn't one of those. Our minorities were Mexicans."

"Ah, so you'll be our expert on the Chicano Revolution. Coming from southern Colorado, you probably know Reies Tijerina. Does Corky Gonzales call you directly?" Dave had no clue what Jonas was talking about.

"Pete, if Denver buses kids across town to new schools, will some of us be reassigned too? I'll retire first," said Susan Bentert.

"Let's not get ahead of ourselves just yet. I'm pretty sure the court will tell us to desegregate, but it just might mean some voluntary plan. I haven't heard anyone suggest we move around our teachers. I just want you all to be aware of the trends along these lines." Cirillo changed topics and his tone after that. He wanted the school year started on a positive note, despite the fact clouds on the horizon were ominous to the veterans. Change was in the offing. "Let's see. It's 2:00 o'clock now, but if you want to leave a little early and get ahead of the Labor Day traffic, I'll be in on Monday, and the building will be open in case any of you want to come in for a little preparation."

At the close of the meeting, teachers stood around in small groups to talk and plan, but quickly they began to vacate the school. Jonas told his new pals he needed to work a little bit longer, since he had missed most of the morning. "I'll join you later."

Back in his room, Jonas stood motionless in front of the heater wondering how to stack the government texts. His hands were doubled up into fists in front of his body. Why had he returned to Colorado? Why did he return to teaching? Finally, he took in a deep breath and unclenched his fists. "You can do this." He breathed heavily again, picked up the first stack of texts, and slid them out of the shelves. He shook his head and then repeated the action until all the books were ready for distribution on Tuesday.

§

On Sunday night Jonas called home. "Hey, Dad, it's me. How's Patty doing?" Jonas' current stepmother was not well, but the doctors couldn't figure out why. After his dad recounted the most recent attempts to get her to feel better, he turned to his son's new job. Mr. Cullen was extremely proud of Jonas. He always had been. He preferred for his son to remain close to home. He never understood Jonas' desire to teach, especially in "one of them big cities with colored kids."

"If Patty wakes up, have her call. Yeah, I know. Don't send any more money; I have a part time job. I'm keeping it a secret; the principal doesn't want us rookies to have one, but I'll be okay. I've never really needed much sleep. A little bookstore in an upscale shopping area called Cherry Creek. It's pretty flexible; the owner just wants some weekend help.

"Dad, don't argue. I'm putting some money away every week to help. It's my call now. Hey, you raised me; it's your fault. Grampa said you were a bit of a hell-raiser yourself as a kid. No, I won't. No, I haven't heard from Abby. Don't hold your breath. Gotta go. This is costing too much. Yeah, you too. Oh, Dad, one more thing. Remember me telling you about my friend Paul Garrity being drafted and sent to Vietnam? Well, he's been listed as missing in action. Yeah, MIA. His parents told me. They think he's a prisoner and not, you know, dead, but I'm not sure that's not just hope. I don't know. Yeah, thanks, I will. Yeah, very angry, but I'll handle it. I'll let you know."

§

Dear Ruth,

Well, it begins again. What an exciting time! As always, Pete has me hopping, but I like the confidence he shows in me. He's such a good man. The students arrive on Tuesday. Help me remember I work for

Pete and the teachers first; you know how protective and distracted I get with the students. There are four new teachers in our building; I think you've seen them in the office a few times. Watch over them because they are all young. Be particularly watchful over little Laura—she's the least prepared for this tough job, but keep your eye on Jonas too, because he's had a run of bad luck.

Annette tucked this letter into a manila folder along with several previous letters and replaced the folder in her lower left drawer.

§

MURRAY OYLER, 1966

"Okay, Murray, it's your turn. You've been quiet all year, and I'm not going to allow you to get through second grade without speaking in front of the class." Mrs. Conduct stands behind her desk at the front of the room and peers over her jeweled glasses at the class's tiniest boy, who sits in the fourth seat in the row nearest the windows. Mrs. Conduct is a taskmaster, a thirty-seven-year veteran of the elementary classroom, a no-nonsense teacher whose students' skills are much better in May than they were in September. Murray's head stays down, and he makes no move to get out of his desk.

"Murray, the class is waiting. I am waiting. Bring your book." The little boy swivels in his chair and drops his feet to the floor. He takes the history book from his desk with both hands and walks deliberately to the front of the room. His classmates know not to giggle for fear of Mrs. Conduct's wrath.

"Murray has chosen to read a shortened version of President Kennedy's Inaugural Address to you, class. It is a difficult speech, and Murray is to be congratulated for attempting it." The teacher pauses, looking at the back of the little boy's head. He turns slightly to look at his teacher, and then he places his book on the corner of her desk and opens to the page marked by a playing card. Tucking his head against his chin, he begins to read in the quietest voice, audible only to Mrs. Conduct and two or three students in the front rows. It takes just under two minutes for him to complete the speech, and at its completion, the boy gently closes his book and walks to his seat, without waiting to be

excused. Mrs. Conduct watches and gathers her words.

"Well, class, let's give our classmate a hand for his brave effort." At his desk, without looking up, Murray smiles ever so slightly.

Four more students present their two-minute speeches before the day ends. Mrs. Conduct excuses her class on this Friday, May 6, 1966, with a warning they are not to forget to make their mothers a card over the weekend. She stands by the door as each student springs by. She is aware that Murray Oyler has not left. Rather than say anything, she returns to her desk, sits down, and waits. She is making a few notes in her planning book when she hears him leave his desk and walk toward her. She waits until he stands at the side of her desk before looking up.

Quietly, and without his book, Murray begins presenting his speech again. "We observe today not a victory of party, but a celebration of freedom . . ." His voice is louder, and although he does not look at his teacher directly, he is aware of her stare. He realizes she isn't surprised, but there is something. Is it a sense of pride for him? He feels a warmth come over him. He pauses after the phrase ". . . the torch has been passed to a new generation of Americans," both for effect and to gauge his audience. He finishes, "And so my fellow Americans, ask not what your country can do for you; ask what you can do for your country." Then he looks up to see Mrs. Conduct with a smile before dropping his head again.

Mrs. Conduct reaches over to him and, with a cocked finger under his chin, gently lifts his head. "Murray, you delivered that with dignity and clarity. President Kennedy would be proud of you."

"Thank you, ma'am."

"Your father will be waiting for you, so you better gather up your supplies and go meet him. Please tell your mother I said hello, and don't forget to make your Mother's Day card."

"Yes, ma'am."

CHAPTER 4

L aura Sanders sat behind her desk on the first day of school going over the pronunciation of her students' names. She tried to give the Anglo names their Spanish form, but Rogelio was having none of it. "I'm Roger, okay!" he said. As she passed out her first worksheet over numbers, she found herself wondering how her *treinta y dos* students would be able to share the *quince* Spanish language tapes.

Down the hall on the first floor, students in Elyse Cottage's Earth Science class were busy completing a worksheet based on pictures of the planet's various surfaces. She abandoned the traditional teaching station behind the science table at the front of the room and cruised the spaces between the student desks. At her heels was a tiny, hyperactive, curly-haired blonde student named Sadie who followed Elyse around the room to every station. "Girl," Miss Cottage said, "take those big dark eyes back to your desk and work on your paper." Sadie tried to obey but could not sit still to save her life. Elyse had opted for a suit for this first day, but already found it to be too hot. By lunch she had discarded the jacket, which was more revealing than any dress in her professional wardrobe. Mr. Cirillo was correct. Several of her sophomores developed an immediate crush on her.

Dave Fallon tossed a baseball from one hand to the other at the front of his classroom. "Can anyone tell me the circumference of this ball? Do you all know what the term circumference means?" Pete Cirillo leaned against the back wall with his arms folded watching Dave begin his career. Students came into math classes with a unique attitude. They were supposed to be worked hard, and they knew much was expected. Dave Fallon intuitively understood this from his own experience. As the year progressed, his stories about his kids would strike Elyse and Laura as fantasy. Dave's students always had their materials; most had their homework completed, and they did not disrupt the lesson. Laura even developed a squeaky robot routine to imitate him. She surprised everyone when she performed "Mechanical Man" at the November faculty meeting. The seven-man math department laughed the loudest.

When he arrived at six, Jonas delivered his lesson plans to Mr. Cirillo, made small talk about the running condition of the Chevy station wagon he was borrowing, and then left to place brown sacks on the desks of his three colleagues. In them were a variety of snacks and a journal. When he taught for four months in Livingston, Montana, in the spring, one of his fellow teachers had done the same for him, and it made a difference in his outlook. Jonas' first class was American History, a required class for sophomores. He began with an update on the upcoming presidential election between Richard Nixon and George McGovern. "Is there only one issue? Does Senator McGovern have any chance?" His students were not old enough to vote, but he asked them if there were any actions they could take to influence the outcome. Jonas had done grunt work as a high school senior for the Goldwater campaign in Montana as a social studies requirement, but by 1968 he was committed to Robert Kennedy. Despite his anger over Kennedy's murder, he put his efforts into the Humphrey campaign in Boulder, frustrated that many liberals refused to make that internal switch. In some ways, he blamed his party for the loss to Nixon. Now he would try to mask his dislike for Nixon and present a neutral position to his students.

Mr. Cullen closed with a note about something called "Watergate," but to his chagrin, only one of his sophomores, a redheaded girl named Rainer, knew any of the details. Then he passed out textbooks and gave them a four-page homework assignment. "Homework on the first day! Come on, Mr. C, give us a break." No undeserved breaks, he told them. They were in high school and had to earn their way.

§

Charles Chartwell briefly observed each of the rookies during the first two periods. Before leaving for the Ad Building, he met with Pete to relay his impressions.

"Well, what did you think? asked Pete.

"They're young, but they were trying. They all had first day jitters."

"I think we hired some battlers. Any concerns?"

"The first day can be misleading, but I'd say your math and science departments will be happy with your choices. Hard to tell with Miss Sanders. Cullen seemed more concerned with current events rather than history while I watched, but I think most social studies teachers are. Their type wants to be the conscience of the country."

§

Jonas shared third period planning time with Archie. On this first day, Archie wanted to know all about Jonas' first two classes. Like most times, Archie's questions were a lead-in to a story.

"Every Friday afternoon around 3:30 during my first year of teaching, old John Grossman would pull a bottle of whiskey from his bottom desk drawer, pour two glasses, and discuss my short-comings with me. There were many. Mr. Gross!Man, as his students referred to him, was nearing retirement at the end of a thirty-year career as a classroom teacher, all in the Denver Public School system, and all except the last six years here at Andrew Jackson in junior high. He began in 1938, took three years off to serve in World War II, and then finished a couple of years ago. During 'His War,' he served as a prison guard in a Missouri stockade, mostly guarding U.S. Army soldiers who were too immature to handle the pressures of military service. 'Great training to be a junior high teacher,' he would say about every other week.

"If anyone would have offered me another job that spring," said Archie, "I would have been out the door, because in all honesty, I wasn't very good. Teaching was not my planned career goal when I entered college, but some things in the Sixties changed my plans.

"Andrew Jackson High was my rookie assignment. Not exactly inner city. All white and high achieving. High expectations for students and teachers alike. When you talked up at your family's place about wanting to teach in the inner city and do something special in education, you reminded me of my reasons for coming into this profession. Like you, I was older than most beginning teachers. My initial schedule consisted of civics and history, six periods with about thirty students per class. My three civics courses were one semester, so I saw a different set of kids in those three classes each semester. For the year I taught 273 students. Looking back, it seems as if I was constantly taking roll, rearranging the seating chart to get Johnny away from Susie, and wrestling with sophomore boys. Either times had changed, or I didn't remember how physical teenage boys were.

"Another thing I remember about that year was Denver instituted a current events policy. Every social studies class district-wide was to include current events as part of the lessons for the day. Read the newspaper and discuss the important events occurring around the world. Most of my students were oblivious to any world outside of Denver, but in each class, there seemed to be a handful of students who relished the chance to debate Vietnam, or Civil Rights, or the Arab-Israeli conflict. In retrospect, it was these cells of *newsheads* that saved me, that convinced me to return for a second year.

"Gross!Man told me not to worry about it, that it would take about three years to be comfortable with it. Then he'd down his whiskey, laugh, and tell me that if I couldn't get a handle on my classroom discipline, the little shits would run me out."

"Any suggestions?" asked Jonas.

"There're all kinds of methods, my boy, all kinds. Personally, I like to use my paddle early and often, but I fear your generation is going to abandon that method. The courts will probably take it out of your hands. A strong kid like you should be able to stand over them and scare the hell out of them, especially with that poorly disguised anger you carry. Still, you can't take anything they do personally. Gross!Man's stare was what caused students to fear him. At sixty, his coal black eyes and silvery mane, along with a bulbous nose and bad breath, kept his students in line. 'Look, King,' he would say, 'I suspect life's been pretty easy for you so far, but this teaching gig is hard. Damn hard. Every day's new and exciting.' There was always a hint of sarcasm in Gross!Man's use of the word exciting. 'You're a smart lad,' he'd say. 'If you stick around for three or four years, you'll get it.' Then Gross!Man would smile at me and end with a single word, 'Maybe.'

"The social studies staff consisted of seven teachers. No aides, no secretaries. Type your own tests. Run them off on the Gestetner. Fortunately, the other members of the department were supportive of my efforts and tolerant of my inexperience. In more positive words, they echoed the same message as Gross!Man. 'Stick with it. Persevere. You have what it takes.' I thought my life experiences and age would make this an easy job, and so I was a bit arrogant at first, but that quickly vanished. I'm still arrogant, just not about the job. Teaching is hard; good teaching is even harder. Those who do it well have my highest admiration.

"My department chair was Flo McMann. She taught mostly world geography to ninth graders. Her students referred to the class as 'Tenth Grade World Coloring,' but it was a valuable class, and she was tough on them. Mrs. McMann saw the district's current events edict as just one more fad in a long line of fads and ignored it. Our conferences were treated in a similar manner. I was just the most recent young teacher to pass through Jackson who was told to pry some world history into tenth graders' thick skulls without doing any damage to their psyches. She advised me to read Palmer's *History of the Modern World* over the summer and take notes on the relevant parts. This little bit of a lady had scared the hell out of me during my first week, marching into my room and warning me not to allow my students to leave before the bell because it made it that much harder for the veteran teachers to do their jobs. While I didn't take notes, I did manage to read both volumes of Palmer's text over the summer, and it did do wonders for my ability to relate history to my charges."

Archie opened his briefcase and handed Jonas two dog-eared books. "You won't have time to read these this year, but next summer when you're lounging by the pool, take it in. It'll do you good." They were his copies of *History of the Modern World*. As he stood to leave the lounge, he asked, "By the way, Jonas, did you finish *The Pentagon Papers?* I noticed you were reading it this summer."

§

At the end of the first day, Elyse wanted nothing more than a foot massage and a margarita. It had been over three months since she had worn pumps on hard tile floors for an entire day. Only the five rooms on the second floor designated for the social studies department had carpeting, achieved through a federal grant that ran out long before its stated objectives were secured. Elyse was pleased, however, by the performances of her students. She laughed frequently and answered a few personal questions posed by curious boys. "Are you married, Miss Cottage?" The boy who asked was booed by his classmates. "It's Miss Cottage, you bonehead." One girl asked if she was a hippie, "You know, the straight hair and goofy necklace." Elyse said that she had flirted with "hippiedom" a little in college, but now she was just a teacher. "Were you at Woodstock?" "No, that took place in New York, and I was going to college in California, but I wish I would have been." Several of the sophomore boys laughed. Little Sadie hung around after class and asked her if she could be her student aide.

Most of her lesson plans were implemented. She spent the required forty-five minutes after her last class cleaning her room and setting out the materials needed for tomorrow. Then she jotted down a few notes in her journal. Jonas' little gift from the brown bag was going to be filled with anecdotes by the end of the year. Laura dragged herself in at 3:30. Her day had not been quite so productive.

"I need a beer." She set her tote bag down on Elyse's desk. "No, I need two beers at the end of this first day of my teaching career.

I'm going to call all future days like this 'two beer days.'" Elyse wasn't sure what to say. Laura looked up and started to laugh. "Shit, have I got a lot to learn," but it wasn't said in desperation, more in determination.

"Well then, let's go see if the boys fared any better." After collecting Dave, they found Jonas glued to a TV in the social studies office. Palestinian terrorists had captured several Israeli athletes at the Munich Olympics earlier in the day, and it was now playing itself out to a tragic conclusion. At 3:45 the ABC crew was cautiously optimistic, and Elyse persuaded Jonas to go with them to a bar over by Cherry Creek called Rick's. They could watch the TV there and have a couple of beers.

In less than a half-hour, eleven teachers from Andrew Jackson High were quietly drinking and watching Jim McKay on the television trying to sort out a vast amount of conflicting information.

"Does anyone know who the terrorists are?"

"Around noon they were calling them Black September, a Palestinian group associated with Yasser Arafat, but I'm not sure if they're still holding to that."

"Isn't Mark Spitz Jewish?"

"He's not one of the captives, is he?"

"No. As far as we know, only Israeli athletes were captured."

Issues from the opening school day should have been the topic of conversation, but they seemed trivial to the teachers at this moment. Even the girl fight, which normally would have drawn plenty of laughs, was not discussed. Everyone's attention was on the hostage situation in Germany. The entire bar fell silent when Jim McKay began his most memorable line in his career as commentator of Wide World of Sports. It was a quarter past seven.

"I've just gotten the final word," McKay said softly. He looked exhausted. "When I was a kid, my father used to say our greatest hopes and worst fears are seldom realized. Our worst fears were realized tonight." Beneath the table Jonas and Elyse held hands. "They're all gone."

Archie King spoke first after the guttural sounds ended. "Let's all go home. We won't get any more solid information tonight, and we'll all have to be at our best tomorrow."

In the parking lot, Jonas and Elyse stood by her Ford Mustang after the other teachers had left. They were still holding hands.

"You knew at school, didn't you," said Elyse.

"I didn't know, but I had a sick feeling."

"How?"

"When I was in high school, I worked part-time in a nursing home. There was this cat that would curl up on the beds of the old people who were dying. When the cat stayed, the people died, but the strange thing was I knew where that cat was going every time. Just a feeling. That's how I felt today."

"Did you ever tell anyone?"

"Just my dad. He said it would be better if I didn't tell anyone else. He also had me quit."

"What do we do now?" asked Elyse.

"We don't do anything. There's nothing we can do about what happened over there. Bad things happen all the time. We just move on."

"Pretty pessimistic outlook, isn't it?"

"No," said Jonas. "You persevere. Isn't that one of the lessons we're supposed to teach our kids?"

Elyse just looked into Jonas' eyes for a minute. In the grip of his hand and the squint of his eyes, she sensed a frustration born in anger. She chose to go in a different direction. "You know rumors about us will begin after tonight, don't you?"

"Let's keep it just rumors for a while. I'm still in the tail end of this other situation."

"Abby?"

"It's just a rumor, but it's a rumor with history."

"You'll let me know?"

"Yeah, Elyse, I'll give you a sign." Jonas leaned in and kissed Elyse tenderly on her lips. "Why did you kiss me that first day?"

Elyse pouted her lower lip before she answered. "Jonas, beautiful women can do whatever they want and usually don't have to explain. Besides, men are never in charge of relationships." She touched her index finger to his lips, smiled, and mouthed goodnight, then turned and got into her car.

On a day when Jonas should have remembered the red-haired girl from first period and the trio of boys in sixth hour who cornered him after class to be their chess club sponsor or the tragic event unfolding in Germany, his thoughts were on two women; one who had distanced herself from him and one who was trying to edge closer.

Chapter 5

"Where's Chuck?" asked Archie, referring to Charles Chartwell. "I need to meet him up close."

"He's only here until noon on most days. The rest of his day is spent at the Ad Building," answered Pete.

"Odd arrangement," said Archie.

"The district's fast-tracking him for personnel or something. I don't think he'll ever have a school of his own. I get the feeling he doesn't want one, but they want him to have this experience."

"Probably a good thing. He seems a little too pretty for a hands-on job like this," said Archie. "You didn't ask for him, did you?"

"Are you saying Pete's not pretty, Archie?" asked Annette.

"That's obvious, isn't it? Chuck evidently reprimanded a few of Jonas' students after class for being too loud outside his door coming out of class. Jonas didn't see it as a problem, but regardless, Jonas needs to learn to handle those things."

"Did he step on your toes too, Arch?" Pete smiled. "If you have time right now, I'll have him come in."

As Archie waited, he teased Annette and tried to disrupt her work. Some things were obvious to the trained eye. Charles came in from the counseling office, and the two men used Pete's office to talk.

"Working here has to be a comfort to you," said Archie.

"What do you mean?" asked Charles.

"Andrew Jackson. Southerner. Southern values." Archie

chuckled.

"I haven't seen too much of that," said Charles. "Pete said you were a Southerner too. South Carolina?"

"Long time ago. How about you, Chuck? What's your background?"

"Charles. I grew up in northern Arkansas, small town near the Missouri border. Poor. Most of us were. I went to the College of the Ozarks near Branson, Missouri. It's a college where everyone works for his tuition."

"All white, I suppose, and Baptist?"

"Not all Baptist. Mostly evangelical though. We called our school 'Hard Work U'. None of our parents had enough money to pay for our college. I was able to attend because of this plan. I made it out of poverty by working hard, like all those black students should do in the poorer schools in north Denver."

Archie kept nodding, kept feeding Chartwell. "I went to a military prep school in Charleston and from there to The Citadel. My parents were rich and well-placed. I didn't pay any tuition either, and here we are, Chuck, together at Andrew Jackson High School. Rich and poor in the same school."

"The Citadel. That's impressive. So, I guess you understand. I suppose you went into the Army as an officer. Vietnam?"

"Family tradition," said Archie. His head kept nodding, and his eyes remained fixed on the assistant principal. "What about you, Chuck? Did you serve?"

"No. My local draft board passed me over since I got my degree and married. No lottery numbers back then, so if you knew someone, you could slide. I started a family and began teaching junior high near my hometown."

"How'd you get to Denver?" asked Archie.

"Wanted something better than being a teacher, so I got my master's degree in administration and was hired here two years ago. My wife didn't like the city, so she moved back. She doesn't have any college, so I send money back each month for the kids."

Archie stood. "I need to get back to class, but it was nice chatting, Chuck. By the way, I'll work with Jonas on his discipline. He's my charge. You don't need to worry about him."

§

Pete felt a different vibe from his teachers, subtle, but there none-the-less. There was money available for supplies, the football team was winning, and school spirit was high, there had been no major fights between students, and the *Post* ran a complimentary article about several of Jackson's seniors who won prestigious scholarships. Still, something.

Today, Pete and his assistant principal were having lunch with the rookies, a chance for the young teachers to share any problems that had built up over the first five weeks of the school year. None had expressed any concerns up to now in the brief Monday morning meetings or during classroom observations. As they sat and ate, they laughed at how tired they were, about how much energy they expended to keep up with their sophomores, and at how quickly the first month had passed. Each fretted about the upcoming parent-teacher conferences.

"I appreciate the energy each one of you is bringing to our building. We're a bunch of old fuddy-duddies, and this is good for us. Shakes the cobwebs off. At this meeting, I want you to relax and think of us as co-workers and not your bosses. Call us Pete and Charles; be a little less formal in this office," said Pete. He nodded to his assistant principal who leaned forward in his chair to speak.

"You guys have been mostly invisible. I hope that's an indication that all is well. Laura, I'm sorry I mistook you for a student in the hall last week. You caught me off guard a bit." As Chartwell spoke, Elyse was sizing him up. On that very first day, when he gave her the building tour, she pegged him as a flirt. He made her uncomfortable. Laura told her about last week's incident, that he seemed to blow her off until she identified herself as a teacher. She had been hurt by it. Charles turned to Jonas. "A couple of the older teachers asked me what revolutionary movement you're a part of. The AP laughed at his attempt at humor. "I told them it was the Boulder Peace Union, and that the FBI was keeping tabs on you."

Pete flinched at Charles' remarks but said nothing. The FBI

topic was confidential, on a need-to-know basis. Pete asked his new teachers for their input, to have them tell a story or share an insight about this first month. Each story was about a student interaction until Jonas spoke.

"I think teaching for those two semesters in Denver and Montana helped me," said Jonas. "They were so different from this; the schools each had fewer than fifty students, and our staffs were only about six or eight teachers, but at least I got my feet wet." He gave them a quick summary of each school and then added, "It's hard to compare, but the teachers at those schools seemed closer, more relaxed, more ready to trust each other. Here, I've been more comfortable in my classroom than in the teachers' lounge." He turned to Charles and said, "If I really was a revolutionary, I wouldn't be here." He paused. "I'd be in jail." Jonas' eyes confronted the AP's eyes.

Pete reminded the young teachers that their first evaluation was coming soon and then sent them back to their classrooms for the afternoon. Charles left to the Ad Building, leaving Pete to consider Jonas' comment. He stood and looked out his window onto the campus, wondering about Jonas' path to Denver.

Pete walked the halls after lunch picking up trash, ordering the stragglers to class, replaying Jonas' observation. Pete found himself near old Marsh Daniel's room, a place where he used to hang out frequently during his first year. Marsh had been his early confidante. It didn't last long. Marsh was now in his final year before retirement, but Pete had encouraged Marsh that first year to retire due to poor health and a lack of energy to be a competent teacher. It caused a rift and now they seldom spoke.

Marsh walked up behind Pete and slapped his shoulder. "Don't just stand there like a lost sophomore. Come in and tell me what's on your mind."

"Planning period?" asked Pete.

"Yeah. Coffee?"

"No thanks. How're doing, Marsh?" asked Pete sincerely.

Marsh took the question as it was asked. "Mostly good, Pete. The hip still flares up some, but . . ." He paused. "You were worrying out there. What about?"

"Something seems to be brewing, and I can't put my finger on it. Any insights?"

"Yeah." Marsh allowed his answer to hang in the air for a moment. Neither man rushed to pull it down. "Anxiety, Pete. Your teachers are a little scared. They work hard, harder than the world out there appreciates, but they're worried that it's not enough. You understand, and that's why they like working here; they know you have their backs." Marsh lowered his eyes and tapped his desk twice with a flat hand. Pete waited for Marsh to continue. "But they aren't sure they'll be here after the court rules on this integration thing. The rumors are out there that teachers will be moved to new schools along with the students. We're a conservative lot, and when some unseen force threatens our students—and our jobs—it's disconcerting."

Pete remembered the rift. He had held Marsh's health problems at the forefront, but he hadn't expressed himself well. He warned Marsh that, as principal, he couldn't allow the students to be adversely affected. Marsh took it as a threat, and they argued.

Marsh cleared his throat and continued. "One of us ought to apologize, you know." The old man smiled. "You're too stubborn, and I'm too vain, so we'll let it pass. But I appreciate that you got me that aide, even though I never told you. It's helped." Pete nodded. "Pete, a couple of things are out there. One, Denver's going to integrate, and that will necessitate change. The teachers understand that, and for the most part, support it. What really scares them is that they don't know how they're going to be evaluated to be reassigned. Evaluations are always scary. They just have a feeling that it won't be you doing it. It will be administrators who don't know them, have never seen them teach, who weren't long in the classrooms themselves. Put yourself in their shoes. Your teachers are in a high achieving high school doing good things, and then bang, they're out and working in a new building for a boss they don't know with kids who don't understand the Jackson Way."

"Where do these rumors start?" asked Pete.

"In this case it's not where they started. The decision from the court on desegregation will cause worry. But it's how these rumors are fanned." Marsh pondered his next words. "You might want to have a talk with your new AP."

§

Pete Cirillo removed Jonas from his classroom on Tuesday morning, October 24. Mr. Cirillo knocked on Jonas' door and called him into the hall. With Pete were Jane Walburg and an unnamed man in a black suit. What Jonas first noticed was a seething Pete Cirillo, but then Jonas recognized the man in the suit. He tensed immediately.

"Jonas, don't say anything and follow my instructions explicitly," ordered Pete. "Miss Walburg will take your class for the rest of the period. Other teachers will cover you the rest of the day. Don't worry about lesson plans." Jonas understood what was happening, and he nodded to Walburg as she entered his room. "Follow me," said Cirillo. With that, the three men marched to the main office.

"No interruptions, Annette," Pete directed and slammed his office door. Inside, the black suit stood silent near the west window as Pete spoke privately to Jonas. "Son, the FBI has pulled your teaching license—for no apparent reason that I can see. Until I can get it reinstated, you'll have to stay home. At lunch, I'll walk you down to your classroom so you can get your stuff and leave. Until then you'll wait in here. This is crap, and I'll take care of it. It's harassment, plain and simple." Pete placed his right hand firmly on Jonas' shoulder and squeezed. The principal then turned to the man in the suit. "Okay, he's out until we clear this issue up." Still with his teeth clenched and his nostrils flared, Pete continued. "I know you're just following orders from your superiors but tell them I said this is pure bullshit! The FBI is messing with a good young man, and this needs to stop." Cirillo turned back to Jonas. "Jonas, go out and get yourself a cup of coffee. Come back in here until I come and get you." With that, Pete left the room.

Jonas sensed that the suit man wanted to apologize and leave, to remove himself from Jonas' glower. They had been in this situation once before in Montana, but there Jonas punched him and wrestled him to the ground. This time, Jonas obeyed Pete's directive, but he didn't take his eyes off the agent.

§

That afternoon Assistant Principal Chartwell returned from the administration building with a list of five social studies teachers who were available for transfer. Cirillo was not expecting him since Charles seldom came back to Andrew Jackson after he left for his other assignment at the Ad building. Chartwell was forced to wait until Pete completed his afterschool duties.

"Sorry to keep you waiting, Charles. Annette tells me you have something for me."

"I thought we could be proactive here, Pete, and replace Cullen with someone who has more experience and isn't so radical; more in line with what a teacher ought to represent these days. Then, if Jonas does get his license back, which I'm not sure will happen, he can be reassigned to another school, maybe a junior high, something that's less in the public eye." Chartwell handed Pete the list and continued while Pete looked it over. "Each of these teachers has at least five years of experience, and each one is in the system at one of our junior highs, so whichever one we take, Cullen could slide into the vacated position."

"Did you make up this list this afternoon?" asked Pete.

"No. I've had it in my desk. I haven't seen much in Cullen. Frankly, I think you might have missed on him, so I've been looking for a replacement for a few weeks. Guys like Cullen don't belong in education. A stint in the military might do him wonders."

"Pete lifted the first page of the list and glanced at the second. He then set it carefully down on his desk and looked up at Chartwell. "Why do you think Jonas won't get his license back?"

"There's been some talk at the Head Shed about his past. Seems like the Feds would like to make Cullen go away. We'd be better off if he returned to Montana and cut wood."

"Is this talk in a memo somewhere or just water cooler talk?"

"Nothing official. I think the Martin fellow on that list could step right in and be a real asset. He's the last name on the list."

Pete nodded slowly. "I interviewed Martin for a job two years back. He's a good man, but I didn't think he was a good fit here." Cirillo paused. "I don't know if you've noticed, but there are quite a few young men with long hair these days. Hard to tell which of them are communists just by that." The principal wasn't finished. "Have you taken the time to sit in on one of Jonas' classes?" It was a rhetorical question. "I've been in several times, and that young man has it going." Chartwell started to speak, but Pete cut him off. "I never know how a first-year teacher will turn out, but I like this one. He has energy and passion about this job and understands that he's here for our kids. Or should I say, 'my kids.' I'm not sure you've quite bought into that philosophy yet; that it's first and foremost about the kids. From what I'm hearing, you've created a bit of a stir among several of my teachers about being reassigned next year because of the desegregation issue too. I know for a fact that nothing has been decided about that, and yet you've given the staff some unnecessary stress because of your loose talk. An administrator, whether it be at the building level or the district level needs to be tight lipped, needs to be circumspect about what information is passed on, needs to know what is rumor as opposed to what is fact. The fact is, Charles, behind my back, you've contradicted the information that I've given them, and I will not tolerate that." Pete took a step into Charles. "As for Jonas, he's my hire, my teacher, and I'll get him back. As for you, don't come back tomorrow. I'll call your boss and have you reassigned to one of the other schools."

As Charles turned to leave, Pete added, "I won't pull any punches with your bosses either. Charm doesn't educate students. Get in the trenches and learn that."

§

On Wednesday Jonas called the Livingston, Montana, high school to inquire about his old job, but was told his license there was suspended too. Pete received a call from the district office on Thursday afternoon telling him that Jonas was cleared to teach again. According to the director, it was a clerical error, that the license had not been properly notarized before it was sent from

Montana over the summer. In addition, Jonas' Colorado license had been sent by the Department of Education and was now on file. Jonas was certain it had been, but Pete told him to let it go, to control his anger and his words. If he needed to talk, he was to speak only with Pete or Archie in the principal's office. Pete directed Jonas to tell his students that there had been a family emergency and leave it at that. How the FBI got involved was a mystery to the district.

§

On Monday, November 6, the day before the presidential election between Nixon and McGovern, Mr. Cullen presented the same lesson to each of his five sophomore classes. While some repetition occurred because many students were taking more than one social studies course, all the social studies teachers focused on the election. In other social studies classes, seniors old enough to vote were identified early in the semester, and nearly everyone had been registered. Now they were being quizzed by their fellow students about their vote the next day. During one of his planning periods, Jonas sat in on Archie King's Senior Problems class.

"Okay, you new voters, come take one of the chairs at the front of the room." Only seven of the twenty-eight students had turned eighteen and were eligible to take advantage of the Twenty-sixth Amendment. Archie turned the desks to face north rather than west so he could turn one bank of lights off and keep the other shining on the panel of new voters. Five girls and two boys. Only three weeks earlier, one of the girls, Liz, admitted to not caring who won, only to be subjected to the scathing sarcasm of Mr. King. Since then, Liz had become an enthusiastic supporter of George McGovern, wearing her beads and peace medallion each day. She even slapped a McGovern/Shriver bumper sticker on her Jeep.

A period of last questions; one last attempt for students to change one last vote. Archie pointed to a student at the back of the room to begin.

"Now that Nixon and Kissinger have announced that 'Peace is at hand,' what platform does McGovern have?"

"How about Nixon's a liar." The boy on the panel high-fived Liz.

"He's been promising peace for four years, and now that there's an election, he says the war is over. You can't believe him."

"The President has been a strong opponent of forced busing to achieve desegregation. It's an issue that will affect our community. Where does Senator McGovern stand?"

The three Democrats on the panel looked at one another for help. Finally, Liz spoke. "First of all, it's an issue that may affect our community. It's not certain. Beyond that, what's wrong with being integrated? Isn't it the law? You guys know as well as I do we get a better education here than they do over at Manual. Is that fair? Nixon's only against it so he can get votes from the South."

Archie assumed the role of teacher for a moment. "Since this class is so overwhelmingly Republican, let me play the devil's advocate." Before he could continue, one boy interrupted.

"Like it's hard for you to be against Nixon, right Mr. King." There was some clapping in support of the questioner.

"Regardless, the President has continued with most of LBJ's Great Society programs. Isn't this a continuation of big government?"

The Nixon panel had dressed up for the debate and was well-prepared. "Mr. King, Mr. King, Mr. King. If you haven't noticed, there's been a war going on, a war, we might add, begun by a Democratic president and then seemingly lost by another Democrat. The Congress has been controlled by the Democrats. Even a strong president such as Richard Nixon can only do so much in four years. He'll end the war in his first term and then tackle the burden of socialism in his second."

Another student continued along the same line. "Don't be surprised if on Wednesday we wake up to a Republican Congress. Then we'll see what happens to big government."

No one spoke for a moment prompting Jonas to ask a one-word question. "Watergate?"

All four Nixon supporters wanted to answer. "It's a nothing. It's an issue carried on by the liberal newspapers."

"Yeah, a couple of loose cannons, overzealous supporters of the President broke the law. Shit, only the *Washington Post* and the *New*

York Times care."

"It's 'shoot,' Norm."

"Sorry, Mr. King. I spend too much time around Coach Steib."

The rest of the period went on much the same, and Jonas slipped out after about a half hour. He later found out that no student vote had changed, which was not reflective of the class as a whole where the vote was twenty-two to six. The following day Richard Nixon won over sixty percent of the popular vote and carried forty-nine states. Only Massachusetts and the District of Columbia supported George McGovern.

§

At the end of the day, Jonas stopped by Mr. Cirillo's to respond to a note from the principal's secretary. Annette told Jonas that his first official observation was going to be in a week, on November 14, and that Pete would be coming to a U.S. History class.

Chapter 6

M r. Cirillo seated himself in the back right of Jonas Cullen's first period U.S. History class on Tuesday, November 14. The students were filing in past Jonas, who stood at the doorway and greeted each one. He generally touched each sophomore on the back shoulder, unless he was rapping one on the head for being a "knucklehead."

"Nice hat, Dale. Now take it off and don't let me see it again.

"You did a great job at state, Terry. Third in number three doubles is quite an accomplishment.

"Rainer, where will you be sitting today?" Rainer was the one kid who chose to ignore Jonas' seating chart and select her seat for the day based on personal whims.

"I don't know yet, Mr. C, maybe next to our two black kids." She laughed and waited to see if she had provoked Jonas.

"Might be a good idea, Rainer. If you get Rosie to sit with you, I'll have all the minorities grouped together."

"Real funny, Mr. C, but I don't think the Census Bureau lists redheads as an ethnic minority." She reached out and poked Jonas in the chest.

"Where's your book, Craig? Go back and get it. You'll need it today."

"But if I go back, I'll be late, Mr. Cullen."

"Yes, and it'll only cost you fifteen minutes after school today."

First period was Jonas' largest class at thirty-three students. At 8:00 o'clock the kids were subdued, and instead of trying to settle them down, Mr. Cullen was trying to get them aroused. When Rainer noticed the principal was in the room, she chose the seat next to him, forcing Alana Ritacco to sit in Rainer's assigned seat in the front row. The class knew and accepted the fact that one of them would be forced to sit directly in front of Mr. Cullen based on where Rainer chose to sit. Jonas liked it because a different student would be available for his antics each day.

As Jonas was taking roll and the class was getting out their notebooks, Rainer asked who the new student was, referring to Mr. Cirillo. "That would be Pete, but we'll be calling him Mr. Cirillo out of respect. Some of you in here know him quite well, judging from the amount of time you spend in his office." There was scattered laughter. "Okay, before I collect your homework, I want you to find your thesis statement in the first paragraph and underline it." He waited for two minutes and then collected the essays. Only two students did not have their homework. "Ian and Jeremy, I'll see you both during lunch, so you can finish your homework."

From there Mr. Cullen had the class do a three-part assignment. "First, I want you to do a drawing showing how King Cotton wielded such power over the politics and economics of the nation in the 1830s and 40s. Second, write a letter as a Southerner to a relative living in the North defending slavery. Make sure you show Southern attitudes toward the Peculiar Institution. Finally, draw a political cartoon using William Lloyd Garrison as the focus. I'll write all this on the board to help you remember, but you can get started with the first part."

The class got busy quickly. After Jonas finished writing the assignment on the board, he walked the aisles noting each student's progress. When he got to the back of the room next to Rainer, she tattled. "Mr. C, the new student isn't doing his assignment. I don't think that's fair to the rest of us." Pete Cirillo laughed.

"Well, Rainer," said Mr. Cullen, "I happen to know he's already passed this class some time ago and probably knows quite a bit about the causes of the Civil War."

Mr. Cirillo leaned over to Rainer. "The problem with first year teachers, Rainer, is they assume too much. I can't recall much about the lead-up to the Civil War. If you'll loan me a few sheets of paper, I'll take a crack at this."

Rainer tore out two pieces of paper from her notebook and then said, "Mr. C, the new kid came to class unprepared. Don't let him get off easy, or it'll set a bad example for the rest of us."

Betty "Friedan" Norton drew her picture as "Queen" Cotton, refusing to allow the male gender to gain any foothold. Jonas could always count on Betty to stand up to the class as the school's leading feminist. When someone began calling her Friedan instead of Norton, she adopted it and signed all her papers Betty Friedan. After grading the papers on Tuesday night, and knowing Betty could take a little teasing, Jonas would display her paper the next day. She had drawn Queen Cotton standing in the Atlantic Ocean reaching out with her right hand and holding on to Florida. One boy said aloud, "Now that woman understands how to control a man." The class got a good laugh, and Betty was embarrassed, but enjoyed the event.

After about twenty minutes, most of the class was working on the letter. Students would lean over to their neighbors and discuss the issues. "Use the Biblical references to slavery, doofus. We talked about it last Friday."

"The first part of the assignment gives you a clue to this part."

"Mr. Cullen, can we make this a letter to the President?"

Many of the students had not completed the assignment as the period ended. "Okay, listen up." Jonas returned to the front of the room and got the class's attention. "Since not all of you are finished, let's do this: Take this home and finish it, and I'll collect it tomorrow. If you're done and want to give it to me now, I'll take it."

"Do we get extra credit if we turn it in today?"

Jonas smiled at the inevitable question. "No, Karla." He returned to the whole class. "Also, you'll need to read the first eight pages of Chapter 17. It talks about the Compromise of 1850 and how it begins to break down." A collective class groan was cut short by the bell, and the students began to file out. Jonas collected a few of the assignments as he moved to the back of the room to speak with Mr. Cirillo. Without offering any feedback, Pete told Jonas he would review the observation with him on Wednesday during his first free period.

Rainer spoke loud enough for Pete to hear. "Mr. C, I think our new student is a slacker. He only tried the first assignment. Maybe he should be placed in the low-level classes." She turned and smiled at the principal and left.

"Enjoy that one, Jonas," said Pete Cirillo. "Her kind only comes around every four or five years."

§

Jonas was late for his appointment with Mr. Cirillo on Wednesday, because he had to break up a fight in the hall between two boys who were dating the same girl. Jonas waded through the crowd of onlookers and grabbed each boy by the hair. The one sophomore was bleeding from the nose, and much of the blood ended up on Jonas' white shirt. He dropped the boy with the nose-bleed off at the nurse's office and took the instigator down to the gym to face his football coach.

Pete Cirillo smiled when Jonas arrived at the office. "I hope that's not your blood." He motioned for Jonas to have a chair.

"No, I kept ducking. Got an extra white shirt laying around somewhere?"

"No, but I do have a sweater in my closet you can wear. I'll get it for you when we finish this." Pete took out a legal pad that held notes from yesterday's observation. "First off, what questions do you have about your presentation?"

"I don't know. Do I talk too loud?"

"Sometimes, but it's not a big deal. It'll come with experience. What else?"

"I don't spend much class time talking about school happenings and things like that. Some teachers do, and the kids seem to like it."

"The less class time you do, the better you'll be. Every once in a while, break the pattern, but keep it at a minimum. The kids will try to get you off track. Don't let them. Before and after class is enough to let them know you're interested."

"You were right about not knowing my stuff. It seems like every night I'm reading just for the next day. Will it get easier next year?"

"For you, yes."

"What do you mean *for me?*"

"Not all first-year teachers get better just because they become second-year teachers. We think you will, and to back that up, I want you to take some classes this summer up in Greeley, classes in gifted-and-talented education. You're doing a nice job with all your kids, but you seem to make a real connection with those top-level students, kids like Rainer and Jeremy and Julia."

"Every teacher connects with Rainer. She's responsible for the yellow cloth banner that hangs above the blackboard. She said my room was too blah and needed some color, something cheery and inspiring."

Pete tilted his head in agreement. "Yes, but not every teacher encourages her behavior like you do. She and I talked during class. She respects you because you challenge her, and she respects you because you challenge all your students in some way or another."

"There's a bunch of them I don't seem to be reaching."

"They're sophomores, Jonas. Hell, I mostly expect rookies to survive them, but you actually have them working hard. There wasn't a single kid who didn't do the assignment yesterday. That's good stuff."

"Thanks. What do I need to improve upon?"

"Well, you're not perfect yet. I wrote down a few things to begin with. Let's see. When you return homework, write comments on their papers. Just giving them a grade isn't enough feedback. I think you're just guessing on their grades, especially on the tweeners, the difference between say a B-minus and a C-plus. The comments will help you in determining those differences." Pete checked off that comment and went to number two. "You seem to be a bit tougher on your boys than girls when you ask questions. Are you missing the feminist movement?" Pete smiled. "Didn't your experience with that SDS radical in Boulder teach you anything?" Jonas knew the last part was a rhetorical question, but his mind began to drift back. "I think you're focusing a little too much on facts rather than on stressing skills, but most social studies teachers do, even my veterans. Get to know your students outside the classroom a bit. Vinny is a curious kid. Ask him about non-history things. Karla was in a body cast for a curved spine for over a year. Brittany and Alex work Saturdays at the Good Will. Like your own history, would your teachers have helped you if they didn't know your background? Finally, you seem to be enjoying this whole experience too damn much. That attitude gives all public school teachers a bad name, makes the public think anyone can teach. Tone it down some, okay."

Jonas smiled and nodded, understanding his boss's humor. "I have to tell you, you watched me on my best day so far. They haven't all been so successful."

"That could be said for any teacher. Some days are better than others regardless of whether you're a rookie or a seasoned veteran. Tell me about Cliff Steuben."

Jonas thought for a second. "He's as smart as they come, and I think he has the top score in my government class. He's got his little clique of friends, and they stay mostly to themselves."

"Jonas, we've had some reports he's bullying several of his classmates, kids who aren't as bright as he is. One girl in particular has been missing school, and her mother blames Cliff. Dave and Elyse say he can be quite a handful and not too respectful to them at times."

Jonas was thinking about his class with that group. "Honestly, I either haven't noticed, or they haven't been doing it in my class."

Cirillo got up and walked to his closet to get Jonas the sweater. "I suspect you haven't noticed, so be alert. By the way, Jonas, how's the coaching coming?"

"I have twenty kids who can't shoot a layup, can't dribble, and don't want to play defense. My best player is five foot nothing and weighs a hundred pounds. But the plus side is they don't know yet that I haven't got a clue."

"How long until your first game?"

"We start before the varsity, December 2nd, Saturday morning over at Thomas Jefferson. One kid plays every minute, and I divide the rest among the other nineteen kids. It'll be an adventure." Jonas checked his watch. "I better get going."

"Jonas, you're doing a good job. Try to catch up on your sleep, though. Nodding off during teachers' meetings is bad form."

"Okay, Mr. Cirillo, I'll try."

§

The pendulum swung for Jonas' Friday classes, and when he met Elyse, Dave, and Laura for beers at the Cherry Cricket, he was exhausted. His friends were already on their second beers when Jonas dropped himself into the booth. "Sorry I'm late, guys. I had to deal with a couple of my little goofballs after school. They wore me out last period when I was already done in. Days like this make me wonder why I chose this profession. I could be driving trucks in Montana for better money." He waved his hand to get the waitress' attention, signaling for the symbolic two beers right away. Then he dropped his head on Elyse's shoulder and moaned.

"Poor baby," consoled Elyse in mock sympathy. "Maybe you're not the badass you pretend to be."

Laura leaned across the table and cuffed Jonas on the forehead. "Jonas, this is how I feel every day." She wasn't kidding, and Elyse knew that Laura had contemplated quitting several times.

It was quiet for a moment before Dave spoke. "I think it's harder for women at the high school level than guys. Maybe it's just that fewer women teach math or science, disciplines that are more structured. I don't have to put myself out there like you and Jonas. Math teachers don't have to discuss the relative merits of formulas or vote on multiplication tables. Math just is, so the kids accept math teachers just as we are. We don't have to prove anything. Laura, your job is so much tougher."

Laura smiled. "Thanks, Dave. I know you're trying to make me feel better, and I appreciate it, but I'm just the weak link here. It'll take me longer to become a good teacher than you three stars."

"Do you see any stars here, guys?" asked Elyse.

"Not me. Just four rookies trying to get by," answered Dave.

"Stars? Nope, just a cluster of black holes trying to get through their first year," added Jonas. He held up his beer glass for a toast.

"To teaching."

"No, to teachers," said Dave.

"To rookie teachers," said Elyse.

"To clueless, rookie teachers," said Laura with a smile.

They clinked their glasses and swigged their beers and called for the waitress to bring another round.

As the evening wore on, the beer made them more philosophical. As usual Jonas and Elyse monopolized the conversation. "You guys ever fly-fish?" he asked.

"Here we go again," moaned Elyse.

"No, really. Sometimes I think teaching is like fishing. We're tied to our students as if by an invisible line, just like the fisherman and the fish. Today, I didn't read the hatch . . ."

"Or the barometer," interrupted Elyse.

". . . *the hatch* . . . properly, and so I wasn't successful. We're all fishing in a new stream, and it takes time to read the water. Our principal has assigned us small fish to catch . . . sophomores . . . but they're still not easy. As I said, we need to learn how to read the water."

"Can't we just net them?" asked Laura.

"Couldn't we just shoot 'em?" added Dave.

"You don't shoot fish," said Jonas.

"You've never gone after carp, have you?"

Elyse laughed. "What fly were you offering your last period, Jonas?"

"That's the point, smartass. It's Friday; it's last hour; I assign them thirty minutes to read their textbook; and I want them to do it quietly. That's not going to work. It's like offering a trout a terrestrial at this time of the year."

Laura opened her eyes and asked, "What's a terrestrial?"

"A grasshopper or an ant," answered Jonas.

"So, it's a metaphor for an assignment, huh?" Laura closed her eyes again.

"What kind of pole are you using?" asked Elyse.

"Small one for small fish," answered Dave.

"Anyone ever seen it?" asked Elyse.

"Where are you going with this?" asked Laura.

"Not far with you guys. All I'm saying is . . . teaching is an art, just like fly-fishing. You can't be successful in just one season, or just one year. It's going to take time, for all of us." Jonas nodded his head as if he approved his explanation himself.

"Do the fish have any responsibility to get caught, or do they get a free pass?" asked Elyse. Dave and Laura laughed.

"Do fly fisherman drink to excess?" asked Laura.

"Oh, yes." Jonas stood and waved to the waitress.

"How are we getting home?" asked Elyse.

"Fishermen always find their way home. Don't you worry about it." The waitress brought four more beers. After two swallows, Jonas excused himself to go to the toilet. He returned in four minutes and slid back into Elyse's thigh. A half hour later, Archie King drove the four rookies home.

CHAPTER 7

"Cullen! Hey, Cullen!"

It's Thursday and Jonas is studying for a French Revolution test, the mid-term exam in his toughest class. His roommate seldom studies yet makes passing grades in every subject. Math majors, thinks Jonas.

"Come on, Jonas. Let's go get a bite to eat. We don't have much in the frig for dinner. You can study when we get back. Besides, Colleen said she'd buy. Can't pass that up." Grabowski goes through so many women Jonas can barely keep up, but Colleen seems to reappear monthly. When she comes, she always brings a friend for Jonas, as a joke, and she is bringing one over tonight.

"Jeez, Grabo, not a good night." Jonas gives himself an out just in case Colleen's friend isn't appealing. The last friend she brought over was a chain smoker.

Abby . . . Abby Archer . . . is shockingly beautiful. She arrives wearing cut-off jeans, sandals, and a men's blue dress shirt rolled up to her elbows with only two middle buttons buttoned. And nothing else. She has long, ironed-straight brown hair, heavy dark eye make-up, and huge breasts, one of two reasons why Jonas' friends will nickname her "Bags." After a brief introduction, Grabowski jokes that Jonas said he has a test to study for and isn't hungry.

Abby jumps right in. "Me neither. Colleen, why don't you and Ray go, and I'll stay here with Jonas and help him study." Jonas smiles at his roommate and deliberately closes his history textbook. Then Abby pulls a five-dollar bill out of her back pocket and hands it to Colleen. "Didn't you say you wanted to see *Bonnie and Clyde*? It's playing on The Hill."

When Colleen and Ray leave, Abby settles herself on the high-backed couch and pats the cushion next to her, a signal for Jonas to join her. From her purse, she takes out a plastic bag and rolls a doobie, lights it, and sucks it in. After a second hit, she hands it to Jonas who waves it away. "So, Jonas, where're you from?"

"Montana. Up north of Yellowstone. Indian country. You?"

"I've practiced this line. I'm from nowhere now. I'm just here." She giggles and takes another hit. "So, Jonas Cullen, you don't smoke dope?"

"Nah. I'm more of an beer guy from Montana. Cowboys aren't supposed to use drugs."

Abby pinches the end of her joint and puts it back into the plastic bag. She unbuttons the two buttons on her shirt. It is 5:45.

Jonas nods at Abby. He stands in front of her, pulls his Denver Bronco tee-shirt over his head, unbuttons his jeans and steps out of them, and smiles.

"I think I've just found my new boyfriend," says Abby with a big grin.

For the next two hours, Jonas and Abby alternately have sex and talk, even arguing over politics. Around a quarter to 8:00 and unable to get it up again for the moment, Jonas suggests they go get burgers and fries.

It is unseasonably warm in Boulder this October in 1967. Jonas and Abby walk the three blocks to McDonald's holding hands but saying very little. The street traffic along Arapahoe makes small talk difficult. At Mickey-D's Abby orders a cheeseburger, fries, and a soda while Jonas gets the Big Mac meal with iced-tea.

"Weener said you didn't have a girlfriend," says Abby as they settle into a booth.

"Weener?"

"Colleen. Just a dumb nickname. Anyway, do you have a girlfriend?"

"Nope, not at the moment, unless I hold you to your words earlier *tonight." Jonas flashes a smile.*

"You can."

"I don't know though. You're just so shy."

Abby looks down into her soda. "Actually, I've always been kind of shy with boys. I just transferred here this semester from Greeley. The girl down the hall is a dealer, and for the last month I've been smoking dope five or six times a week."

Jonas thinks about that for a moment. "Are you coupling that with sex like we did tonight?"

"God no! This was a dare." Abby wonders if Jonas is buying her story, even though it is all true. "I've seen two boys since I've been here, but it was nothing like this. Weener said she had this routine of bringing over a girl for you whenever she dated your roommate and asked me if I'd come. A couple of our friends at the house said you were good looking and nice, so I said yes. Then we smoked a few joints, and the shit-talking began. These aren't even my shorts."

"Why'd you transfer?"

"Greeley's boring. I come from a family of activists. In high school, I was the anti-war leader, and that was '65. My parents are union leaders, run a soup kitchen in downtown Chicago, and are in charge of collecting a slush fund in case of strikes. Activism is in my blood."

"Why'd you start at Greeley then?"

Abby finishes her soda. "I need a refill. Want anything?"

Jonas nods and pushes his change across the table to her. He watches as she stands at the counter to get the drinks. Somewhere she has found a black bra. Why a woman like Abby is available is a mystery to him.

Back at the table Abby slurps an ice cube out of her soda and tucks it inside her cheek. "Northern Colorado has a reputation as a teachers' college, and I want to teach in the city. Also, Greeley is a meat-packing town that needs union agitation. And it wasn't Chicago. Seemed like a good decision at the time."

Jonas puts his chin in his cupped hands and smiles. "Well, girlfriend, I'm glad you came here." He pauses, and they stare at each other. In a moment he asks, "Is there a time when you have to be back in the dorm?"

"In theory at midnight, but since my grades are good and I'm a

junior, they never check on me. There's no rush. Are you ready to walk back?"

Traffic has quieted, and now they continue. Jonas tells Abby he will most likely fail his history test, but it's a good trade-off.

"Jonas, if you're going to be my boyfriend, you've got to help me with something."

"What's that?"

"I need to cut back on my marijuana use. I don't want to quit, but maybe just on the weekends. Okay?" Abby stops walking and turns to look at Jonas. "I'm serious."

Jonas puts his hands on her shoulders in a mock pose of seriousness. "We won't have to cut back on the sex, will we?"

Abby doesn't go back to her dorm, and she doesn't smoke any more dope. Over the next two school years, more than any other activity, Abby and Jonas argue politics.

§

By November, Abby is preaching to Jonas about the anti-war move-ment and is frustrated because he has refused to become as involved as she is. By December, her frustration has turned to anger. To her, it seems only logical her boyfriend should be as committed to radical politics as she is.

"You must take a stand now, Jonas! NOW!"

"No, I don't, Abby." Jonas doesn't know whether to pretend anger or act cool and aloof. He knows either attitude will piss her off. He chooses anger. "You tell me, what's a leftist? I don't know! Because of your parents, you understand socialism more than the rest of us, but I don't, and neither do any of your fellow radicals."

"Fuck you, Jonas, you coward! You don't have to be a radical leftist to know what America is supposed to stand for and what it actually is today don't coincide. The war is . . . "

Jonas interrupts her. "What do you really know about the war? It's a guy thing. Guys get drafted; guys go to Vietnam; guys get killed. You're being taken in by grad students. Co-opted, duped, used."

"Jeez, Jonas! That's why you have to commit. Most guys will drop out of the movement when the war ends, but we need some white boys

with a backbone. You're against the war, so why not stand up? What are you afraid of?" When Abby's anger rises to this level, two things happen. During the argument, she blinks her eyes excessively and bobs her head. When the fighting stops, she can't wait to jump into bed with Jonas.

"So, white boys' activism is only about the draft?"

"Hell yes! You guys will drop out and return to the Republican mainstream when the war ends. Women and blacks will continue because our repression is real and continuous. White boys are just pretenders!"

Jonas is thinking about this, even as he resists. "So why do you need me?"

Abby's head stills and her blinking stops. She takes a deep breath and walks into Jonas. "Because, my dear, I want you to. You're this incorruptible dude that people listen to. You're not like the rest of the guys in the movement."

"Oh yeah, me and Mario Savio."

"Shut up, won't you. You're a presence, Jonas, and you could make a difference."

"Bags, I just don't believe a revolution will happen. Any changes will take time. You've convinced me I can make a difference, but it won't be by storming the barricades."

"You'll see, Jonas. It's time for violence." The time for arguing has ended, and the time for sex has begun. Jonas will tell his roommate that arguing with Abby is just foreplay.

§

Jonas brings the terrible news of Dr. King's murder to Abby while she is studying at the library. He knows where to find her because earlier in the day, he dropped an encyclopedia from the balcony onto the table where she was studying. For the first three months of 1968, they have avoided one another, but Abby has asked Jonas if they can try it again after spring break. She is using new drugs, and they scare her, and only with Jonas does she limit herself to marijuana. "A sex addiction is better than a drug addiction."

Abby admires King but believes he has become mostly irrelevant.

Only his position that the civil rights and anti-war movements should be fused keeps him viable. Instead of joining the university candle-light vigil on the night of April 4, Jonas and Abby light candles at his apartment and talk about America while watching Walter Cronkite on TV. It is one of the few times she doesn't end up screaming at Jonas.

"I always try to act like such a tough ass here, Jonas. I purposely never asked about your life before we met, but tonight, I want to go back to the America before all this shit occurred." Jonas is holding Abby's head in his lap rubbing her temples, as they sit on the floor. "I was a happy kid. I started piano lessons before I started school and dance lessons shortly afterward. I was good too. Maybe even gifted. I loved the recitals. So did my parents. They were proud of me."

"I suspect they still are." Jonas tilts his head to look at the enigma who is again his girlfriend.

"Yeah, Unitarians tend to be pretty tolerant, and I'm the second kid. Mom says second kids are always a bit rebellious, so she puts up with it."

"I never even thought about whether you might have brothers and sisters. How many?"

"I'm one of five. Two brothers and two sisters. My older sister is five years older than me; the rest of us are kind of bunched up. Jackie married a Quaker right out of high school and already has two children. Not for me." Abby looks away, far away, and Jonas waits for her. She changes the subject when she returns. "I'm a pretty good tennis player too."

Jonas sits up. "I'll play you for dinner sometime. Do you think you could take a beating and not yell at me?"

Abby doesn't answer the question. Instead, she nods her head at the television and moves back to the King murder. "Doesn't look like the black community is following the Doctor's prescription for non-violence, does it."

"Where have you put your anger tonight?"

"It's never far away, Jonas. I don't know where it comes from either. Every time I sense stupidity or deceitfulness, I just explode." She shakes her head.

"Which am I, stupid or deceitful?"

"Neither. I don't know why I take it out on you." Abby sits up and gives Jonas a kiss on the cheek. "Not fair, is it?"

"I don't think either one of us believes in the concept of fair. What happened tonight to Dr. King isn't fair. Besides, you more than make up for your tirades with me in other ways."

"Now you're being suggestive."

"No," reacts Jonas, "I don't mean it quite like that. You're," he pauses, "this is going to sound corny, but you're my best friend these days. I know I disappoint you, but I am going to be a teacher . . . in the inner-city, and that's partly because of your influence."

"So, you're not going back to Indian country and teach in your hometown?" Abby is reacting in mock surprise.

"I say something serious, and you make fun of me. You only understand one thing, huh. Would it be disgraceful to have sex on this day?" Jonas hesitates for an instant and then tackles Abby.

She smiles. "Tonight, be gentle. We'll try it a new way."

§

The phone at the Cullen house in Livingston, Montana, rings just after three in the morning on June 5, 1968. Jonas answers, knowing it is Abby. "Where are you, Abby?"

"Oh, Jonas! Are you watching? They just shot Bobby!" Just after winning the California primary, a Palestinian-born Arab who has lived in America for a decade guns down Bobby Kennedy. Despite advocating a complete revolution for America, Abby loves Kennedy.

"Abby, where are you?"

It's obvious Abby is crying, nearly hysterical, but Jonas' tone seems to calm her down. He can hear her trying to gather herself, sniffling and gulping for air. "I'm in Los Angeles. I was at the hotel until a few hours ago but left to march in the streets. Jonas, he won! Bobby won!"

In a very calm voice, Jonas responds. "I know, Bags, I've been watching all night. My family stayed up until they announced the results. I just woke up my dad. Maybe Bobby'll be okay."

"I heard he was dead. Everybody's saying they killed him."

"No. They're taking him to the hospital. We don't know yet. Abby, can you get to the airport?"

§

Jonas meets Abby in Great Falls, Montana, the closest airport she can fly into on June 6. The drive from Livingston has taken just over three hours, but the return trip at the speed limit the next day takes over four. They stay at the Motel 6 in Great Falls, the only night Jonas ever remembers when they stay together and don't have sex.

Back in Livingston the "Explosive Abby Archer" is introduced to the Cullen clan and begins to unwind. She stays until the end of June before flying back to her home in Des Plaines, Illinois. When she leaves, Jonas' current mother cannot understand how she got the nickname "Explosive," but Mrs. Cullen knows Abby has some demons.

"Jonas, there were times when you and your father were at the mill, and I would find her curled up on the couch or on the porch just shaking. As soon as she'd notice me, she'd jump up and offer to help with whatever I was doing, but I could tell she was upset at herself. I tried to talk with her about it, but she wouldn't say. She kept asking when you would be home." Mrs. Cullen looks at Jonas for answers.

"Patty, I've spent hours and hours trying to figure her out. You've seen her on her best behavior. She needed to be here, and I think it's been good for her, but honestly, I don't think she'll change. Next time I see her, especially if it's in Boulder, she'll go off."

"About what?"

"The first thing she disagrees with, which can be just about anything."

Jonas' dad, the silent Cullen, shakes his head. "That's about the prettiest woman I've ever seen, but she scares me. She's on edge every moment. She was holding herself in the whole time."

"Jonas, are you all right with all this? Do you need to step away from her?" asks Patty.

"Yeah, I'm okay, Patty. And, no, I won't abandon her." He smiles both sheepishly and with determination.

CHAPTER 8

On Friday, December 15, Andrew Jackson High School held its traditional pre-Christmas faculty meeting, a gift exchange in conjunction with an after-school snack. Women who drew women's names bought candles, clothing, or jewelry. Men who drew men's names bought books and sporting goods. The humorous moments came when a man drew a female faculty member. Pete Cirillo drew Laura Sanders, but he had his secretary for guidance. Laura smiled at her new Eiffel Tower in winter jigsaw puzzle. Mrs. Bentert rolled her eyes when she opened a box containing a copy of the December issue of *Playboy* magazine and a silver boa, compliments of Archie King. In good humor, Jonas traded his Christmas candle for the magazine.

The assistant principal handed out duty assignments for second semester, and Coach Ragni made a general plea to the staff to give his star player, John Bosley, every possible benefit on finals so the basketball team would have a chance to make it to the state playoffs in March. He promised the staff one of his wife's famous spaghetti dinners if they did. As Pete Cirillo took the dais in the library for his message, he kidded the basketball coach for his "shameless groveling."

"Well, people, good job this first semester. We have four days to go, but I've been proud of you up to now. A couple of you have been in to ask about what's ahead for next year with the desegregation thing hanging over our heads, so I thought I'd address the question with the entire staff." He took a drink from the eggnog, smiled, and toasted the home economics staff. "As you know, the U.S. Supreme Court heard arguments about Denver's overall plan in October. They're supposed to render a decision in the late spring. I don't have a crystal ball, but I've been in touch with Superintendent Johnson and Mayor McNichols." He paused. "Yes, I hobnob with the bigwigs." He continued, "They both seem to think the Court will rule Denver is not in compliance with desegregation guidelines. It's a pretty liberal court. If they do, our demographics will certainly change. We've all seen an inkling of white flight, but we expect more of our kids to move out of our district and into the southern and western suburbs. No plan will be put in place for next year, but the school board will act fast, so maybe for the fall of '74, and I think we're looking at busing. I tell you this not to alarm you, but I know some of you are not interested in teaching . . ." Cirillo searched carefully for the right phrase. "I know a few of you would be more comfortable teaching middle-class kids." A low murmur spread across the library as the principal paused.

"Superintendent Johnson does not believe any high school teachers will be reassigned to other buildings. Maybe, at first, some elementary teachers will, but not secondary. Again, I don't know for sure what the Supreme Court will decide or how our school board will react, but I'm giving you a heads up in case you'd like to pursue a different teaching venue. Any of you who do will have my complete support, and I can guarantee you I'll write a fair recommendation that does not include any comments on this issue." Cirillo had a handle on his staff and knew most of them would not be affected by which kids showed up in their classroom. They would work hard and teach them regardless of race or economic background. "Any questions?"

"Pete, is there any chance Denver will simply annex areas to help prevent white flight?"

"They've been doing that to some degree, but the problem is simply the more affluent just move farther out. Hard to say."

"Mr. Cirillo."

"Yes, Ellie."

"If all this happens, will training be available for us who are . . .

how should I say this . . . inexperienced?"

"No doubt. If the District doesn't do it, we will here."

The woodshop teacher, Gary Dessins, stood to make a comment. "Pete, you know as well as I do that forcing this on Denver won't improve our schools or lessen tensions. It's judicial social engineering, and it's not gonna work. How do we stop it?" He remained standing after his question.

"Gary, I don't know that," said the principal. "Maybe our kids will learn better in a multi-racial school, and by our kids I mean the new kids, the blacks and Chicanos. I believe you guys are the best teachers available. We'll have some obstacles to overcome, certainly, and there will be bumps in the road, but we'll continue to offer a great education for whoever walks through our doors."

Dessins didn't back down. "You know I'm not leaving, but damn it, we'll look back on this and see it for what it is, a damn experiment." He sat down.

"It is that, Gary. It is an experiment, and we're the guinea pigs."

Cirillo looked around the library for other questions, but there were none. Dessins spoke out again. "I didn't mean to stifle discussion here. I'm just an old fifteen-year guy who hates change. If you got a question, speak up."

From between the stacks, from the 800 classification on the Dewey Decimal System, a redheaded student appeared. As she began to speak, all faculty heads turned. "Mr. Cirillo, if the Court says Denver has to bus black kids to Andrew Jackson, does that also imply that some of us will be bused into town? Could some of us students be sent to, say, Manual or North?"

"Ah, Rainer, nice to see you catching up on the latest literature." He smiled at her. "For those of you who haven't had the pleasure, this is Rainer Brecht, our most precocious sophomore. Yes, Rainer, that will happen. We focus so much on whether or not blacks will come here, but it will mean we'll lose some of ours."

"I'm not going! I'm not prejudiced, and I'll be happy to have blacks here, but this is my school, and I'm staying. I just live ten blocks from here."

Jonas was sitting near where she was standing. He stood and

walked over to her. "Mr. Cirillo, I'll adopt Rainer if that will help." After the laughter died down, along with a smattering of applause, Jonas gave her a pat on the back.

Pete Cirillo held up his hand for order. "We've been here much longer than I anticipated, so let me close. Rainer's sentiments reveal a great deal about what's ahead. Many of those kids from the inner city won't want to leave their neighborhoods either. They'll feel uncomfortable here. If the Court forces us to integrate rapidly by any means, there will be some real hard feelings. But I have this feeling Andrew Jackson will be up to the task. Rainer, somehow we'll make sure you stay."

Jonas led Rainer to his seat and stood behind her. Cirillo nodded to the choir director to lead them in a parting Christmas song. Darkness had fallen on Andrew Jackson as the faculty softly sang *Silent Night*.

§

Pete, Archie, and Annette sat in Pete's office long after the teachers left, drinking a scotch and winding down. Archie's glass was empty except for the ice, and Pete asked him if he wanted a refill. Archie declined.

"Thanks, but me and Annette gotta get going. You've got a nice staff, you know."

"You're right there. Dessins can be a horse's ass, but he always seems to step up. He's a foxhole guy, that's for sure."

Annette had her legs extended out from Pete's swivel chair, looking as if she could nod off at any moment. "The redheaded student was pretty impressive. I thought for a minute it might have been your kid, honey."

Archie reached over and squeezed Annette's hand. "She does have some spunk, doesn't she?" He turned his head to Pete. "They're gonna take this out of your hands one day, you know. Give it up to politicians and judges. It'll go in the tank then."

"It's already happening. They don't care like we do; like Gary or Marlene or Cyndy or Johanna or Mike do. I honestly don't know what the right answer is, but I do know their criterion is votes. We need to do a better job of integrating our schools, but hell, nobody really wants busing."

Archie sat up a little straighter. "We've always bused students, but it was in the direction that whites wanted to go. If this new busing isn't done correctly, they'll rip the soul out of the public schools, but it's long overdue."

Pete shook his head in disgust. "Some Washington politician will get on the education bandwagon and come up with some slogan like 'Educating Every Kid,' but won't ever really fund the program where it needs to be. His kids will probably be educated in some expensive, private school too."

Annette opened her eyes again. "Does your wife ever get to see you, Pete?"

§

After treating Rainer to a quick burger and fries, the rookies decided to meet at Elyse's apartment. Jonas and Laura drove Rainer home, Dave went for snacks, and Elyse went home to "straighten up the place and make it presentable." Her apartment was decorated mostly in purple and smelled like olive oil. Unlike Jonas' and Dave's places, Elyse's furniture matched. Then again, her parents lived in a south Denver suburb and were financially able to help support her. Of the four first-year teachers, only Elyse had original pictures on her walls instead of posters.

"Are the roads getting any slicker?" asked Elyse.

"Starting to. We'll all just have to stay here tonight," said Dave.

As they settled in, the four young teachers talked about their first semester, their successes and their failures. They laughed at themselves, about their ignorance in handling situations, about their favorite students, and about those kids who should be locked up, which, when they dissected them, were very few. All seemed happy with their choice to become a teacher, even Laura, who was still struggling with discipline. In time the conversation turned toward the faculty meeting and Mr. Cirillo's remarks about busing.

"I didn't choose Andrew Jackson. It chose me," said Jonas. Archie came and got me. He won't tell me how he knew I was in

Livingston; says he will someday, but he hasn't so far. I didn't want to remain in Montana. I liked to work outdoors, the idea of working alone--it's how I was raised--but many Montana men get stuck driving trucks or working at a sawmill or a lumberyard. Andrew Jackson might become the place where I hoped to teach when I was in college."

Elyse scrunched her forehead. "How's that?"

Jonas was sitting backward on a straight-backed chair at the dining room table. He got up and moved the chair closer to the group. "During my junior year, I decided I wanted to teach in the inner city. It became my thing. I'd often thought about teaching, but it became a more focused pursuit at CU. My girlfriend was a flaming radical, always frustrated I wouldn't join the revolution, but she did influence me a bit on doing something about social change. Maybe this was the path of least resistance."

"Was this the mysterious Abby Archer?" asked Laura.

"Yep, I was a reluctant warrior. I never made the connection between a good education and equality. I simply wanted to stand in front of my class and teach history or something. Abby pulled me into the movement up in Boulder, but I never was totally committed to her revolution. Teaching for me was what I had experienced as a student. I didn't see the social change part."

"Any new word on her?" asked Elyse.

"Nope."

"What about you, Laura? Are you going stay?" asked Dave.

"I don't know yet. The nice thing about being a Spanish teacher is I have lots of options. School districts are dying for us, and there are lots of jobs in the business sector." She was nursing her beer. "Remember what Cirillo said to us that first week, that if we survived, he'd have us back?"

"He's been a rock for me," said Elyse. "I have a catty group of girls fourth period. Haven't been able to teach very effectively because of them, but he's supported me. And there's Cliff Steuben. Devious little turd!"

Jonas shook his head. "I've never told anyone about this, kind of embarrassed, but the third week of school I had a little kid tell me to 'go to hell.' I thought I'd give him a chance to apologize, so I asked him 'What did you say?' He repeated himself, so I grabbed him out of his desk and carried him into the hall. He just wouldn't stop swearing, so I picked him up and held him against the lockers. Just then, Cirillo walks around the corner. I'm sure my face was on fire, which is how it gets when I really lose my temper. I thought for sure I'd be fired. He looked at the kid, then at me, and said 'Nice job. Keep up the good work.' As he walked away, with me still holding the kid against the lockers, he told me to see him in his office later in the day. I've got this temper thing."

Dave laughed. "What did he tell you then?"

"Just the same thing. I was doing good things, and sometimes the class needed to see I had a limit to my tolerance. He did suggest I try to tone it down a notch though. He asked me if he needed to call the kid in, but I told him no. That kid hasn't been a problem since."

Elyse leaned forward on the couch. "Okay, guys. Best class."

Dave went first. "Easy. Sixth period Algebra I. Those little sophomores are smart. Eighteen boys and seven girls, but the girls are battling every test to make the top scores. Because of that, no girl slacks off. Danny Castle still gets the highest score on each test, but the gap is closing. Rainer's in that class, and she's really improved her math skills. It's just fun every day."

As Laura and Jonas thought, Elyse spoke. "I thought it was going to be my biology class at first, but it's not the subject matter that determines it. It's the makeup of the kids. My earth science classes are all good, but third hour is the best. They're the class that played the prank on me, about the phony earthquake in California. As it turned out, they did it because they liked me. My mama's been my biggest supporter. As I think I've told you, she was a teacher for a while and encourages me to hang in there during these first few years, and that I will get better. Focus on my strengths and put most of my energy there. Sadie's in that class as my aide, and she's such a precious little thing. She won't allow me to stay in a bad mood."

"No contest," said Laura. "First hour. They're the quietest, but I have some good students in each class. I just need to learn how to quiet my classes down without showing my frustration, but it's so much better than it was a month ago."

It was Jonas' turn, but he had a dilemma. All his classes were enjoyable, even if they were a bit rowdy at times, especially his afternoon classes. He liked teaching both history and current events. He was smart and prepared, and he had a great supervisor in Archie King. They talked almost daily about methodology, about situations, and about the profession in general. His dilemma was he didn't want to brag in front of Laura. "Does it have to be a class, Elyse?"

"I guess not."

"Well, my biggest surprise has been my coaching. What I mean is we've actually won three games out of the five we've played, and it just blows my mind. My kids are having fun, and they all know I'm a dunce out there. During games, I just rotate them in four at a time. Only little Jack Winge plays all the time. He's just the glue."

"Are you going to take Ragni's place when he retires?" kidded Dave. "Did you ever even play basketball?"

"Not really, just a little in high school, but don't tell Ragni. I just played some intramurals at CU."

"So, you're faking it?" asked Laura.

"Yep, but Pete saw through it right away. He knew I didn't have to be a college player to coach underclassmen."

Elyse wanted to add one more thing. "Surprisingly, sort of like Jonas' coaching, I'm enjoying my lunch duty. It's like what high school really is. I'd forgotten how much I liked lunch when I was in high school. The way kids move around, where they sit, who interacts with whom. It's such a laboratory! Our classes are so regulated we don't see what's really going on in the minds of our students. I don't think I'll want lunch duty my whole life, but this has been so interesting to me."

"I'm hungry," said Laura. "What do you guys want? Ellie and I will throw something together."

"How about cheese sandwiches?" said Elyse. "I can do those."

The boys agreed anything would be fine. Once the seed had been planted about spending the night, the crew settled in and continued to drink. After four months of sharing problems, they were comfortable enough to say almost anything.

"I need to talk now, before I pass out like I always do. You'd think I'd get better at this, but it's always two or three beers and 'Goodnight, guys, for me." Laura was already slowing her cadence.

"What do you think, Laur? Do we talk about you when you're passed out?" Dave was stretched out on the floor in front of the couch.

"I would hope so. I'm such an interesting case." Laura was being sarcastic.

"The boys don't know about your musical background. Can I tell them?"

"Sure, Ellie. They'll be surprised I'm competent at something."

"Shit, Laura, don't be so hard on yourself." Jonas was serious. Listening to Laura criticize herself each weekend got old to him.

Elyse realized this and jumped in. "Anyway, Laura was the bass guitarist in a rock band while she was in college."

"Pretty damn good band, if I say so myself."

"What was the band's name?" asked Dave.

"Great Lips. Ever hear of it?"

Jonas sat up. "I'll bet I saw you play in Boulder."

"We played there a lot before we broke up in '69."

"You guys were a hellacious band! Why'd you break up?"

"Drugs." Laura was fading fast. "Two of the band members were in such bad shape, they'd miss gigs. On stage they got so bad we'd get booed at FAC."

"That is pretty bad," said Dave, but Laura probably didn't hear him. Her head had fallen back against the high-backed occasional chair.

Elyse grabbed Jonas' eyes. "You need to lighten up with her. She's having a hard year. She's the kid here, unlike you with all your worldly experiences. She can tell when you act like that. She already feels bad enough about her inadequacies."

"She doesn't have to whine about it every weekend. None of us were guaranteed our classes would be filled with angels. We all have our problems." Jonas caught himself and backed off. "You're right.

I need to have a little empathy. Sorry."

Dave sided with Elyse. "Just don't roll your eyes at her. Look away if you have to."

"No, I really do need to lighten up and try to understand. I do, I think, I just get frustrated when she continually brings it up."

Elyse reached across the couch and touched Jonas' thigh. "Just try, okay?"

§

Elyse put a blanket over Laura who was out for the night. Dave got a pillow and a blanket and slept on the floor, saying the couch was too short, giving it up to Jonas. Dave fell asleep quickly. Elyse and Jonas sat on the couch and continued to talk. The conversation turned serious and very quiet.

"You hide your anger pretty well most of the time, you know," said Elyse almost in a whisper.

"You don't miss much, do you?"

"Women's intuition." Elyse reached up and turned off the switch for the overhead light. Then she slid into Jonas' shoulder. "Where's it come from?"

"That's a hard one. In high school, I was always angry. Lots of fights." He turned to show Elyse the scar under his chin and the one along his left eyebrow. "You probably noticed my nose isn't entirely straight."

"Doesn't matter, you're still cute." She thought about kissing him again but restrained herself. "What hurts, Jonas?"

She allowed him to think about his answer. Finally, he spoke. "Because, I think, maybe because I'm lonely. Always have been." He immediately wished he hadn't said it, but now it was out, and like once before, he decided to take a chance. "My mom disappeared when I was a baby. Just disappeared. Nobody knows where or why. I don't know to this day whether she's alive or dead. My dad worked a lot just to survive. I spent lots of days by myself when I was young. One day, I think when I was in about sixth grade, my dad brought home a new wife and told me I had a new mother. Nice lady. Lasted two years, then one day she just left. At least she had the decency to say goodbye. I called her mom, but it never felt like she was. Then there was Doris. She's my brother's mother. Never called her mom." Jonas shook his head, amazing himself with the details. "Doris left during my first year in college. My current mom is Patty. I like her, but she's just another woman in the house. She tries, and I think she'll stay. My brother likes her."

Elyse spoke softly. "Anger from loneliness. I never thought about that."

"I'm not sure it's just that easy. In grade school the kids called me Joanie, just to tease me. I was kind of withdrawn for a while. We moved around a bunch. We didn't live in the same town for longer than a year or two until my high school years. We always rented. Another way you and I are different." Jonas withdrew for a moment and Elyse waited for him. "Anyway, around the fifth or sixth grade, I got bigger than most of the guys. I got even fast. My dad kind of encouraged it."

"Encouraged what?' asked Elyse.

"Fighting."

"When was the last time you were in a fight?"

"Freshman year in Montana, if you don't count the little tiff with the FBI guy. That's part of the reason I transferred. The dean said it might do me good and would help me go. It's funny. It was one of the only times I really thought someone was looking out for my best interests. My part of Montana's pretty macho. I played into that concept to the max. I've pretended to be a badass for a long time."

"Poster boy, huh." She smiled to let Jonas know she was sympathetic and wanted to hear more.

"Yeah, that's a good way to put it. Problem was that in school, I just absorbed the information. I loved school, but I still acted out. Mr. Kerrigan, my principal, suspended me lots, but he had to. Never even suggested I be thrown out permanently. I ended up number one in the class. Class only had seventeen seniors, but still, I was number one, the valedictorian."

Elyse joked again. "Did you get to give the graduation speech?"

Jonas flashed his biggest smile of the night. "As a matter of fact,

I did. The faculty was a little worried about what I might say, but Kerrigan said I earned the right. I thanked my teachers and the town for putting up with me. Pretty standard speech."

"You and Abby must have been quite the pair. It sounds like a good match."

Jonas thought quietly about Abby, and Elyse wondered if she had taken the wrong avenue in the conversation.

"No, it wasn't. Abby's anger was so much worse than mine. Seeing her made me realize how destructive anger can be, and it's a part of the reason I've tried so hard to rein mine in." Jonas turned into the light so Elyse could see his face more clearly. He took her hand and put it on the scar over his eyebrow. "Feel that? It wasn't a high school fight. It's where Abby hit me with a piece of pottery during one of our fights. She broke a part of my skull off. That's not healthy."

Elyse's eyes registered her concern.

"I don't know where her anger came from either, but I understood its depth. As deep as the ocean. It's what made me step back. I couldn't be angry anymore and help her." He paused again. "She realized I was holding my anger in and began to bait me. In the end, I had to kick her out of my life. That's when she left for California. Her anger put her in jail for five or six years. I sort of got control of mine. I don't really know how I did it. But it's still there, buried in here somewhere." He pointed to his torso. "I'm a little less crude than I used to be. I've been filtered through CU, you know, liberal university culture, but Montana is still there."

Elyse put her arms around Jonas' chest and hugged him. "You're good for me; I'm too refined." She didn't know what else to say or to ask, but she knew she wanted to hold him and let him know. Something.

CHAPTER 9

John Bosley remained eligible, and the Andrew Jackson Generals basketball team was in first place in the Denver Prep League at the end of January 1973, the first time in over a decade it had been so successful. Little Jack Winge was elevated to the junior varsity, leaving Jonas without a point guard for his C-level squad. They had not won a game since his departure. The U.S. Supreme Court ruled the 14th Amendment insured a woman's right to an abortion in *Rowe v. Wade.* President Nixon announced an agreement with North Vietnam bringing the war to an end. On January 27, the North Vietnamese delegate gave the U.S. a list of over 550 prisoners of war, one of whom was PFC Paul Garrity. And on January 30, two Watergate defendants, James McCord and Gordon Liddy, were found guilty for their part in the break-ins.

While Jonas and Elyse had been flirting most of the school year and were at the center of faculty rumors, except for a half-dozen kisses, they had not sealed the deal. Jonas was about to change that. After school on the last day of January, he wandered into her classroom. "Hey, Elyse, how'd your day go?"

"Hi, Jonas. Pretty good. One of my girls scorched her textbook with a Bunsen burner sixth period, but the alarm didn't go off. Thank goodness! Cliff Steuben gave me the evil eye when I warned him to leave one of my girls alone. What about yours?"

"Good too. There's so much happening with current events I have a hard time getting through the prescribed curriculum in history." He wandered over to her desk. "I was wondering if you'd like to go to a movie with me this weekend. Maybe Saturday."

Elyse, who was putting away lab kits in the glass cabinet and had her head turned away from Jonas, stopped abruptly. She smiled, then suppressed it before turning around. She closed the cabinet and locked it with the key hanging from her neck. She turned and asked, "Should I check with Laura and Dave to see if they'd like to go too?" She had her eyes locked on Jonas'.

"Ah, no, I just thought maybe you and I would go."

"Are you asking me out on a date?" She knew.

"Yeah. It's about time, I think."

§

At his apartment that afternoon, Jonas opened the letter from Abby Archer.

Jonas,

This will be short and direct. Through several sources I have been able to ascertain that Paul is alive and will be released in the next few weeks. I have been unable to learn about his health. I didn't know him as well as you did, but he seemed like a quality guy, and he stood up for some of the things he believed in. If you have any information about that, I would like to know. He should have gone to Canada.

I still have over three years to go here, even under the best of circumstances. While I haven't responded to any of your letters, I do read them and appreciate the sentiments. Yes, Jonas, I'm still very angry.

Abby

PS. Not that it's worth anything, but I'm proud of you for teaching in the city, even though your school isn't in a poor section of Denver.

§

At Elyse's apartment on Saturday night, the couple listened to KIMN and cuddled. After the movie, they had dined on burgers at 1421 on Larimer Street in downtown Denver and talked shop for the better part of two hours. Now they were sipping coffee and relaxing to the music.

"Do you think any of these groups will be around when we're

old?" asked Elyse.

"I'm not growing old."

"Seriously?"

Jonas shifted on the couch. "I hope not. Can you imagine sitting at home or driving around in the car listening to these songs when we're sixty. How pathetic."

Elyse smiled and kissed him gently. "Why would that be pathetic?"

"Because it's rock 'n roll. It's supposed to be about youth and energy. It's a commentary on these times. It's not supposed to be nostalgia."

"Just suppose we're together when we're sixty. Couldn't the music remind us of these times? In a good way?"

Jonas nodded his head in a contemplative way. "Maybe." He paused again. "So, who's going to last?"

"Carole King, for sure. Eddie Holman. Always the Beatles."

"I'm not listening to The Carpenters though."

"Why?"

Jonas scratched his nose and then drew Elyse into the crook of his shoulder, so they could not see each other directly. "When I was in jail, the guards played them over and over just to drive us crazy. 'We've Only Just Begun' was their favorite. Jekyll walked around the block laughing, saying, 'Get it, girls. You've only just begun.'"

Elyse pulled her legs up onto the couch, which tucked her in closer to Jonas. "Who was Jekyll?"

"Our schizophrenic nightmare. He relished strip searches, especially looking up our asses."

"Cavity searches?"

"Yeah, anyway, his real name was Fortner, I think. We just called him Jekyll because he transformed in a second to Mr. Hyde. Violent SOB." Jonas shivered and his face showed that he was moving back in time for an instant.

Elyse waited until he returned. "Did he ever hit you?' she asked gently.

"Remember those earlier stories about jail that were funny?"

"Yes."

"This isn't one of them." Jonas breathed in heavily. "Jekyll was often part of the night crew that was bored. They left me pretty much alone, but there were others who truly were victims. Stupid guards abuse stupid prisoners. They seem to resent smart maggots, but they left me alone." Then Jonas added, "Mostly."

"Maggots?"

"Prisoners. That's what they called us."

Elyse sat up where she could see Jonas' face. "I've heard guards didn't like war protesters."

"No shit. I can't imagine how bad it's been for Abby. Because they were trying to turn me, I think I got better treatment. The Feds wanted Abby."

"Have you had any contact with her recently?" asked Elyse.

Jonas hesitated. "Not really. I wrote her a few letters telling her about teaching, but I know the guards read them, so they're completely generic. Just want her to hear something positive."

They were quiet. Light from Elyse's candles cast shadows on the west wall, and the radio seemed to catch the mood by playing love songs. *Since I Fell for You. Then You Can Tell Me Goodbye.* Until that moment every kiss Jonas and Elyse shared had been standing up. Jonas turned slightly, and Elyse took his lips readily. Unlike every other kiss between the two, there was no hesitation or apprehension.

At Last

CHAPTER 10

Two weeks of mindless drivel about the industrial revolution in America in the four decades after the Civil War. Jonas suffered through it as a high school student ten years earlier, and it was no more interesting or exciting on his side of the textbook. It felt as though he was losing his students, and if they had to follow this up with U.S. imperialism in the Caribbean and Pacific or the Populist-Progressive Era, he might never get them back. His high school history teacher had rushed through this period, substituting lessons about the Indians' struggles to keep their lands from American colonization. Archie's instructions at the beginning of the second semester were to "get through the book." Jonas wondered if anyone would complain if he just skipped over to World War I. Now there was a period of history that he could make relevant.

He got up from the couch and turned off the radio. He opened his lesson plan book and tore out the week's plan. Jonas wondered what Archie would do. Archie approved those plans on Friday afternoon, but on Monday they would be completely different. Gavrilo Princip would get a second opportunity to strike at the ruling dynasty of a corrupt and oppressive empire. Nicholas II would be given another chance to call off mobilization. Would the German general staff keep the right wing strong? Would the sleeve of the last German soldier get wet from the spray of the English Channel? For America, and for his students who were to learn of these events over fifty years in the past, would President Wilson order "Black Jack" Pershing to remain in Mexico in search of Pancho Villa, or would he be recalled so America could claim its destiny across the Atlantic Ocean. Jonas would send his own students on a journey "to make the world safe for democracy."

At 4:15 the phone rang. It was Elyse. He was supposed to have called her at four, but in his excitement to create new lessons, he had lost track of time. "Hello."

"Let me guess," she said, "you're having second thoughts about this relationship already."

Jonas sensed she wasn't serious. "Oh, no, it's just that I told my dad everything about last night, and he was disappointed in me. You know, sex before marriage. So, I thought maybe I shouldn't see you outside of school."

Elyse laughed on her end. "Yeah, my mom told me the same thing."

"I'm sorry. I put off calling like you asked, and then this afternoon I started redoing my lesson plans and, well, I lost track of the time. Sorry."

"If that wasn't such a stupid excuse, I'd call you on it, but I've watched you teach, and it's probably true. Let's see, since your government classes are all about this Watergate thing, my guess is you changed your history plans."

Jonas liked Elyse's insightfulness. She demonstrated it in his relationship with Abby, trying to be patient with him while he worked out his own understanding of his feelings toward her. Elyse had been raised as her father's kitten and often reacted as a subservient female, but she was every bit as capable in the classroom as Jonas. Elyse touched him just often enough to let him know she was interested, just often enough to keep him aroused and curious, but not so much as to make him feel uncomfortable. Elyse was at ease in her own skin, confident in her ability to get what she wanted when the time came. He had the feeling she had determined the course of this relationship more than he. "Yeah, history. I've been pretty boring the past couple of weeks."

Elyse changed the subject. She wanted to talk about last night. "What time did you leave me this morning?"

"I left about two, I guess, then I went back to bed over here.

Slept until about eleven. For some reason, I couldn't sleep at your place and needed to think."

"I got up at noon. My parents cooked an early dinner. Jonas . . ."

"Yeah?"

"Last night was great." Elyse said this so gently that Jonas barely heard her. "I don't know how else to say that. I know you want to go slowly," she laughed lightly. "Boy, do I know! But it was a wonderful start, and I want it to continue. I'm not referring to the sex part exactly, but just to the being together part. Does that make any sense?"

"It does. Me too. Can we be discrete at school?"

"Everyone already talks, especially the faculty. With the kids it's just teasing, but the staff is already planning our wedding."

"I think a lot of it starts with Laura and Archie. I guess it's all right. You should know, though, people will question your taste if they think we're a couple. The guys will just slap me on the back and say, 'Way to go, Jonas!'"

§

The Generals played the Denver East Angels on February 16, a game to determine the league championship. Since the C-team finished up a week earlier, Jonas was attending the varsity practices and sitting on the bench during games. At first, he sat next to Coach Dudley and Coach Ragni, but since he never offered any advice and wasn't asked, he began to sit with the reserves at the end of the bench.

Milt Simmons and Rick Parris were sophomores up from the JVs and hadn't yet been put into a varsity game. Milt was quick and tenacious, a defensive stopper who drove the starters crazy in practice. More than once he had his nose bloodied by a senior for taking a charge, but during the games he was their biggest fan. Rick was a strange bird. He had been the best player for the JVs, and Jonas felt he was good enough to start for the varsity, but since they were winning, Coach Ragni was reluctant to alter his lineup. During timeouts Rick would wander out onto the court, talk to referees, check the official scorebook at the scorer's table, or look for people in the crowd. During the games Jonas, Milt, and Rick talked about basketball, the nature of competition, or a person's place in the universe. Rick, in particular, viewed the game apart from the score, and Jonas enjoyed his insights. Milt tried to converse on Rick's plane, but the game always seemed to distract him.

"What makes a man want to be a referee?" asked Rick after a particularly odd foul call on East's center brought the wrath of their crowd down on the slender, balding official. "I suppose I'm asking why a man, any man, does what he does."

"Oh, in this case I suppose a guy wants to remain part of the game and earn a few extra dollars." Jonas was keeping foul stats for both teams and signaled to Coach Ragni the East center now had three personals.

Rick didn't get a satisfactory answer. "No, there has to be more to it. It doesn't seem as though anyone respects them. Players don't seem to, and the coaches sure don't show it if they do. They get called the most awful names by half the crowd on every call. I don't get it." He had a searching look on his face, and the game score at that moment was not of significant importance.

Jonas leaned toward him. "They're a cult, Rick. Referees meet in secret, unannounced bars after weekend games and congratulate themselves for being in charge, for being the real factor in all of this. They intentionally wear those silly shirts just to make us think they're goofy."

"Seriously, Coach, don't they see how they're treated?"

"Rick, all these guys have other jobs. Some are businessmen, some are insurance agents, and some are educators. Well-respected somewhere else. I think they really do feel like they're providing something valuable to the youth of America. I have to think the jeers bother them at some level, but most rationalize it, especially after they've been in the game for a few years." Jonas realized he really didn't know what he was talking about but remembered Archie had told him a good social studies teacher was a first-rate bullshitter.

East went on a seven-point run to build its lead to eleven, and Coach Ragni called a timeout. When Jonas looked up from the huddle, he saw Rick talking with one of the officials near the scorers' table. The ref was shaking his head and pointing for Rick to return to the Generals' bench. When the buzzer sounded for play to resume, Rick took his seat next to Jonas again.

"What did he say?" asked Jonas.

"He told me someone had to do it. Then he said if I didn't get back to my side, he'd give us a technical."

"So why do you think someone would be a referee?" asked Jonas.

Rick yelled out for one of the Generals' guards to set stronger screens. "Probably for the reasons you said, but psychologically, I'll have to give it more thought. I just wonder why people decide to do whatever they do, besides money or prestige."

Jonas checked off another foul. The Generals cut their deficit to nine as the third quarter ended. "You're not done yet, are you, Rick?"

At this huddle Rick stood on the periphery and watched the East crowd taunt one of the referees. When the reserves took their seats again, he resumed the questioning. "Coach, why'd you decide to teach?"

"For the money, Rick," Jonas answered.

"I know you're kidding. That's why some of the older teachers teach, but not you. You're different, so how come?"

Jonas was rescued from an immediate answer when one of the Generals' forwards went down with a sprained ankle. Trailing now by twelve with just over five minutes to play, Coach Ragni conferred with Coach Dudley and then walked down to Rick and told him to check in.

§

The faculty met downstairs at 1421 in downtown Denver as they usually did after an athletic contest. Despite Rick's ten points down the stretch, the team came up short, 74-67. Still, the staff was upbeat because Andrew Jackson would enter the District tournament as the second seed. Jonas arrived a little late. He had stayed after the game to talk with Rick about both his play and his life questions. Archie was with his second "roommate," an older lady named Judith who was a painter living in Morrison, an art commu-nity in the foothills west of Denver. Judith tended to be the public girlfriend for Archie. He poured Jonas a beer from the pitcher he was holding. Jonas didn't ask whether Archie was drinking directly from the container. Ben Lucas and his wife Linda were standing nearby taking it all in while they drank martinis. Ben was a light drinker, the watchdog on nights like this.

"You have some catching up to do, Jonas," Archie said referring to the late start on alcohol. "Your friends are over in the corner waiting for you."

Ben smiled as Archie slurred his words and motioned with his head in the direction of Jonas' young colleagues.

When he worked his way over to the booth after exchanging small talk with other faculty members, Laura got up to let Jonas slide in next to Elyse. Under the table she slid her hand onto his thigh and squeezed. Observant as usual Elyse asked, "So what were you and Rick Parris talking about so intently on the bench?"

Jonas shook his head. "Life. How do we steer that boy toward philosophy?" He reached across the table for a nacho and salsa. "He did make an interesting comment though. He asked why we become teachers."

"God, I ask myself that every day," said Laura.

"No, seriously, guys, why did we choose this profession?" Jonas persisted.

Dave raised his hand and grinned. "I'll give it a try. I was a good student in college, but not a great one. Solid, you could say." He turned to Elyse for his next statement. "Jonas and I have talked about not wanting to be our fathers in the sense their jobs are dependent on others. They aren't their own bosses. A teacher is, or at least can be. There is a measure of stability once you find your place, which appeals to me. A good teacher has a measure of respect, at least in small towns. I'm trying to decide if it's true in the city." Dave paused and took a drink from his mug. He shifted to Jonas. "Coaches are important too, and I always wanted to be a baseball coach. Mine were sure influential to me and my buddies. I guess what I'm trying to say is I believe I can make a little bit of a difference." He would never have been so open without the beer, and now he felt a little self-conscious.

Laura put her head on Dave's shoulder. Jonas smiled and did a slow clap. "That's well said, buddy. Pretty cool." Elyse's eyes seemed to look past Dave's shoulder.

"I could do other things, I suppose," said Dave. "But when I went to college, that was my thinking. My parents are pretty proud of me, and that's a good feeling. I'm not sure about the big city, though. I just took a chance coming up here, and the pay was better, at least on paper."

Laura rubbed Dave's arm and took a drag from her cigarette, her "social habit." "We won't let you leave. For me, teaching is what I've always wanted to do ever since I was a kid. School has always been my place, and I like kids." She smiled a private thought. "I'm struggling, but I'll figure it out."

Jonas looked to Elyse to see if she wanted to talk, but it seemed like she didn't, so he jumped in. "I'd played with becoming a teacher when I was in high school. I even wrote a paper, one of those career research papers, on it. I interviewed a couple of my teachers. One in particular said I'd be good at it. Somehow my principal heard about my paper and encouraged me in this direction. Still, when I went off to the U of M, I wasn't sure." Beneath the table Jonas and Elyse were holding hands, and at this moment he slid his other hand on top of hers and rubbed it. "At CU I had a professor who was in a wheelchair, a political science professor, and he talked about it every day at the end of class. He'd close each lecture by urging us to think about being a teacher. Dr. Johnson said he knew we hadn't come to CU to be teachers, but he wanted us to consider it anyway, that it was an important job. That's when I decided."

Elyse challenged Jonas a bit. "I thought it was the mysterious Abby Archer who convinced you."

Jonas didn't flinch, but he didn't attack either. "Nope, she came later. What she did was urge me to join the revolution, and she felt the only way I would join the proletariat was to push me where I was already going. No, Dr. Johnson was my epiphany."

Laura shook her head. "Why is the wheelchair a part of his

epiphany?" she giggled at Dave.

"It's not. Long story short, I had two Dr. Johnsons, and I always referred to this one as the wheelchair Dr. Johnson. He was the older one, in no particular hurry anymore, had already done his research and writing, and was only interested in teaching. Loved his students and it showed."

"Jeez," said Dave in mock disappointment, "I thought this was going to be a cool story." They all laughed and drank for a moment.

"What about you, Elyse?" Dave finally asked.

Elyse let go of Jonas' hand under the table and used both hands to lift her beer in front of her face. "Just sort of drifted into it. Rich girl without direction, so she decides to teach for a while. Teach for two or three years and then get a real job."

Jonas felt the mood swing like someone had opened another door and allowed the wind to pass through the room.

"Oh, come on, El," said Laura, "it can't just be like that."

"Yeah, Laur, it can. Unlike Jonas' professor who lauded the profession, my advisor called me in and told me my grades didn't indicate a professional science career and suggested I might consider being a public school teacher. How's that for an epiphany?" Elyse's eyes had no focus, and Jonas noticed she was sliding her tongue behind her lower lip. "Let me out for a minute, Jonas," said Elyse. She was already pushing against him. Jonas slid out of the booth, and Elyse quickly headed for the ladies' room. Laura followed close behind.

"What was that all about?" asked Dave.

"She's not like us. She's not like anyone I know. We all chose this profession at some point. She thinks by being a teacher, she's compromised herself. It's what her dad tells her, and it's evidently what her college advisor told her."

In time Laura and Elyse returned to the booth. Jonas got out allowing Elyse to slide in. Laura just pushed Dave against the wall and sat next to him. Jonas took Elyse's right hand, leaned into her ear, and asked if she wanted to go.

"No, I'm okay. I just needed to have a little pity-party for myself. It's over now." She rimmed her beer mug with her right index finger.

Dave was uncomfortable with Elyse's forthrightness and tried to ease his own tension. "You wouldn't leave us and all this fun we're having, would you?"

Elyse smiled weakly but did not answer.

Laura rescued her. "Interesting? Yes. Challenging, for sure. But not always fun. She's not going to leave us."

Elyse sniffed and swallowed. "I could. I just don't know."

"You make teaching look easy and enjoyable," said Dave. "Everyone at school says, 'Look at Ellie, she's going to be one of the best.'"

"Thanks, Dave, you're a sweetie. I try."

Elyse deflected more questions from Dave and Laura, but Jonas stayed silent, trying to catch the unspoken meanings from Elyse. Around midnight Archie ambled over. "You kids gonna be able to drive yourselves home tonight?"

Laura nodded and then asked, "Archie, why are you a teacher?"

He didn't take her question seriously. "Cause I can't paint; I can't administrate; I don't want to sell insurance; and I don't have the time to run a small business. That's too much like work." He winked. "Those who can't, teach, and Pete won't allow me to run the school yet."

§

Elyse and Jonas did not talk on the drive back to her apartment. She was glad he had not asked any questions after she told of her abrupt path into teaching, but she knew he had some. They were in no hurry to get out of the car when Jonas parked in front of her apartment. Finally, he asked gently if she was okay.

Barely audible, she replied, "Yeah, thanks." Jonas waited. "I fight my emotions, Jonas. I want to be logical and reasonable like a scientist, not a flighty girl, but I'm at odds with that all the time. Tonight, I lost."

"Letting your emotions show is not losing. I act out at times for reasons I'm unaware of and that, frankly, confound me. Part of me believes I can simply change my behavior by logically thinking things out. But then I get to a place and wonder how I got there.

More and more, I think even when we're logical, our emotions have guided us there." Jonas paused. "Does that make sense?"

"Not really, at least not tonight. I know you're trying to be gentle with me just now." She snuggled into his shoulder where he couldn't see her face.

"Do you need a tissue?"

"No, I'm cried out for tonight, but thanks. Jonas, I'm not a destiny person; I try not to be, but my being a teacher in a city school sure doesn't seem logical to me."

Jonas put his arm around her and squeezed. "Ah, yes, that would explain us; angry, ugly kid from Montana dating a beautiful, brilliant, rich girl from Denver. Yep, destiny!"

"You're looking to get punched, you know," Elyse said.

"Tough girl, huh. Maybe that's what I find so attractive in you."

"Oh hell, that and my big boobs."

"Yeah, well, those too."

They kissed tenderly, but with great passion, and when they pulled back, Elyse said, "Let's go inside."

CHAPTER 11

On March 4 Jonas learned that his friend from college, Paul Garrity, had arrived home in the United States after being held prisoner in North Vietnam. He was one of the third group of Americans released as part of the peace agreement for the Vietnam War. It was Sunday, and even though it was snowing lightly, Jonas decided to go to City Park to be alone and think about the end of the war.

Like nearly every young man in America over the previous seven years, even before the draft lottery, Jonas had wondered what his role in the conflict should be. Duty, conscience, honor, cowardice, freedom, hair. Until October of 1967, Jonas' hair was pretty standard for his age group, even parted on the left. But his association with Abby and his feelings against the war led him to grow it out as a small symbol of his anti-war stance. It had been long ever since. Maybe it was time to cut it. It would certainly make his dad happy, even though his dad had opposed the war too.

Jonas wanted to see Paul, but Paul's parents said he wasn't yet ready to see too many people; he had some healing to do. Jonas wasn't sure he would know what to say anyway.

Who Jonas really wanted to talk to, however, was Abby Archer. Vietnam and Abby were intertwined. From the time he enrolled at Boulder in the fall of 1967, every event related to the war was linked to Abby. Escalation, TET, Rolling Thunder, Agent Orange, the Cambodian Incursion, napalm. The Universal Soldier. Every event was played out under the white-hot anger of Abby Archer, and now as the war was coming to an end, he needed that anger. Abby held nothing in, whereas Jonas was holding everything in.

"Damn it, Abby," he swore aloud as he walked along the park lane near the gorilla house. *You were right in your indignation. You were right in your anger. Visceral anger,* he thought. Jonas recalled the night in May of '68 when she learned of the death in Vietnam of one of her high school boyfriends. She had come to Jonas' apartment not to grieve, but to retaliate. Abby made Jonas go with her to buy red paint and then drive her across campus to the ROTC building, where she painted KILLERS on the east wall. "I want the sun to rise on that word." She had taken the remaining portion of her can and poured it on the steps.

The next day she exploded on her government professor, blaming him for teaching lies about the American government. "No fucking conscience!" was what she screamed. "Ted Klaussen is dead, and you don't care!" The professor did not seek academic sanctions against her. What Abby did best was personalize injustice. War killed her friends. Racism held black children hostage. Segregated schools prevented students like her from living out their dreams. And because she was an American, its sins were her sins.

Jonas wiped the snow off a bench, sat, and stared blankly at the African gazelles. Near the end of their relationship, Abby often pleaded with him to "Let it out. Let your anger out. I know it's in there." He refused, but it was there. He didn't know how long he sat at that bench, but around 3:30 he realized he was cold. Jonas walked back to his car and drove south on York Street to Colfax and then west to the downtown area.

For two of the months Jonas spent in jail, Abby occupied a cell in the same building. Although he couldn't hear her yelling, he certainly received reports about it from the interrogator. She was extradited to California and found guilty for her part in a bank robbery. "Urban warfare" was what she called it. Not much of a defense. Jonas parked his car along the street and got out to get the feel of the federal building where he was held, where they were held, one guilty and one not guilty. At least not of bank robbery. He couldn't recall where exactly he had been held inside the massive brick building. Somewhere. Suddenly, he had a tremendous desire to talk to a guard, to reconnect with someone from inside who shared the experiences of those days. Not Hyde-Jekyll, but maybe Hanscom, the nice guard. Jonas smirked, "Screw you, Hyde, I'm teaching."

"The war is over, Jonas. Go home now. You've got lesson plans to do," he said to the reflection in a smoky window. He had just controlled the anger that once would have taken over him. It was still there, but he had controlled it.

§

At 8:00 that evening, Jonas called home. Patty had recovered from whatever was making her tired, which was a relief. She was back working her two jobs, one as a housecleaner and the other as the nighttime receptionist for the Livingston police. Jonas' brother had given up baseball to run track with the hopes of getting faster for football.

"Dad, my friend Paul came home this week. I guess he's okay, but he has some emotional baggage. His parents are protecting him just now." Each time that he paused, his dad would offer a short response. Jonas did most of the talking on the phone. "He's hurting right now, and it'll take some time, but if I know Paul, he'll be back at something pretty quick. He's not the kind of guy to sit around. Probably pestered the North Vietnamese for books the whole time he was over there." Jonas paused and allowed his feelings to pass through the phone lines unhampered by sound.

"Dad, I'd like to see Abby. With the end of the war and all, I'd kind of like to visit with her. She still has a few more years to serve, but, I don't know, at this moment, I'd like to see how she's doing." Jonas was not seeking approval from his father. "Yeah, I know. She had no idea they'd put me in jail too."

After ending his bi-weekly call home, Jonas went out onto his balcony to switch gears. He still had an hour of planning to do, but now he wanted to talk to Elyse. His apartment balcony faced north, and with the leaves off the trees in winter, he could glimpse the Denver skyline. Funny, he thought, a small-town boy teaching in the big city. Struggling to teach in the big city.

He popped the tab on a soda can and dialed Elyse's number. She had been sent to Albuquerque from Wednesday through Sunday for a science conference. He knew her parents had picked her up from the airport and had taken her to dinner.

"Hello."

"Hi, Elyse, it's me. How was your trip?"

"Really interesting, but I missed you. Come over and finish your lesson plans with me."

§

Along with the lists of POWs came the realization for many families that their sons would not be coming home. Many held out hope these MIAs would still be alive, but most understood they weren't. With the end of the war, searches for them, or their remains, would end. "Any day now" would now be "Never, Mom."

Near Bismarck, North Dakota, Barbara Deaver read her son's last letter one more time before she went to bed. Jason Deaver enlisted in the Marines in 1967, wanting to do his duty for his country. During his second tour, he was listed as missing-in-action in the Central Highlands of Vietnam. For over three years, Mrs. Deaver held out hope he was a prisoner. She prayed for a miracle, that when the war ended, he would be coming home. Somewhere in her gut she knew it probably wouldn't happen, but always she held out hope of his return. Now, with the release of all the names of the POWs, she accepted the fact. One of her twin sons would never be coming home.

She carefully placed the letter back into its envelope and into the cedar box on her dresser. Then, just as she had for twenty-five years, she dropped to her knees and said a prayer for her other son, the son for whom she had never returned home.

CHAPTER 12

"All right, who can tell me what this latest development in the Watergate episode means?" Mr. Cullen asked his sophomores.

Episode! Jonas tried to stay neutral about Watergate and let the events play out, even though he was convinced President Nixon was at the heart of the Watergate scandal. Since September, when the federal grand jury brought indictments against the Watergate burglars, Jonas kept his students in both the history and government classes up to date on the subtle maneuverings of both the participants and the media. His best students enjoyed the judicial proceedings. These kids knew Ben Bradlee, Martha Graham, Woodward, and Bernstein.

In September, when the burglars pleaded guilty, these kids learned that by doing so, the burglars could not be questioned by the prosecution about the case. Information about their pleas seemed to be vaulted. In October, when the *Washington Post* linked the burglary to a larger political sabotage campaign against the leading Democratic candidates, Jonas challenged his students to understand that dirty tricks might lead to inferior candidates in the general election. Senator Sam Ervin and Judge Sirica were admired by many of Mr. Cullen's students.

Kristen and some of her fifth hour peers refused to believe the scandal went all the way to the White House. Erin skipped her dance class one day to sit in on fifth period and argue with her good friend. The month of April was one news revelation after another, and nearly every class wanted to discuss the latest happenings each day. Jonas urged his students to tune in on the President's nationally televised speech on Monday, April 30, and see what their gut instincts would tell them. On Tuesday, his classes were electric.

"The President wouldn't have let his closest advisers go if he wanted to find out the truth," argued one side.

"Come on! Can't you see what he's doing? He's distancing himself from those men who are bound to be indicted."

"Where's your proof? You guys are still pissed Nixon destroyed McGovern in the general election."

After each statement, a partisan response followed: clapping, cheers, boos, and hisses.

Among the faculty, emotions ran as high. The lounge filled before and after school to debate the events, with Republican supporters still in the majority. More than a few teachers had their feelings hurt in these discussions, and some nasty comments were made. Jonas kept his words at a minimum, but he never missed lunch on the "battlefield."

§

Jonas' students knew he arrived early to school, and it was the best time to talk with him about their concerns. Once the bell for first period rang, Mr. Cullen focused on his classes and was seldom distracted. As he approached his second-floor room on Wednesday, May 2, he was greeted by Rainer, Erin, and Ian.

"Good morning, Mr. Cullen. Did you sleep in this morning?" Jonas hadn't, but Rainer played the game anyway. "We need to ask you some questions about Watergate, and we're not going to allow you to play the devil's advocate. We've earned the right to get a straight answer."

Jonas unlocked the door and held it open for them. "Come in and tell me what's on your mind."

"We brought you breakfast, Mr. C," said Erin. "My mom cooked it, but it's probably cooled off some." It was French toast and bacon. Erin also brought a thermos of coffee. She laid out the spread on his desk and held out his chair.

"Fork?"

Erin handed over a plastic fork and a napkin.

Jonas took his first bite of the toast. "Yum. Tell your mother I appreciate this. I could get used to it." With food in his mouth, he spoke. "Okay, I'll answer as honestly as I can."

Rainer jumped in first. "What am I missing? There was a burglary and some dirty tricks. Obviously, some people are lying, but is it worthy of all this attention?"

"Yeah, Mr. Cullen, are Kristen and her friends right? Is it just payback for losing the election?" asked Ian.

Jonas poured coffee out of the thermos and into his Dodgers cup. He was deliberate in his response. "Two things first. I'm better at asking questions than answering them. I tend to hide my thoughts and feelings."

"Ah, Mr. C, we know you love us. You don't have to actually say it."

"Thanks, Rainer." Jonas squinted and made a face at her. "Next, I have my biases on this just as some of you. I don't have to tell you I'm not the President's biggest fan." He looked for confirmation. None of the three were in Nixon's camp either. "That said, I'll answer you as directly as I can, but it's between the four of us for now. In class I go back to being plain jello." He tucked his chin into his chest and looked at them with stern eyes.

The kids looked to one another and then nodded. "Blood oath," teased Rainer.

"Okay then. It's much more than a burglary. This whole thing, as I see it and from what I can gather in the papers, is an assault on the democratic process. It's the corruption of our most basic democratic procedure, the right to free and fair elections. I know politics are tough, but I still expect the other party to respect the nation enough to allow for the best opposition candidate to be nominated. We want the best people running in November. Secondly, the President takes an oath to follow and defend the Constitution. If he protects his people, even out of loyalty, but if he protects the guilty by the use of his authority, then he's breaking the law. We can't have that from our President. Disagree with him, yes, but I've got to be able to trust him. We're a nation of laws, not of men."

Ian held up his hands. "Too fast for this sophomore. From what I'm hearing, you say Nixon tried to get the lesser Democratic candidate to get the nomination?"

"Yes."

"And now he's protecting guilty people because they work for him and are his friends?"

"Yes, maybe not personally on the first part, but he's ultimately responsible. On the second part, I just think he knows all about it now and is going against the law."

Rainer unclenched her teeth. "Will we ever know for sure? I couldn't stand it if we didn't."

"Sorry, Rainer, but I don't think we will. Most people just want this to go away. I'm afraid it will in the end."

"That's not fair!" she cried.

"I agree with you there, but fair hasn't been the strength of this administration."

The three kids were silent, their minds racing. Finally, Erin spoke, "Mr. C, we have another problem."

"What's that, Erin?"

"Ever since elementary school, counselors have split the three of us up. They say we're too dominant and don't give our classmates a chance. They did it to us this year. Is there anything you could do to get us all in one of your classes next year, together?"

"If I'm teaching all sophs again, you won't have me, but I'll see what I can do to get you all in the same AP history section."

They all went silent again, and Jonas put the last piece of bacon in his mouth.

Rainer picked up her books and tucked them under her arm. "I'll work on your schedule. You work on ours. Let's go guys. By the way, Mr. C, did you have time to read my poems?"

"Yes, I did, Rainer. Pretty deep. You'll need to explain them to me."

"We'll talk soon. See you in a while, Mr. Cullen."

§

On Saturday, Elyse lounged with Jonas at his apartment listening to music, one of the few times neither one was preoccupied with some aspect of school.

"Where's Digit?" she asked.

"I haven't seen him all week. On Monday, he's just gone; must have had a higher calling."

"I have a slight allergy to cats. Have you been out looking for him? Don't you miss him?"

Jonas laid his head on the back of the couch. "Yeah, a little. It wasn't like he was the most affectionate animal. Besides, nobody controls cats."

"Sort of like a Montana cowboy, huh?"

"Have you ever heard the term 'truck cowboy,' Elyse? Not a flattering term. It's a cowboy who pretends, one who doesn't know where he belongs. For me, is this the right school or even the right city? I'm still searching."

"I thought I was the only one asking those questions." Elyse said.

"I've become pretty docile, pretty tame." He grinned and shook his head. "I haven't hit anyone since the FBI guy a couple of years ago."

"You know, in civilized society that's a good thing. Is that the same guy who pulled you out of class earlier this year?"

"Yeah. I'm afraid I'm losing the cowboy in me."

Elyse looked at him hard. "I'll bet I can ride horses better than you, and that doesn't make me a cowgirl. I have a feeling that, at heart, you never were a cowboy. You were born to do *this*."

Jonas remained silent, but Elyse knew he was considering her words. Shortly, he turned his head back towards her. He rose and then straddled her on the couch. "My turn to ride. Maybe this is my place. Am I too heavy?"

Elyse put both hands on his face and drew him in for a kiss. "I'll let you know, cowboy," she whispered. "I'll let you know."

§

The week before spring break Jonas challenged his students to find examples of where the Supreme Court had used the Fourteenth Amendment to protect basic rights for all citizens, but particularly the rights of minorities as the civil rights movement was ramping up after World War II. His class would have the spring break week to discover any examples, but being sophomores, Jonas did not expect many of them would delve into vacation research, so he made it an extra credit assignment, and they would discuss their findings after the break.

On Monday, March 26, Teacher-boy Cullen received another present from the immensely gifted Rainer Brecht.

"Mr. Cullen, can our examples about the use of the Fourteenth Amendment by the Supreme Court be about current issues? I know you wanted something from the 1950s."

Jonas nodded and stepped to the side of the room, forcing Rainer to turn into her classmates and speak louder. "Of course, Rainer, if it's relevant."

"Well, I was reading the newspaper, and there was a story about the Supreme Court deciding a current case called *San Antonio School District v Rodriguez*. It caught my attention because it sounded like Denver's case before the Supreme Court. The *Keyes* case." Rainer paused to turn her desk around so that it faced the class, so she wasn't at a weird body angle.

Jonas was aware of the case but didn't know it had been adjudicated.

"Anyway, a poor school district on one side of San Antonio felt its students were being discriminated against because of how money was raised to fund schools. Property taxes mostly, I guess, so they sued and won in the federal court for West Texas. The school district argued that education is a basic right and not funding it properly is a form of discrimination. I think they called it 'wealth-based discrimination' and that low property taxes created inferior schools." Rainer stopped here to pull several newspaper clippings from her notebook. She stood, grabbed the stapler from Mr. Cullen's desk, and proceeded to staple the clippings to the bulletin board at the front of the room. Jonas and the class waited. Rainer had earned their patience. Then she walked to the chalkboard and wrote the name of the case on the board. *San Antonio Independent School District v Rodriguez, et al.* She looked at her classmates and said, "You might want to write that in your notes.

Jonas raised his hands for protection and nodded to his students to do as instructed.

Rainer continued. "This suit was started in the Sixties. Gad, it takes forever for the courts to get anything done. Anyway, last week the Supreme Court gave its ruling, and it overturned the Texas decision. Here's where the Fourteenth Amendment comes in. The Texas court used the Fourteenth Amendment to rule that this type of funding was unconstitutional under the equal protection part of the amendment. Get this, the Supreme Court agreed that the system was unfair and that poor students were getting screwed, but ruled that no federal laws had been violated, so it was not going to uphold the lower court's decision. The state of Texas had to fix it on their own." Rainer looked to her teacher. "Where's the justice in that? They agree that it's unfair but say that it's okay?"

From her side of the room, Erin said, "It's as if the Court is conspiring against public schools, at least making it hard for them to operate on an equal footing with rich schools."

Rainer nodded and continued. "The Court also said that education isn't mentioned in the Constitution anywhere, so it's not a protected right. Is that true, Mr. Cullen?"

Jonas pushed himself off the heating unit and walked to the front of the room next to Rainer. "That's probably true about not being specifically mentioned—I'll have to check—but the judges' reasoning sounds crazy to me. Funding for public schools has always been at the crux of education; it's at the base of the *Keyes* case. It seems to me to be a missed opportunity to move America closer to one of its great promises, that of equality of opportunity." He put his hand on Rainer's shoulder. "Marvelous job, young lady." Turning back to the class, "I'll duplicate the articles on the bulletin board and give them to you all tomorrow. I guess we have two court cases to follow now."

The bell rang and the class filed out. All except Rainer. "What do the poor and minorities do when the Supreme Court fails them, Mr. Cullen?"

"You lean on the legislature to change the law. That's slow too and not certain."

CHAPTER 13

Elyse Cottage could pass for a model. Her dark hair was just long enough to rest on her shoulders and her observant hazel-blue eyes, her "German infusion," accentuated her Mediterranean skin. People of every type gravitated to Elyse. She was the center of attention, which Jonas liked because he could stay in the background. She practiced, it seemed to Jonas, the subtle art of tilting her head slightly when she listened. Students worked for her, sensing she expected they would. The brightest girls saw her as a role model, while low-achieving students loved her for her consistent encouragement. Even in her first year, she became the sponsor for the science club. While she was not particularly concerned about the daily details of world politics, she did know her science, especially her earth science. But to her rookie partners, it was her knowledge of people science that was her forte.

For Jonas it began with that first day kiss. For Dave it was the box of Bronco pencils and a Big Chief tablet during the first week, and for Laura it was Elyse's habit of always buying the first two beers for her on Friday afternoons. Early on, Elyse formed a bond with her buddies, and she seemed not to need anything in return. She suffered through first year teaching difficulties just as Laura, Dave, and Jonas did, but when the bell rang at three, she seemed able to walk away from the stress and look forward. Gary Dessins, the staff's eternal pessimist, nicknamed her "Morning Star" for her optimistic, bubbly demeanor.

Elyse's gifts did not go unnoticed by Pete Cirillo either. He was more than pleased with her classroom performance and was looking for a teacher to represent Andrew Jackson at District meetings in anticipation of the enrollment changes. Who better to be the face of Jackson than Elyse. He picked up his phone and buzzed Annette.

"Annette, would you have Ben and Archie meet me for lunch today. I have something I want to run past them. We need to tie that young lady to Andrew Jackson."

§

May, the home stretch. For teachers who taught seniors, the great reward was at hand. Graduation. For teachers of underclassmen, the last four weeks seemed more like four months. Laura Sanders was struggling. Discipline in three of her Spanish I classes had deteriorated to the point where one of the counselors was sitting in to help. Cirillo called Laura in for a supportive conference in late March, telling her he was still in her corner and next year would be better. When he had told the rookies that if they tried, he would want them back for the next year, he meant it. Laura's year-end evaluation was much tougher, however.

"Tough year, huh, Laura? You seem to have given up some these past few months." Cirillo's face showed both concern for the first-year teacher, but also a determination. "You don't seem real happy."

Laura stayed quiet for a moment. "I guess I haven't been. I've been looking for the end of the year for several months."

"Well, let's see if we can look forward here. Laura, you have some real skills and connect with many of our students. Still, I'm not sure you wouldn't be happier at the junior high level. Don't jump to conclusions, but I want you to think about it. If you decide to stay, if you want to give it another try next year, we'll do everything we can to help. If not, I have contacts in several towns where you could get a junior high job. I know that Ellie would want you to stay."

§

Dave Fallon's evaluation conference was easy. His second observation of the second semester had been quite good. Cirillo watched twenty-six sophomore students work through three activities which included guided practice, small group learning, and creative word problems.

"Dave, I still need you to teach three algebra classes next year, but I'd like to reward you with two junior level courses. Are you up for the trig-pre-calculus classes?"

Dave smiled his crooked smile. "Yes, sir, I think I can learn trig over the summer. Thank you."

"What do you have planned for the summer?"

"I'll be busy. I'm taking two classes at DU, you know, working on my master's, and I'll be working nights at Safeway to make a few extra dollars." Dave was not a warm person, but he was an effective teacher and Cirillo liked him.

The principal signed his evaluation and passed it across his desk for Dave's signature. "You can see most of the categories are marked positive. The others are satisfactory. You've done a superb job for a first-year teacher. I look forward to working with you for many years to come." While Dave skimmed the paper, Cirillo smiled to himself. Cirillo believed math teachers were part of a small foundation of teachers upon which the excellence of a school was measured. He wanted to keep this one. "By the way, I'm hearing rumors about you and an elementary teacher from Bromwell."

Dave slid the signed document back to his principal and smiled sheepishly. "Not many secrets even in a district as big as Denver, I guess."

§

The third evaluation took place the next afternoon, on May 2. Elyse had agreed to act as Jackson's co-rep on the "integration committee." In Pete's office Elyse spoke first. "I know my work has suffered this semester, especially these past few weeks, but I have to be honest, Mr. Cirillo, I'm worn out. This is the hardest job I've ever done."

"What other jobs have you had, Elyse?"

She raised her eyebrows. "Mostly summer jobs like life guarding and swimming lessons. I've always been a student, but this is much tougher. No days off."

"Do you remember what I told you back in September, that this year was Andrew Jackson's? Well, it's almost over and you've not only survived, but grown. You can be proud of that. Besides, none of us have noticed any drop-off in your performance. What I'll bet is that you tend to be your own worst critic. You've been very good in all areas."

"Jonas and I talk about it all the time. We laugh at all our shortcomings. It's been a survival course, that's for sure. We've talked about how tired we've been these past few weeks, about other jobs that would be easier and pay more money."

The principal stretched his arms behind his head. "Elyse, my staff and I go to great lengths to hire good people, but there are no guarantees. Your crew this year has more than lived up to our high expectations, and to a man, we want you back."

"Thank you." It was a genuine response and Elyse's eyes welled to tears. She took a tissue from her purse and blew her nose. "By the way the phrase is 'to a person.'" Both laughed.

Cirillo was used to first year teachers, tired and spent from their first full year of teaching, breaking down during this evaluation. He asked his usual last question, "And what are your plans for the summer? There are some very good science seminars you could attend."

Elyse regained her composure. "Sleep first. Then I need to read up on this stuff on Denver's integration plan. I don't just want to be a silent observer, you know, a pretty face on that committee." She hoped the principal saw her humor. "Seriously, I do want to learn more about all that. I'm also going to do an internship at the School of Mines. It's just four weeks, but I'm really looking forward to it. It's aimed more at the business side, but I think it will be valuable in time."

He passed her evaluation across the desk and asked her to look it over. "Any questions?"

"There's nothing here about Jonas."

§

Jonas' year-end meeting with Mr. Cirillo took place on Friday after school, the last of the four rookies to receive his evaluation.

"Well, son, what do you think?"

"It's been a tough year, but a good one. Maybe in a couple of years, I'll be a teacher."

"Yeah, maybe." Both men smiled. Unlike the other three rookies, Jonas had become friends with Pete Cirillo. The nature of his hiring, the jail thing and the ongoing FBI investigation, the car fire, and numerous odd occurrences that struck Pete as funny had brought them close. Jonas learned Pete had been a football coach in his early years but was now a motivational speaker in great demand around the region. He contributed articles to educational journals on leadership skills and being an effective principal in the Seventies. Coach Cirillo. And more.

"Jonas, we've found the money to send you to school this summer up in Greeley. If you're up to it, I think there's even money enough for you to take a seminar on being an AP teacher too. Mrs. Froman's retiring this year in anticipation of busing. That would be a heavy load, but I think you can do it."

"Archie sort of told me about all this. Why doesn't he take the AP classes? There are a couple of others in the department who would like these classes too." Jonas was deferring to his department elders.

"Archie only wants to teach government. He's on a mission to reform America by teaching the Constitution. Besides, growing up in the South, he was inundated with history, Confederate history, and he doesn't have the regard for it a true history teacher should. As far as the others in your department go, they have their specialties." Pete's words were decisive.

"I was planning to work down here, but if you think I can do all this, then I'm game. I'll have to work up there some. Money's a little tight."

"I know some people. We'll get you something. I know money's an issue, so what if I set you up to live with a friend of mine—for free?"

Archie King entered without knocking, carrying three Dixie cups.

"Hey kid, Pete and I thought we'd expose some secrets to you." From his hip pocket Archie removed a flask and lined up the cups on Pete's desk. "FAC in here. Hope you and your young friends don't have plans."

Over the next half-hour, Jonas learned Archie had been on the board of directors for the Emma Goldman alternative school, even a minor financial contributor. While he had never observed Jonas teach, he read the reports of those who did. Nine teachers lost their jobs when the school folded, and all were committed to educational reform. "I knew those other eight, Jonas, all great teachers. They were all confident they would get new jobs, and they sang your praises." Archie looked at Pete with scrunched up eyes. "Did I just say, 'sang your praises'?"

"You did."

Archie shook his head. "Annette's gonna need to drive me home. Anyway, I knew we'd have an opening in social studies soon. Fortunately, it didn't happen until this year, time enough for you to get out of jail."

Pete shifted to claim the floor. "Archie came in last year around Christmas, right after Christmas, I guess, and asked me if I had any connections in Montana. I did. In Livingston. Archie convinced the guy to give you a chance, to get you back into teaching." Pete took Jonas' eyes. "I told you when we first met that I trust this guy implicitly. He was right on with you."

"Yes, I was," said Archie proudly. "While you're a rookie here, those months at Goldman and in Montana were effective training grounds, sort of gave you a leg up."

"Those were pretty different environments compared to Jackson. They did help, especially Goldman. I saw teachers willing to take chances, and they absolutely believed in what they were doing. It was fun for me to be around them," said Jonas, "but I wasn't on their level as a teacher."

"We're going to have to wrap this up, but I want you to know you've seen your last full load of sophomores. You're good with those kids, but we think we've found our man for the upper-level history classes. So, next year you'll have the two AP U.S. History classes and possibly two history electives for seniors. You also have a couple of persuasive students in your corner who pushed for you to move into the AP classes."

"And you thought you were busy this year. Pete here just threw your ass into the ring."

Pete raised his cup. "A toast. Here's to you, Jonas." Pete then walked behind his desk where he pulled out a used leather briefcase, which he handed to Archie.

Archie passed it over to Jonas. "You've got to stop looking like a rookie, carrying around that folder you call a notebook. It's falling apart. You need something more substantial. My dad gave this to me for college, but I've sworn off everything I got from him. If you'll ignore my initials on it, it'll work out fine to carry all those important papers you have to grade. Now get out of here and spend time with people your own age."

§

"I thought you were finally going to tell him," said Archie as he poured another round into his cup.

"I decided not to. He has enough on his plate," answered Pete. "He takes responsibility for everything he's connected to. Anyway, it's under control."

"Damn FBI! They can't admit they made a mistake when they arrested him. I know they're still trying to connect him to some revolutionary activities, to tie him to that girl in jail. They kept him from getting a teaching job until you used your contact in Montana, and now they keep tabs on him here. I wouldn't be surprised if they're behind his car problems."

"Arch, put away your conspiracy theories. You got him down here, and he's doing well. That government trouble is a thing of the past. They haven't called in over a month." Pete looked over his paper cup and nodded with finality.

"I sure wish we could relieve him of his worries over that girl in the California prison. She's an anchor around his neck," said Archie.

"Somehow, he feels responsible for her too, but he'll work it out. I'm pretty sure it's not a love thing anymore. I'm not sure it ever was."

Archie shook his head. "It's not. He's completely gone over Elyse, more than he even knows yet."

CHAPTER 14

Sitting in the teachers' lounge together that first month of their careers, Jonas waved Dave's cigarette smoke from his face during an idle conversation. Dave asked if it bothered him, and Jonas replied that it did, "a little." Dave's simple response, "Okay, then I'll just quit," gave Jonas his first glimpse into the make-up of his rookie comrade. Dave didn't just quit smoking that cigarette; he gave it up as a habit.

Both were small town kids with all the rural baggage, but only Dave was teased about being unsophisticated, especially by Laura. Jonas filtered his small-town upbringing through a major university, while Dave went to the nearest small state college. Growing up in Del Norte, Colorado, with a college stop in Alamosa at Adams State, Dave took the job in Denver alone and friendless. Maybe in another time or place, they would not have hooked up, but at Denver's Andrew Jackson High School in 1972-1973, they became close friends.

Had Dave started his teaching in a town of five thousand instead of five hundred thousand, he would have moved easily into various leadership positions. When the tardy bell rang and Dave closed his door and stepped up to the blackboard, he was home. Students could have told Jonas and the rest of the faculty just that: Mr. Fallon knew his stuff and genuinely cared about his kids. Unlike the other rookies on the Jackson staff, Dave was seldom tested by his students, and his classes had a calm, working atmosphere.

Two weeks prior to graduation, when Jonas pondered his living arrangements for the summer and following school year, Dave suggested the two of them get an apartment together.

"It would save us quite a bit of money."

Jonas laughed. "Our take-home pay is about $420 per month. What's to save?"

"I don't know about you, but my rent is $165 each month. By getting a two-bedroom apartment for $200 a month, I could save $65. That works out to about $800 for the year." Dave raised his eyebrows. "Of course, you could move in with Elyse and maybe pay no rent. You'd save a bundle that way."

Jonas shook his head. "We're not quite ready for that, yet. Our living arrangements are just fine for now." He and Elyse had briefly discussed it a few weeks earlier but decided against it. "My lease is up this month, then I'll be up in Greeley for the summer rent free, but if you want to get something beginning in September, I'd be up for it."

Information about Dave's childhood came out slowly, and there was no great event like Jonas' Abby Archer episode. Over pizza one evening at Elyse's apartment, Laura had asked all the rookies to reveal something about themselves that people wouldn't suspect. Dave removed his glasses and rubbed his eyes before speaking. He told the group he had been the star of his high school baseball team, a two-year all-conference first baseman who could "hit the stuffing" out of the ball. "It was small school stardom, but lots of fun. I couldn't have even made the team at one of these big schools here in Denver." His friends laughed, calling him modest.

"Why would you think we wouldn't suspect you were an athlete?" asked Laura.

Dave stood in profile and replied, "Is this the body of an athlete? I may have been the only college student in America who liked dorm food. I've gained over fifty pounds since the glory days of high school." Then he patted his belly.

Using the investigative prowess of Archie King, Jonas found out Dave was being modest. He was every bit the high school star he had said he was, and he attended Adams State College on a baseball scholarship and had a successful first year. His career ended abruptly when he was beaned in the last game of the season against Western State and suffered permanent vision problems, which necessitated glasses and left him unable to gauge the curve ball.

Given his own background, however, what was most admirable to Jonas was Dave's work ethic. Teaching was not a 7:00 to 3:30 job at Andrew Jackson. Teachers were assigned students and given the task to teach them. Dave did this, and if that meant fifteen-hour days and the weekend, then so be it. It was just what it was. Get the job done.

§

With a week to go in the semester, Dave continued to funnel formulas into the minds of his students. Jonas backed off Watergate, sensing he might have overdone it in his classes. As usual Jonas went downstairs to get Dave for lunch, and they joined the staff in the teachers' lounge. Seating charts could not have ordered the lounge at noon more than seniority already had, and even though the year was at an end, the rookies still sat next to the copy machine at the back of the room.

"Ever wonder why all these guys became teachers?" Jonas was mostly just thinking aloud and didn't expect the question to be taken seriously, especially since their conversation about it earlier in the year.

Dave put a potato chip in his mouth and clasped his hands in front of his face. "Probably for the same reasons I did. You guys think it's a calling. Who knows? Maybe they had an epiphany like you did. Not me, and don't get me wrong here, but it's a job." He looked directly at Jonas. "My dad, and I think yours, have worked dangerous jobs all their lives. My pop's missing two fingers on his left hand and limps from a bad hip where he got caught between two trucks. In the winter, he works outside in some pretty rough weather. I didn't want that. This is a physically safe job."

Laura smiled. "I never really thought of it that way but look at the older teachers. They're all in pretty good health."

"Not in very good shape, but good health."

"You would notice that, Elyse," said Laura. "What about

Walburg though? She could pass for your older sister."

"Or me in ten or fifteen years," said Elyse.

"Except that she's an English teacher and writes poetry," kidded Laura.

"What do poets know anyway?" Elyse shook her head ending this detour in the conversation.

"So, there's no greater cause for you than numbers packed into your students' heads?" asked Jonas.

"There is some. I like what I do. I'm coming back next year, but if this school changes and I don't like it, I'm out of here. Southern Colorado has lots of small towns that need a math teacher who will coach baseball."

Elyse reached over and took Jonas' candy bar from his hand, eating the last bite. The staff knew they were dating, but in the building, they were circumspect.

Laura took things personally, one of the reasons disruptive students caused her such stress. "What about friendship? I guess I see the four of us together for a long time."

"The odds are against us all being here for a long time, Laura," said Elyse, "but I think we'll be friends wherever we go."

"Geez, I hope I get better treatment than you've given me this year," kidded Dave, and the others laughed.

"Did you see where Cirillo gave us all parking lot duty for graduation?" It was the traditional duty for first year teachers who would have to wait for a year to get invited into the actual ceremony.

"That's okay," said Elyse, "we don't know any seniors anyway. Walburg's giving the speech, though, and I'd kind of like to hear her. She can be so funny, and she's always insightful."

"You and Laura can sneak in. Jonas and I will hold down the parking lot while it's going on. Jonas is such a car guy anyway!" said Dave.

§

In the afternoon Elyse made the climb up to the second floor to talk with Jonas. "Are you still giving homework?" she asked when she sat down in the desk that was assigned to Rainer.

"Nope, I've got a few kids who are borderline, and I'm trying to get them ready for their final on Tuesday. We're just reviewing pretty hard in class. You?"

"No, but it's because I'm just pooped at the end of each day. My mom was right when she said I'd wear down as the year came to a close."

"I don't remember if you told me, but did she teach?"

"Yeah, for a few years before she got pregnant. My dad wouldn't let her keep working. Very traditional." She paused while Jonas taped the cover back on an old atlas. "Jonas, we came up with a lot of reasons why we shouldn't live together next year, and I know I agreed we shouldn't." She stopped there.

"Your parents were the biggest reason. Are you having second thoughts?"

"Yeah, especially when I heard you and Dave were getting a place. Your place is sort of like my favorite place." She smiled coyly. "Lots of great memories recently."

"Tell you what. I won't get rid of my squeaky bed. We'll make more memories." Jonas looked at the door, and seeing nothing, walked over and kissed Elyse.

"We'll have to make a real effort to see each other this summer. If you're staying with one of Cirillo's friends, I doubt if I'll be able to sleep over."

Jonas put his government textbook in his briefcase. "Come on. Let's go get a drink." Jonas felt Elyse's need for reassurance, but he was unsure as to how to do it. It was a different kind of reassurance than what Abby used to demand. Elyse's need was about heart—hers and her concern for Jonas' heart. Elyse was unselfish. Jonas thought the summer separation could be handled, that they could get together intimately on a regular basis. Maybe being a solitary person all his life led him to this conclusion, but he didn't know exactly how to explain it to his girlfriend. Elyse had never been a solitary person. She had been raised with rules and expectations, and now one of her expectations was he would follow those rules of hers. But, and he shook his head, he didn't know those rules.

In the hallway Archie stopped them for small talk. "Annette is hosting some people over tomorrow night for a little end of year get-together. You're welcome to come."

"Thanks, Archie, we already know," said Elyse. "Annette told us last week. We'll try and make it."

"Jonas, I'll need to have a formal meeting with you sometime next week. Froman's going to sit in and give you some tips about AP History. Elyse, your beau here will be really busy next year. You won't get to see him much." Archie laughed at his tease.

In the faculty parking lot, Jonas looked at Elyse to tell her where to meet for that beer, when he noticed her tears. "Now I'm confused."

"What Archie said about not seeing you much. I've just loved this year, hanging out with you and Laura and Dave. Working on my own, feeling good about what I've done, you know. I just don't want it to change."

"Let's go to your place. I'll pick up some KFC on the way over. I'll be there in twenty minutes."

§

Extra crispy. Mashed potatoes for Jonas, coleslaw for Elyse. Elyse didn't have any beer in the frig, and she didn't want Jonas to go out again, so they drank sodas.

"So, continue with my education about women." Jonas smiled.

"I'm just too sentimental. I'm fine." She pushed back from the table and took him to the couch. "Radio or records?"

"Records."

"Ever since we talked about why we got into this profession, I've been thinking. Dave's a pretty straight-forward guy. He knows why. I still don't," said Elyse.

"You're good at this, you know." Jonas believed his words; it wasn't meant to be a pep talk. "We're different, Elyse. I want to do this. I can do this. I'm not real good yet, but I will be. Maybe here at Jackson, maybe not, but somewhere. You haven't committed to it yet. That holds you back some. You're still looking for a more glamorous profession." Several times over the recent months, Jonas had watched Elyse from a distance and saw the teacher she was becoming. He wished he could transfer that vision to her, because he wanted her to succeed in her own eyes.

"Sometimes I do. You grow up with an idea, and it's hard to get rid of. Until my senior year, I never imagined myself as a teacher." She shifted on the purple couch to see Jonas better. "My mom taught; I loved school, both high school and college; school's always been easy. Did I just automatically take the next step?"

"Does it matter?" asked Jonas.

"It does to you." She put her hands on his thighs.

"Yeah, but what I mean is maybe it doesn't matter what brings us to the classroom. All that matters is that we give our kids an honest education. Really, that's what teachers do, isn't it?" Sometimes Jonas' simplicity was insightful.

Elyse patted her hands on his thighs. "Yes and no. All of us need to do our jobs, but schools need passion. If I continue to do this, or if I go into administration, I want to be passionate about it. Like you or Mr. Cirillo."

Jonas smiled. "From what I hear, you're a ball of fire in the classroom. Singing, dancing, crazy lab experiments. Kids love you."

"I don't know. I carry my students around, especially my girls. They need to be taught adult social skills, but they're so wrapped up in being boy-toys. That behavior doesn't serve them well after high school. I need my princesses to become queens. I keep thinking I could do more." She paused. "I just don't want to be blasé."

Jonas believed it was neither possible nor desirable for every teacher in the profession to possess that *fire*. Grinders like Dave were as important as stars like Ben Lucas. The chemistry of a staff had to meet the various needs of the student body, and not all students responded well to passion. "I think you don't want to be like me in the classroom. I tend to get frustrated too easily and that pushes kids away. At 3:00 when the last bell rings, it seems like you can leave it behind. I bring it home and stew."

"Seems that you all think I just walk away every afternoon. Elyse leaned in and kissed him, signaling the conversation was closed.

They didn't make it to the movie. Jonas did not fall asleep as quickly as Elyse did. He was confused about what his responsibilities were in this relationship. Maybe he should write her notes. She had written one to him earlier in the semester trying to explain her behavior on a night when he had continued to work on lesson plans when she wanted his undivided attention. At the end of the note, she attached a smiley face with a postscript which said, "If you add a smiley face at the end of a statement, you can get away with almost anything." Jonas hoped that Elyse understood him more than he understood her so their relationship could continue. He leaned over and kissed his sleeping girlfriend, shook his head, and whispered, "Goodnight, Baby. I love you."

§

ELYSE, 1963

Elyse Cottage introduces her parents to several of her counselors on the last day of camp. All of them are gushing in their praise of Elyse.

"Such a talented girl, Mr. Cottage. She won the three highest awards for horsemanship, and her campmates voted her favorite camper of the summer."

"You must be very proud, Mrs. Cottage. Your daughter always seems so happy. She also won a blue ribbon for taking care of the rabbits."

"She's a very strong swimmer. She tells us she's been taking lessons and wants to swim in high school. She'd be a welcome addition to our camp staff in a few years."

After each compliment Elyse's parents beam.

In the car on the ride home, Elyse's parents listen to their daughter tell of her two weeks away. It is obvious she has had fun and wants to return the following summer.

"What was that about the rabbits?" asks her father.

"One of the projects was to build cages for the bunnies. I couldn't do that so well; a couple of the boys had to help me with the chicken wire, but I seem to have a knack with the bunnies."

"What do the counselors do when camp is over?" asks Mrs. Cottage.

"A couple of them are teachers and just do this in the summer, but I

really don't know about most of them. Do you think I could work here when I grow up?" asks Elyse.

"Oh, I think it would be a good summer job for you when you're in high school or college, but not for after that. You'll have a real job and won't get your summers off," answers Mr. Cottage.

CHAPTER 15

Not every member of the Andrew Jackson staff attended Annette's year-end blow out, although the invitation was open to all. The teetotalers avoided it because of the abundance of booze. A handful of others refused to come because of run-ins with Archie over the previous years. Jane Walburg did not attend this year due to her long-running feud with Susan Bentert. Mrs. Bentert was the informal guest of honor due to her pending retirement. Jane believed Bentert used her age and longevity to bully students and staff to get her way. She also deemed Bentert no longer competent in the classroom to the detriment of her students, and that should not be celebrated. But those who came always had a great time, if they could remember it. The food was spicy, always a Mexican potluck with prizes for the hottest and most original.

Jonas and Elyse went as a couple. Both wore Hawaiian shirts and leis since neither owned any Mexican garb. Dave brought his elementary school teacher girlfriend, Katey Turpa, who was five feet three, one hundred and five pounds of energy, enough for both of them. Laura was now dating a stockbroker, Kevin Tappy, who wore a suit. By nine both were drunk in the downstairs bedroom. Thereafter, Kevin's nickname became Tippy, but he accepted it with good humor.

Pete warned everyone in attendance that school talk would not be permitted, but nobody paid any attention to his threats. Departments generally clustered in groups in different rooms and talked shop. Students were the chief topic of the night. As at school the top and bottom students received the most attention, with the average kids barely being mentioned. The entire staff got together in the family room just once. Annette had an extensive 45 rpm record collection, and from eight to nine she played requests, but only about fifteen to thirty seconds of any record. Because this had become a tradition, several of the older teachers brought in their 45s and donated them to the Jackson Oldies. Most of them were severely scratched, but no one seemed to care. At precisely nine Annette ended the session with *The Battle of New Orleans* in honor of Andrew Jackson. The faculty sang along with Johnny Horton, drowning him out by the end of the song. Tradition is important to schools. "I never want this to get old. Leave them wanting more rock 'n roll." Then, Archie stacked several albums on the spindle, and the staff returned to their department cliques.

Afterwards, many of the staff began to drift away, while the remainder calmed down and de-briefed the year. Elyse took Jonas' hand and led him to the upstairs hall where they could still hear the music but wouldn't be bothered. She brought along a nearly empty bottle of scotch from Archie's kitchen, and they danced slowly.

"Pretty romantic, huh."

Jonas was not a great dancer, but he liked this and tried. "Boys from small towns don't do this well, you know."

"You're doing just fine. When I retire, I hope I'm as feisty as those two retirees."

"I hope I'm still alive when you retire. We'll be nearing sixty. Can you imagine thirty-five more years of this?"

It was a rhetorical question, and they remained silent. Their dancing resembled more of a slow-moving hug with frequent kissing. Occasionally, they would sip straight from the bottle.

"Did you drink in high school?"

"Yeah. Small town boy, remember. My dad is a heavy drinker and didn't care if I did. What about you?"

"Very little. Drugs?" asked Elyse.

"Not until college and then not much. As you've noticed, I'm kind of a beer guy. You?" Jonas asked Elyse to answer her own question.

"Just a little in college. A couple of times I tried LSD. It really scared me. Sex?"

"Right now?" Jonas knew what she was asking but made it a small joke to buy some time.

"No, I mean did you have sex in high school?"

"No, you're the first," joked Jonas.

"Liar! Tell me the truth."

"Yeah. Again, small town boy. We had lots of time and opportunity."

"Lots of sex?"

"No, but don't tell anyone. I want to have a reputation." He kissed her. "Is this going anywhere?"

"No, just alcohol talk. I probably won't remember your answers in the morning anyway. Aren't you going to ask me about sex?" asked Elyse.

"No."

"I'm going to tell you anyway." She took another sip from the bottle. "I've had four lovers before you, my high school boyfriend, two one-night stands, and my college boyfriend. I almost married him, but he kept pushing me, and it didn't feel exactly right. He wanted to control me. Made me uncomfortable. Anyway, those were the only four. Not quite the stereotypical, sexually charged, college girl of the late-Sixties."

"You had me fooled."

Elyse tucked her head into Jonas' shoulder and remained quiet for several minutes. Without looking up at him, she asked, "Why do you hesitate with me?"

Jonas spoke slowly. "For lots of reasons. We share this, this year, but that's about all. When I got out of jail, you know I went back to Montana. I hired on with a company repairing fences all over the state. The company gave me a truck and a trailer. I would be gone for two to four weeks at a time. I became obsessed during the day with those fences—perfection—tight wires and correct spacing. In the evenings, I read and wrote down my thoughts. Lots of Louis L'Amour and Kurt Vonnegut, some philosophy, and even a little of the Bible. I asked myself lots of questions. I didn't come up with the big answers to the universe, but I did figure out one thing. I wanted to get back to teaching someday. It didn't have to be right away, but someday. There were some tough nights out there by myself, but, I think, on the whole, it was good for me. Elyse, my life to this point has been pretty messy. Andrew Jackson has given me some structure, maybe for the first time ever. We're very different in our paths to this place. You're rich. I'm kind of poor. You're outgoing, and I'm not so much. You're a beautiful woman, and I'm pretty average looking. You've got better options than me . . . and I know you're looking beyond teaching to a different career."

"I didn't kiss you that first day because you were average looking. I wouldn't have kissed Dave. I thought you were a stud."

"It was cool."

Elyse looked up into Jonas' eyes. "I thought so too." She held him with her eyes. "Is there any other reason why you withhold yourself?"

"Timing. I could fall completely in love with you, but we both have this job that consumes our time. It won't get easier next year." Jonas remembered telling Elyse he loved her while she was sleeping, but he panicked as her eyes were locked on his.

"And . . .?"

Jonas knew what she was asking. "And there's Abby. It's not what you think. She's not my girlfriend in any sense of the word. She was once, but it wasn't love. It was . . . the time. Abby was the revolution, and I liked being a part of that, a rural outsider holding on to the eye of the hurricane. It's hard to explain it to you because I can't really explain it to myself." He stopped dancing and pulled his head back. They were joined at the hips. "Come on." He led her to the steps and sat her down. "I'll try, but you have to try and see what I'm trying to say and not just hear my words."

"Strange request, but okay," said Elyse.

"Evidently, Abby isn't communicating with anyone. She doesn't speak or call her parents or anything. She's been in prison now since September of '70, and since her transfer to California, she hasn't spoken to anyone. Prison officials can't figure her out. They've contacted me three times trying to enlist my help. I've written letters but she doesn't write back. It's just she's out there alone for at least another three years, and I feel somehow responsible for her. The crazy thing is I know I shouldn't be." Jonas realized Elyse was squeezing his hand tightly.

"I don't know what to say."

"The whole thing is weird, I know. Let me ask you. Are you in a hurry with me?"

The question caught Elyse off-guard. "Maybe I am."

"Do you have to be? We have a good thing going just as it is."

Outwardly, Elyse nodded an acceptance, but inwardly, she drew back slightly.

§

JUNIOR WARREN, 1970

Mr. Elzey will not be mistaken for a coach, what with his round body and coke-bottle glasses, but he is thoroughly a teacher. He has volunteered to teach the "disciplined challenged" when he arrived at Aurora's North Junior High in 1965 and has made it his class. Junior high students are challenging enough, but to group twenty-eight ill-behaved fourteen-year-olds and expect them to learn? Mr. Zachariah, Elzey's best friend at North, can only shake his head in disbelief whenever Elzey plans another outing for his kids, but then he too will board the bus in support of his friend. Both men are science teachers, but the D-C class learns all subjects from Mr. Elzey.

On this particular day, Saturday, February 23, Elzey and Zachariah load the class into a bus and take them to play a basketball team from the Park Hill neighborhood in Denver. As north Aurora becomes more black in its demographics, Mr. Elzey thinks it a good idea to show them how an upscale, integrated neighborhood functions. What he has not planned on is that the game itself will be so one-sided. Coach Elzey plays all fourteen of his boys who have expressed a desire to be on the team. He has dyed tee-shirts blue and spray-painted numbers on the back for the entire class, while the Denver squad has full uniforms. The score on the board reflects the difference in talent, and at the end of the third quarter, Park Hill leads North 71-23. One of Park Hill's guards, a smallish black kid named Junior Warren, has scored more points than the entire North team combined. This kid confidently walks over to the North bench, says, "Let me help," and puts the North squad into a zone defense. He tells them to cut to the basket after each pass on offense and not to be timid to shoot. "Don't be afraid out there!"

Junior sits on the player side of Mr. Elzey and talks while he stares onto the court. "Life isn't a field trip, Coach. Your kids need to get after it. They're falling behind." Junior stands and yells at a North player to get in front of his man. He sits again. "Four or five of your kids could be pretty good, but they're lazy and content. Not a good combination. Someone needs to push them. That's what good coaches do, sir." Mr. Elzey listens without being intimidated. The Park Hill kid continues to talk and coach for the entire fourth quarter.

On the bus ride home, Mr. Elzey quizzes his students about their experience. "What did we learn today?"

"How to get our asses kicked!"

"Rich uniforms are nicer than poor ones!"

"We need to practice harder at lunch?"

"We should have let the girls be our cheerleaders." Even Mr. Zachariah laughs at that comment.

"Shoot, Mr. Elzey, I'm pretty sure that Candy, Jean, and Micki could have played better than us."

Mr. Elzey raises his hands as a show of enough. The bus goes quiet. He smiles before he speaks. "Well, maybe Micki could have helped, but Candy and Jean can't even guard me." Micki blushes and the boys giggle. Then he asks, "Did you have fun today?" The boys admit they did. "I did too. You guys are my guys, you know," and he loosens his tie and unbuttons his white shirt to reveal he also is wearing a blue-dyed tee-shirt with the number 29 on it. The bus roars with laughter. Mr. Elzey looks to Mr. Zachariah and nods. Zach removes his tie and shirt to reveal the number 30.

Mr. Elzey turns to the front of the bus and yells to the bus driver, "Norm, take us to get some hamburgers!"

§

At his home in Park Hill, Junior Warren's mother asks, "What did you learn today?"

"That you have to get after it early. Once you get behind, things get really difficult. Those kids from Aurora are already struggling."

CHAPTER 16

The noise from the halls grew louder as more students poured out of their classrooms with the early dismissal announcement from Mr. Cirillo. It was only forty-five minutes on the last Friday, but the students were grateful, as were the teachers. The graduation ceremony would be held the next morning, May 26, in the gym. Three hundred and fifty-three seniors would be receiving diplomas and heading off to college or out into the "real world."

Laura was hosting a first-year celebration for her gang, but the dinner wouldn't commence until 9:00 on Friday night. As a science teacher, Elyse especially had materials to inventory and store over the summer, but all the rookies had to get their rooms in order and go through an official checkout. Jonas was busy counting textbooks when Rodney Petersen walked in carrying a grocery sack.

"What's up, Rodney? How come you're still hanging around? Isn't there a swimming pool calling you?"

Rodney was one of those students Mr. Cullen had to work overtime with just to get him to pass. It hadn't been easy for either one of them. Rodney's IQ was below three digits, and it was obvious his family's goal for him was simply to graduate. At parent-teacher conferences, Rodney's father expressed his gratitude to Mr. Cullen for helping his son and promised to make sure Rodney would spend time on his reading every night. "But he's not a good reader. None of the Petersen clan really is."

"Hey, Mr. Cullen, I'm not disturbin' ya, am I?"

"Heck no, come in."

"Mr. Cullen, sir, when I told my dad I'd passed your class, even though it was a D, he let out a holler. So, we decided we wanted to get ya somethin' to say thanks. I got ya this." He handed Jonas a thin box wrapped in plain white paper. Inside was a wide, blue tie with pickup trucks on it. Before Jonas could say anything, Rodney held out the brown paper sack. "This is for you too. My dad thinks you deserve it for puttin' up with me all year."

Jonas opened the sack and immediately smiled. Inside was a six-pack of beer. "Well, Rodney, thank you, for both gifts. Tell your dad thank you too." Then Jonas did something he seldom did as a teacher. He stepped forward and hugged his student. Later, he wondered if he would have done that if Rodney was taller or more mature and decided that maybe he would have.

"You have a good summer, Mr. Cullen. I'll see ya next year."

"And the next year after that, Rodney."

§

"Miss Lake, can I ask you something while I wait to check out?" There was one teacher ahead of Elyse waiting to see Pete Cirillo, but he was near the door away from where Elyse stood.

"Ellie, you're no longer a rookie, so how about if you call me Annette like the rest of the staff does."

"Okay. Annette." Elyse didn't like her name shortened to Ellie, but she seldom corrected anyone. "How do you accept that Archie …" she paused, and Annette finished her sentence.

"Shares me? You'd never ask me unless it was personal. Is this about Jonas?"

Elyse smiled. "Yes."

"Honey, our situations are different, but I'll tell you. I like Archie a lot. I also know it's a temporary condition, and someday I'll leave and find someone else. I stay because he's so much fun." Elyse looked perplexed, so Annette continued. "Ellie, I met Archie at a strange time in my life. Things were kind of upside down. He's helped me through some troubles, but he has never been my soul mate. If he was, I'd stay through the darkest days. I mean that. If he was my soul mate, I'd wait forever. You and Jonas are young and talented, and from all I gather, he's not sharing you. What he's doing with Abby is providing a lifeline. That girl is messed up. He can't make a commitment just now."

"Do you think he'll be able to at some point?"

"I do, but I don't have a crystal ball as to the timetable. I do know most men resist being kept too tightly. See what the summer brings. Don't smother him. In a strange way, a perverted way, I think that Abby chick did."

Elyse nodded. "Thanks. I'll try to let him breathe."

"Ellie, I think if you allow him to become the teacher he can be, the teacher he wants to be, if you're there to support him in his endeavors without the pressure, you'll become his all-the-time lady." Annette gave Elyse a long stare and then reached over and squeezed her hand. "And you'll become the teacher we think you will, and that's a damn fine one."

§

As Jonas and Elyse touched and hugged throughout dinner, Dave shook his head. "You know, it doesn't seem quite fair on the last day of school, you guys are with your sweetie, and Laura and I are stag."

Jonas got up from the table, walked around to Dave, and gave him a hug. "We told you guys to bring Katey and Tippy, but Laura said she just wanted us on this special day." Dave swatted him away.

"Toast!" They all stood for Laura's toast. "To the best three friends I could have wished for in my first year. I could never, and I mean never, have handled this without you guys." They clinked wine glasses and drank.

"My turn." Elyse looked to her friends. "To next year. May it be easier." Laura responded with a hearty head nod toward Elyse.

Dave and Jonas looked at each other like immature junior high boys and started to laugh. Jonas realized Elyse was offended, so he tried to explain.

"We aren't laughing at your toast. Really. We were laughing because we both thought it was expected we were to give a toast, and we don't have one. Really."

Dave nodded. "Really. We're drinking wine for god's sake, and I'm from Del Norte and he's from Montana. We're not the most sensitive of guys. You both know that."

Elyse leaned over to Laura and whispered something into her ear. Then she spoke. "Unless you come up with a toast, a sincere toast, you won't get dinner. And, Jonas, you won't be getting any sex tonight." Both Laura and Dave laughed at that.

Jonas kept the game alive. "Quit laughing, you dickhead, this is serious. If we don't come up with a toast, we don't get dinner." He smiled at Elyse. He took Dave by the arm and escorted him into the hallway.

Elyse put her arm around Laura's shoulders. "We're not going to let them off easy."

The boys returned, and boys they still were on this night. They picked up their wine glasses, raised them, and waited for the women. Jonas spoke. "Okay, toast."

Dave interrupted. "Ah, whatever Jonas says, that's me too."

"As I was saying, a toast. To Laura and Elyse, our partners in education at General Andrew Jackson High School, who shared our occasional triumphs and many troubles. Who mocked us at teachers' meetings and at 1421. Who locked us out of our own apartments, without coats, on that terribly cold night in February. Who stole our lesson plan books on the Monday morning when we were all meeting with Cirillo." Jonas was not done, but the girls were starting to giggle. "Who dressed up as cheerleaders and came to my first basketball game. Who captured the bull frogs and put them in our desk drawers on April Fools' Day. Who taped the Playboy playmate on the blackboard behind my world map—and the naked pig on your chalkboard. But through it all, to you guys who are now our lifelong friends." Then Jonas bowed, and Dave patted him on the back.

"What do you think, sincere enough?" asked Dave.

Laura had both hands over her mouth and had tears in her eyes. "I guess. What do you think, El?"

Elyse paused, and then pointedly to Jonas said, "Hell, yes."

Laura came around to Dave while Elyse went to Jonas, and they hugged together.

"Dinner is served," said Elyse, "and there will be dessert."

§

Graduation for the Class of 1973 was held at 10:00 in the morning on May 26. Jane Walburg gave the commencement address, an honor voted upon by the senior class. Her closing words to her seniors were to "Take risks and don't be afraid, travel and learn about the world, volunteer, and give back. Remember that you will always represent this school and this community. Make us proud." There she paused and looked over the students for a few seconds, holding them with her eyes and her heart. "Finally, love your people and make sure they know it."

§

For Jonas Cullen, Dave Fallon, Elyse Cottage, and Laura Sanders, it was the end of a trying, but occasionally rewarding, year. Over the summer Annette Lake moved out of Archie King's house in southwest Denver and into her own apartment in Aurora. John Gross!Man died of a heart attack. Mr. Elzey and Mr. Zachariah were in a serious car wreck, and Elzey would be forced to give up teaching. Mrs. Conduct finally took that vacation to Washington, D.C., and remembered a little boy who gave a speech about President Kennedy to her after school. Pete Cirillo hired new teachers to replace Mrs. Froman and Mrs. Bentert.

In Los Angeles, California, Abby Archer neared the end of her third year in jail. She had not spoken in over two years. She continued to receive letters from Jonas, one about every three weeks. He wrote only about his students.

Rainer, Ian, Kristen, Erin, Stu, Betty, and Rick were all scheduled into Mr. Cullen's second hour AP History class. Messi, Julia, Danny, Martha, Sandy, and Stacey were in the sixth period AP class. Cliff Steuben and three of his friends transferred to Cherry Creek High School in a southern suburb.

II
SUMMER 1973

Chapter 17

On June 21, 1973, the United States Supreme Court released its decision regarding Denver school desegregation. The ruling would fundamentally change how education, both public and private, was delivered to students in the entire metropolitan area. The petitioners' claim was that in one neighborhood in particular, Park Hill, deliberate segregation had occurred. The petitioners were eight families--five black, two Anglo, and one Hispanic--who claimed intentional segregation in one neighborhood meant the entire Denver school district was segregated. For Denver this issue had been simmering since the late-1950s.

Brown v. Board of Education of Topeka Kansas, 1954, ruled segregated public schools were "inherently unequal" and should be desegregated with "all deliberate speed." This ruling seemed to be focused on border and southern states, and it did not immediately impact northern, urban schools. It did, however, energize and raise the awareness of blacks across the country.

In 1962 the Denver school board had organized a committee to examine racial patterns in the city and make recommendations. The Vorhees Special Study Committee on Equality in Educational Opportunity urged gradual integration of the school system should begin first by redrawing boundaries. Instead, the school board massaged the boundaries to protect white schools. When progress on this recommendation proved too slow, a second study group was formed. In 1966 the Berge Committee recommended more direct action.

In 1968 the Denver Public Schools school board, behind the lead of Rachel Noel, the first black to sit on the Denver school board, directed the superintendent, Robert Gilberts, to prepare a "comprehensive" plan to desegregate the entire system. Gilberts' plan included busing some students across traditional neighborhood boundaries to achieve "racial diversity." The Denver school board accepted his plan in April 1969.

Immediately, opposition to the plan erupted, enough so the election held in May was basically a referendum on the Denver school board. A record turnout resulted in the overwhelming defeat of two incumbent school board members who had supported the superintendent's plan of school busing. By June the new school board had thrown out the busing plan in favor of a voluntary desegregation plan. Gilberts was on his way out too.

Ten days later the eight families filed a suit to "enjoin" the implementation of the superintendent's plan. They also wanted the federal court to declare the abandonment of the plan was a violation of the Equal Protection Clause of the Fourteenth Amendment. Few people trusted the Denver school board. The suit asked for the courts to direct the desegregation of the Denver schools. Many white families, especially in the Park Hill neighborhoods of northeast Denver, were already deserting the system in favor of neighborhoods in south Denver and the southern and western suburbs. Cherry Creek was one of these areas.

The United States District Court granted the injunction saying the public schools in Denver had intentionally followed a segregationist policy for the preceding decade in Park Hill. Judge William E. Doyle also stated schools in central Denver were segregated with substandard facilities, and they needed to be "overhauled" throughout the system. In effect, the Court ordered busing for racial integration beginning in 1970. The new, divided Denver school board appealed.

It was the official position of the school board that no proof of "purposeful discriminatory action" on their part existed. Instead, de facto segregation of neighborhoods had resulted in segregated schools. The Tenth Circuit Court of Appeals issued a confusing decision. It ruled the Park Hill neighborhood needed to be desegregated, but not the core city schools. "Deliberate segregation of one district was not proof of deliberate segregation throughout the school system." The city, the school board, and 95,000 students were operating without direction.

The parents eventually appealed to the U.S. Supreme Court, which heard arguments on October 12, 1972. A decision would be rendered the following year.

§

On Friday morning, June 22, 1973, Pete Cirillo sat in his office at Andrew Jackson High School pouring over two days copies of the *Denver Post* and the *Rocky Mountain News*. He read every word of the stories from the Supreme Court decision, then pushed back from his desk and left the office. Somewhere in the otherwise quiet halls, he could hear the janitor singing softly. Carlos Herrera had a nice voice, and old school hallways allowed for excellent transmission of sound, but Pete couldn't make out the words. Often Pete and Carlos were the only two people in the building. Pete walked his building, a building that would be transformed in yet unknown ways in the years to come.

There would be lots to do over the next year preparing his students, their parents, his staff, and the neighborhoods around Jackson for the desegregation of his school. He knew every day for the next four or five years would be focused on that task. As the principal of one of the two Denver schools closest to the southern gateway to the suburbs, he knew his school would be scrutinized. Even the name itself, Andrew Jackson, with its historical connotations related to the South, would be called into question.

Pete knew this decision was coming. Even though Denver did not have official policies to segregate the schools, subtle practices over time had prevented the system from becoming integrated. "De facto segregation, my ass," he muttered to himself. Real estate practices, covenants, public funding, and clever boundary changes all conspired to keep blacks and Hispanics isolated. It had been especially true for the elementary schools in north and west Denver. In his first year as a principal, one school board member, who no longer sat on the board, told him, "We don't segregate. We just minimize."

Pete's favorite place to analyze his concerns was the tower—quiet, isolated, above the fray—the old music studio for a principal with no musical talents. "Above the fray . . ." After unlocking the door leading up the circular stairs, he pushed open two windows in order to cool the area down. He pulled a chair over to the west-facing windows and sat down. He took a cigar out of his pocket and lit up. The smoke curled around his head before being drawn to the outside air. Pete smiled to himself thinking how the scene might be apropos of the oncoming months.

The upcoming school year would be filled with detailed planning. The school board could appeal certain aspects of the Supreme Court's decision, and Pete was pretty sure they would. His private discussions with the school board members convinced him they would stall and delay as long as they could. Still, some forced busing would begin in the fall of 1974. It would push hundreds, maybe thousands, of middle- and upper-class white students into the suburban schools or into private academies.

"Mr. Cirillo, is that you up there?"

"Yes, Carlos, come on up. I've got another cigar stashed away."

The janitor sat next to Pete and held the cigar in his mouth while Pete struck the match. "Thanks, Mr. Cirillo." The two men puffed in silence, enjoying the view of the Front Range.

"What do you think, Carlos? Is this busing thing going to help or hurt?"

Carlos did not look at Pete. He blew a smoke ring before answering. "That's a tough one, Mr. Cirillo, but forcing this city to integrate isn't gonna go over too good. Lots of people will fight it."

"You're right there."

They smoked in silence some more.

"If people give it a chance, then maybe." Carlos and Pete had held these talks before. "But it's the right thing to do, Mr. Cirillo, and I don't think there's much of an alternative."

"I think so too, Carlos, I think so too. But will people give it a chance?"

"I doubt it, sir, not citywide, but maybe you can get your school to."

"Our school, Carlos, our school."

Neither man spoke for several minutes, taking deep drags on their cigars and watching the smoke drift upwards. In time Pete asked a question. "How did your daughter finish up the school year?"

"They refitted the brace, Mr. Cirillo, so she's walking better."

"No, I meant with her grades."

"Oh, she wouldn't let a little accident slow her down there. She got all the work in."

"Is she still number one in her class?"

"I think so, Mr. Cirillo. She was a little worried about calculus."

"That's quite a girl you have there, Carlos. Tell her I said hi and congratulations."

"Thank you, Mr. Cirillo. I will."

Pete finished his cigar and put the stub in the Folger's ash can, but he made no move to leave, allowing Carlos time to finish his smoke.

As his cigar dwindled down to less than an inch, Carlos spoke again. "You know, Mr. Cirillo, everyone talks about the blacks, but there's a whole lot more browns out there that aren't making noises. You might want to keep tabs on their growing numbers. They're mostly content with their situation, but there are some Chicano leaders who are making noises. It'll spill over into education at some point."

§

In the afternoon Pete spoke by telephone with principals from South High School, George Washington, North, West, and Thomas Jefferson. Pete was surprised to learn there were more Hispanics in the system than blacks by a few percentage points. He hadn't given it much thought before Carlos' warning. Growing up in Pueblo, a tough steel city two hours south of Denver, he had lived around many students of Mexican ancestry, and they seemed to be mostly integrated. What isolated students in Pueblo was poverty, not race.

Participation in school activities seemed to be the main criteria in the Fifties. It would be key to creating a family environment at Jackson in the years ahead also.

Pete's family stopped by around four to say goodbye. They were heading to Grand Lake for the weekend to do a little hiking and boating. He had three children: a boy, Petey, age twelve, and two daughters, Hannah and Lindsay, age nine and eleven. Pete and Colleen worried about Petey in school, especially as he approached his teen years. He was so gentle, an easy target in secondary schools. *So unlike me at that age*, Pete thought.

"Come with us, Daddy," begged the girls. It was tempting, but he wanted to be around this weekend to soothe worried teachers or students. He walked them out to the station wagon, kissed them goodbye, told his wife to call him later that night, and then turned to Petey.

"You take care of the girls now, you hear."

Archie King was waiting for Pete when he returned to the office. Pete had expected him to show up earlier. Instead of staying in the office, Pete led Archie out to the kitchen where he kept summer snacks in the massive metal refrigerator. From there they went to the cafeteria and sat at a circular table.

"Damn school board's going to fight this, Pete. Perrill and Southworth aren't going to give in without a fight."

Pete took the last bite of his fudgesicle. He measured his words, knowing Archie was spoiling for a fight. "Probably, but the writing's on the wall." Archie started to speak, but Pete cut him off by raising his hand suddenly. "Judge Doyle's not going to allow any bullshit now. He's got the Supreme Court behind him. If the board delays, he'll step in and take over. This isn't about the school board any longer; it's about the court directing Denver's system, and Doyle wants to do it. Busing at the elementary schools is already occurring and will continue this fall. I'm sure the entire system will have busing by next year. That means us."

"It's about time," said Archie forcefully. Coming from the South where segregation was deliberate throughout all systems, he saw Denver through those same magnolia-colored glasses. "This is no different than *Brown*, just the logical extension, and God knows, our country is long overdue."

When he was a classroom teacher, Pete had held these same views, but as a principal, he hedged on busing. The short history of court-ordered busing in Boston and other eastern cities told him how destructive it could be for neighborhoods and communities. "So, everything we do here gets a backseat to integration?"

"Damn straight!" responded Archie. "Schools are a vivid cross-section of what's happening in the community, the composition, social, and economic trends. Why not let it be the other way around and let the schools lead the way?"

"Desegregation will lead directly to citywide integration then?"

"Don't bait me, Pete. It's part of the process. Sometimes, a person has to be clubbed over the head to see what's right."

"You always take the high moral ground, and anyone who doesn't agree is the villain. This could work, and you know I'll try my hardest to make it work, but there might be other results. Denver's middle class might just vote with their feet. Then we could become even more segregated, not less."

"Just annex their asses! It's what Denver's been doing over the past decade anyway."

"That works because they wanted Denver's schools, which up to this point have been pretty good. If they see us struggling with this busing plan, people may just oppose annexation. Then Denver gets locked in by the suburbs."

Archie was quick to interrupt when Pete paused, which annoyed Pete who was trying to be thoughtful. "That's their problem. The Supreme Court will deal with them too."

"Not just their problem. I didn't check my morals at the door, Arch, but how do we pay for this education when the tax base heads south and west? Private schools will accept thousands of dollars in tuition from their new students and keep them away from the *huddled masses*, and I hate that, but how do we maintain over the long run if we lose money?"

"You're being short-sighted, Pete. All those families that are leaving are just racist. If they were leaving a poor school for a better one, maybe I could excuse them, but to leave Andrew Jackson is just racism. They're running scared. Besides, the legislature will find a new way to fund public education. Property taxes won't be the foundation of school funding."

Pete laughed out loud. "I don't think they're looking for our permission, and I disagree with you that they're all bigots. But I do think many of them are fearful for no real reason." He paused. "A new way to fund our schools other than property taxes? You're talking about the same Colorado legislature that sits up on Capitol Hill?" He shook his head in disbelief. "I hope you're right, Arch, I hope you're right."

CHAPTER 18

July 9, 1973

> *Dear Mr. Cirillo,*
> *I suspect you have already heard about my resignation from the district, but I wanted to let you know how much I appreciated the opportunity you gave me last year and the support you constantly supplied. While you never said so, I think I let you down. My fear was that this year, I'm not sure I would be any better, and to tell the truth, if they start busing in students from some of the other, tougher schools, I could get worse.*
> *Mr. Cirillo, I'm scared of what might happen, and I couldn't control those kinds of kids. I'm sorry, but it's the truth. So, I've accepted a position in a small junior high up north of Longmont.*
> *I appreciate the recommendation you wrote for me and the contacts you made to get me the interview. Thank you again.*
> *Sincerely,*
> *Laura Sanders*

§

When Elyse told Jonas that Laura was not coming back, Jonas put aside his studies and drove back to Denver from Greeley. He and Elyse took Laura out to dinner to say goodbye, but his primary reason was to be with Elyse, as she was losing her best teaching friend. He allowed the girls to monopolize the conversation, did not bring up his classes at Northern Colorado, and laughed at the appropriate times. After dinner they walked Larimer Street and had beers at 1421, where they met up with Tippy. Around ten Elyse and Jonas left for her apartment.

In bed that night, in the gentle stillness after sex, Elyse whispered to Jonas, "*You* are my best friend, you know, and the most influential person in my life. Can you handle that?"

Chapter 19

Jonas' summer home was in the basement of the principal of a Greeley high school. The principal had taught with Pete Cirillo in the early Sixties in Denver, and they developed a mutual respect during those seven years, if not a close friendship. Plus, they were both Pueblo natives and tough Italians. Jonas spent little time there. Between his classes, doing research at the library, and traveling to Denver to see Elyse on the weekends, there were scant moments to make small talk with Pete's former colleague.

Elyse's fears for the summer proved to be unfounded, while Jonas' lack of concern for the summer separation now seemed justified. She managed to make it up to Greeley frequently for dinner and a movie, and Jonas drove to Denver each weekend and stayed at her apartment. It was during these weekends Jonas' feelings for Elyse began to connect with a future. He realized he was walking a fine line with Elyse by maintaining contact with Abby. Elyse would need to be tough and patient.

It happened again. Near the end of July, on a Tuesday afternoon when Jonas stopped at a 7-11 near the Northern Colorado campus to get a soda and a sandwich, his car was stolen. He left the keys in the ignition figuring he would be back soon. The car was found the next morning in a field east of town, minus tires, stereo, and back seat. Otherwise, it was drivable. He bought new tires and went without the music and back seat. He had visions of the FBI suitman jumping into the car and driving it to the open field and dismantling it.

His graduate classes and the AP seminar were demanding, but valuable. Archie warned him before he left for Greeley to keep his bullshit antennae active, but they weren't needed. Jonas kept up on the legal happenings surrounding school desegregation, as had most of the Jackson faculty. Unlike most of the faculty, Jonas was excited for the busing to begin, convinced it was the right thing to do, and anxious to relate the proceedings to a certain prisoner he knew, who, he was sure, would also believe Denver was doing the correct thing. The idealism of the Goldman teaching staff seemed to be affirmed.

The eight-week summer courses ended the second week in August.

§

The Watergate probes continued to dominate the news. On July 16, 1973, Alexander Butterfield, an aide to H.R. Haldeman, President Nixon's chief of staff, publicly revealed to the Senate Watergate Committee that conversations in the White House had been recorded. Within days, the Special Prosecutor and Senator Ervin demanded that Nixon turn over the tapes for inspection. The President refused. By the end of July, the first article of impeachment against the President was introduced into the House of Representatives.

§

August 12, 1973

Abby,

I'm sorry I haven't kept up with the letters as frequently this summer. Since I've been at summer school, I haven't seen my kids. Rainer and Stacey and maybe Kristen came by school to see me and talk about Watergate and busing, but I wasn't there. Mr. Cirillo told me they came by. Next year should be really interesting—and hard. It will be the last normal year for Denver schools for quite a while. I hope to be at least competent with the AP classes. Mrs. Froman's scores were so good, mostly 4s and 5s, so I'll have my work cut out for me. There're enough kids for two sections. My other two classes will be sophomores again—history, not government, so I'll have three preps. I thought I was getting two senior electives, but Pete had to give them to a teacher with more seniority. Still, two AP sections!

Andrew Jackson is hardly inner city, as I'm sure you're aware, but things will change in a year. Cirillo said we may get as many as 300 black students. I don't know how he knows. He also wondered if I would be interested in transferring to one of the high schools in north Denver. I'll put in a good word for you for when you get out. (That's only partly a joke, Abby.)

I talked briefly with Paul yesterday. His parents have allowed him to take phone calls again. He said to say hi. I think he's doing pretty good, all things considered. He said he lost lots of weight but is gaining it back now that he's home. Technically, he's still in the Army, but I think he gets discharged this fall. I'm going to go see him later this month. Anything you want me to say to him? He said he'd like to write to you.

If the time comes when you want to talk, let me know. I'm sure I can still piss you off quickly. Last year, I was so busy, the year passed by in an instant. Stay really, really busy for the next three years, Abby.
Jonas

CHAPTER 20

Bryson City students in North Dakota would begin the 1973-74 term on September 4, the day after Labor Day. The town was informed in May that one of its graduates had been added to the list of those killed in Vietnam. Jason Deaver, from the Class of '65, had been listed as MIA until the list of prisoners was released by North Vietnam in the spring. Those teachers who worked at the time remembered him fondly as a big, gentle boy who excelled in wood shop and auto shop. His death came as little surprise since no information about him had been received by his mother, who was employed at the school as a cook during his years on the missing-in-action status. The black MIA flag had been flown at the courthouse since Jason went missing in 1970.

Jason graduated from Bryson City Central, but it burned down four years later. Afterwards, students were bused the twelve miles west across U.S. 94 into Bismarck. Now, a new junior-senior high school was nearing completion and students would be staying in town beginning in January. Small town schools are at the center of all doings, and for a town to do without a high school for over three years meant it didn't control its destiny. While Bryson City felt like it was regaining its soul, many of its students were stressed about leaving friends and classmates behind in Bismarck. Two Bryson City boys were members of the Bismarck state championship basketball team from 1972 and now, as seniors, they were being counted on to lead the Patriots back to glory. However, the state athletic association ruled they must play for Bryson City, which was already fielding athletic teams for the upcoming winter season.

Bryson City hired a principal over the summer to prepare the school for students and to hire a staff. Jorgen Andersen was of Norwegian stock from the farming region just west of Fargo and about 120 miles east of Bismarck. A native North Dakotan, he was well-known in Bryson City. He and his four brothers had denied Bryson City Central football championships in the Fifties. A towhead who stood six-foot-five, he was a commanding figure. He believed his most important hires would be the agriculture teacher, the boys' basketball coach, and the two science teachers. Graduates from BC went back to work on their family farms. Often, like Jason Deaver, they spent a few years in the military. Those who did go to college most likely attended one of the schools in the Dakotas.

All totaled, 176 students would be returning to Bryson City from Bismarck in January. For the first half-year, Jorgen Andersen would be hiring fourteen teachers and a counselor plus a secretary and a nurse. There would be no food services until the following year; students would be expected to bring their lunches. Volunteers would see to it some breakfast items were available. Every one of the new teachers would be required to coach or direct extra-curricular activities. Andersen was going to assist with the football team in a year and start up the student government in January.

Mr. Andersen attended a professional conference in Omaha, Nebraska, over the summer. A featured speaker was Pete Cirillo, who spoke on being a high school principal, and the title of his session was "You Are In Charge. Know Your People!"

Chapter 21

"Junior, are you ready?" asked his mother. It was the Friday before the Labor Day weekend, and school would start on Tuesday.

Junior Warren decided over the summer to transfer from Denver East to Andrew Jackson, a difficult decision to understand for everyone who knew him. East High School was regarded as Denver's premier high school, and Junior was among its brightest students and a promising athlete. To hear the students and staff at East describe him, Junior was one of the elites at East, even though he was just entering his junior year.

Warren's college-educated parents moved to Denver from North Carolina in the mid-Fifties. They bought a home in the Park Hill neighborhood, solidly in the upper-middle class. His older sister was attending Cal Berkeley, and Junior indicated he was looking to attend an Ivy League school and become a lawyer.

"I still don't understand this!"

"Mom, we've been all through this. I don't intend to sit this out, and if I wait another year, it'll be someone else's fight. It's my fight; it's our fight."

"At least promise me you'll listen when we talk to Mr. Cirillo. He seems like a sensible man." Mrs. Warren was grasping at straws. She knew her son had made up his mind, and nothing either she or his father would say now was going to change it. "At least you could've chosen Abraham Lincoln High School. That man was on our side."

III
FALL, 1973

CHAPTER 22

On August 31, the Friday before school was to begin for the 73-74 school year, Pete Cirillo did something he never did at teachers' meetings. He sat down.

"I think," he started slowly, "Tuesday will be the last normal opening day of school we will have for many years." He allowed that to sink in. Had his principal been standing, Archie might have given a sarcastic response. Pete continued. "I also believe a year from now, this staff could look considerably different because some of you may choose to leave. That saddens me because you're a terrific bunch, but I understand. This year, our stress will be from anticipation. I still don't know how this whole busing scheme will be played out, but it will come. There's talk that some changes will be put in place at the semester, but I'm sure that won't happen for us. It'll be next year." He resisted his urge to stand, wanting to show just now he was one of them. "With only two or three exceptions, I think I have given you a schedule you will have for the next few years. My thinking is if you're teaching new classes this year, you can concentrate only on their curriculum before we get hit with the desegregation experiment. I'll do my best to buy whatever materials and textbooks you think you'll need for optimum success, and you can plan your classes to the last detail this year. In May I'll sit down with each one of you and go over what you need for the following year." Pete pursed his lips in a determined manner. "We teach kids to be prepared for the unexpected, to pay attention to details, to have a positive attitude going into difficult situations." He scanned the room, looking into the eyes of several teachers. "Well, that's what I'm going to do, and what I'm asking you to do. Andrew Jackson is going to make this work. We're going to be the model to the other Denver high schools. American democracy is rooted in the public school system, and all we're doing is taking it to the next level. So, let's be proud of what we're doing and what it is we're preparing for next year."

The library was silent for only a moment. Then from several places in the room, the applause began, and everyone stood. The principal finally stood and with his hands, asked for quiet.

"Thank you. I appreciate that. Annette wants me to remind you all to stop by the office and pick up your packets if you haven't already. I think we've spent enough time here this week, so why don't we all meet for a cold one over at the Cricket. For those of you who don't drink, I'll buy. For those of you who do, Archie'll pick up the tab."

§

Annette was sitting in the office with Mr. and Mrs. Warren at the work desk completing the transfer papers when Pete returned from the teachers' meeting. Junior leaned on the counter, separating the secretary's desk from the student waiting area. He was reading the Andrew Jackson handbook.

"Good afternoon, Mr. and Mrs. Warren. I hope I didn't keep you waiting. I was just finishing up on our last meeting before I sent everyone home for the holiday." He shook both their hands and turned to their son. "It's nice to see you again, Junior. Shall we all go into my office?" Annette led the march, followed by the parents, with the principal and the student bringing up the rear. Mr. Cirillo put his left hand on Junior's shoulder.

When they were all seated, Pete spoke. "We've enrolled you in a pretty tough couple of classes. Two AP classes, English and history, and our top-level mathematics. Your transcripts indicate this is where you belong. I got a call from the counselor at East, and I have to tell you, she's not happy about your coming over here. They're pretty proud of you and want you to stay." He paused to allow for either

Junior or his parents to respond. The silence was uncomfortable.

Finally, the young man spoke. "All of your other black kids live near the school; it's their attendance area, and they're from middle-class families. *Brown* gave them the right to attend their neighborhood school, but now everything's been turned upside down, and it's going to cause a stir because you're going to get poor black kids. To be honest, Mr. Cirillo, my parents are against my coming here, but I don't want to be left out of all the excitement."

The father spoke softly but firmly. "Junior, be respectful."

"No, no, I respect your son's straight-forward response." Pete turned back to Junior. "Go on, son."

"My father has taught me to be respectful, and I will be. But I'm here for a purpose. I won't be invisible, and in my classes, especially those where we're supposed to discuss these types of issues, I'll speak out." He smiled. "Maybe I can ease the transition into next year a bit, not just for the other black kids, but for your white students and your staff."

Annette wasn't sure Junior Warren's words signaled an offer or a challenge, but she liked his presence: confident, blunt, and honest. She was sure her boss did too.

"Well, I'm glad you chose Andrew Jackson. Can you tell me why you've selected us instead of one of the other high schools?"

The young man had a disarming smile. "Yes, sir. One, I talked with my old principal at East, sort of before he knew I was planning to transfer before the busing started, and he recommended you. Not your school, but you. The other reason is you have a pretty good basketball team, but you need a guard if you stand a chance at beating East."

Mrs. Warren shook her head slightly. "If it was basketball, you'd have stayed home or gone over to Manual. That's where real basketball's played."

"Well, son, I'm glad you chose us. If you'd like, I can introduce you to some of the kids who'll be in your advanced classes. We've got a good bunch."

"Thank you, sir, but I'll meet them on my own."

The meeting broke up with Mr. Cirillo reassuring Mr. and Mrs.

Warren, and with Annette taking her new student on a brief tour of the building; there were some things the secretary wanted to say to him.

"You're grown up beyond your years, but there will be days when it won't be easy. And this year could be a lot easier than next. I think you're aware of that." She paused while they walked. "Know that Mr. Cirillo will treat you fairly. He's committed to his students, and I've never known him to be arbitrary. You might not always see it at the time, but you'll see. What you said in there in front of your parents was brave. I could never have done that at your age."

Junior looked straight ahead. "Miss Lake, ma'am, I'm not brave; I'm just curious as all get out. It gets me in trouble sometimes, but it's who I am. You might want to warn Mr. Cirillo."

"In your second hour AP history class, there's a red-headed girl you might want to meet. Her name is Rainer Brecht."

§

One of the many statistics given to Elyse during her training to be Andrew Jackson's liaison to the district's committee on court-ordered desegregation showed Anglo enrollment in Denver had actually been declining since 1963. White flight to the suburbs was a decade old. The head of the committee, an elementary teacher on special assignment named Betty Germany, said it didn't matter whether whites were leaving because of racism or because of the desire to have their children attend better schools. She said she wasn't able to look into the minds and hearts of those who moved.

That statistic did not correlate to Andrew Jackson. Its white population had only shown a slight decline last year. But it was obvious when the teachers received their new roll sheets for the 73-74 school year that a real decline had occurred. Jonas lost four of his AP students before the first day, including Alexis and Stuart, neither of whom returned to say goodbye.

Jonas received mixed messages from his two mentors, which he mentioned to Elyse. "On one hand Archie says good riddance, but Pete is hurt by their departure. He says those are just the students the Supreme Court wants the minority kids to mix with."

Elyse curled her lips inward and looked guilty. "Jonas, can I tell you something without you saying anything about it just now?"

Jonas put his apple down and stepped toward her. "Of course. What?"

"You know where my house is, in Greenwood Village. We moved there when I was in fifth grade. Before that I lived in Park Hill. I always told people it was so we could have horses, but that was a lie. My parents moved to get me away from the blacks. I graduated from Kent Girls School. There's not a whiter school in the state than Kent. I was a part of that early white flight."

§

Elyse shared all her committee information with Jonas and Dave, which led to lengthy discussions on those evenings after her meetings. While they talked about it at times, Jonas seemed mostly intent on his daily and weekly lesson plans, on grading papers, and on his extracurricular activities. He seemed to accept the inevitability of busing and welcomed it. Jonas could tell Elyse was changing because of her new assignment; she was personalizing the experience, and it was creating a new level of stress in her life.

Chapter 23

Ian was bullshitting Mr. Cullen in response to his questions. He had not read the assigned chapter, but being so bright, he believed he could fool Jonas. "The Puritans came to Virginia to support John Smith who had set up several churches there in opposition to the Church of England." Ian waited for another question. Receiving nothing from the teacher other than a stoic look with crossed arms, he continued. "It was the Puritans who established the House of Burgesses, the first form of representative government in the New World, they and wrote in the idea of church and state in their charter." He smiled sheepishly.

"Ian, sit down! I don't even know where to begin correcting what you just said, but I do know b-s when I hear it. This will be the very last time you come to this class unprepared. If it happens again, I'll run you out and into one of the regular history classes. And that goes for the rest of you also." Jonas had never dressed down a student with such quiet resolve, but he wanted to set the tone for his first advanced placement class. "Oh, and Ian, you'll spend lunch in here reading and outlining the chapter. What you don't finish at lunch, you can complete after school. Tell your parents to expect my call."

When Jonas turned his back to walk to the front of the room, Rainer smirked. "Way to go, Ian. Get us all in trouble."

Jonas eyed Rainer sharply. "Bad timing. You correct some of Ian's errors."

Rainer stood and nodded. "The Puritans, also called Separatists, obtained a charter from the English government and shrewdly transferred both it and a large body of the congregation to Massachusetts. During the decade of the Thirties, that's the 1630s, *Ian*, a period of time known as the Great Migration, over 20,000 Puritans crossed the Atlantic. Avoiding a democracy . . ." She was interrupted by Jonas.

"Thank you, Rainer. Good. Continue, Junior."

The class's only black student rose. "The Puritans established a theocracy, I believe, and wanted all the residents to worship in a like manner. The Puritans were Calvinists. Anyway, the first governor of the Massachusetts Bay Colony was John Winthrop. This colony was not a democracy, nor did it allow for substantial religious freedom."

Jonas was pleased. "Well done, Junior." The teacher looked directly at Ian, then moved on. "Your homework for tonight is to make a chart of the New England colonies in the Seventeenth century. You decide what the categories should be. Then compare and contrast these colonies." He looked around the room to the fourteen AP students to check for understanding. When he was satisfied, they understood the assignment, he had them take out a clean sheet of paper. "In the last few minutes, I want you to write a paragraph explaining Calvinist beliefs. If you don't know, write that on your paper and sit quietly for the remainder of the period. When the bell rings, hand me your paragraph and head off to your next class."

While the class wrote, Jonas walked back to Ian. "Bring something in to eat during lunch. I'll be out of the room at the start of lunch, but I'll be back in case you have any questions." Jonas' threat to remove him from the class was calculated. He knew the phone call to Ian's parents would resolve the problem because they had been so supportive of Jonas during his first year. Ian's mother was an associate professor in English at Denver University, and his father was a pharmacist who had graduated from Andrew Jackson in the Forties.

§

Jonas ate lunch with Elyse and Dave--except on Wednesdays when he monitored noon basketball in the gym with Coach Ragni.

Jonas wanted the period after lunch open so he could scrimmage with the students, but it couldn't be worked out by the counselors, so on these days he talked hoops with the head coach.

"Do you ever find a sleeper during noon ball, Coach?" asked Jonas.

"Actually, I have, especially young kids. The seniors think it's too lame to play at noon. They're upstairs or in their cars with the girls, but the young-uns will get out here and scrap. Besides, if a kid hasn't been a player until he's a senior, he's probably not good enough anyway." He nodded at the three-on-three game at the far end. "That black kid is gonna help us a lot. Played JV over at East last season."

"He's in my AP history class. He's pretty sharp and confident, but I didn't know about his basketball skills. Some of the other kids in my class say he came over to pave the way for next year's kids. Pretty gutsy, I say." Jonas had become comfortable with Coach Ragni in his year of apprenticeship.

"Well, Jonas, I'm gonna slip out for a smoke. Hold down the fort."

§

Because the fight after school on Thursday was clearly racially motivated, Pete thought it best to meet briefly at lunch with his faculty on Friday, so they wouldn't be left in the dark over the week-end. "Sophomores!" he muttered under his breath, almost as if it was a cuss word. Five boys were suspended, three whites and two blacks. It started in the hallways with an intentional bump, then some words, stares, and threats. At least the knuckleheads were smart enough to go across the street into a backyard, off school grounds, but the fight stirred the tension already simmering just below the surface. Pete explained this all to his staff and then allowed for questions or comments.

"Who started it?"

"The bump was intentional. The Vanhaverbeke kid admitted to it. Some of you know he's not at all like his older siblings, who were model students. This one's a jerk most of the time. His parents are appalled at his behavior. They're on our side."

"What led up to it?"

"As far as we can tell, it was just done as a dare. None of the students knew each other. That's why we have to get a handle on it right now and not let the rumors get started."

"I heard there was a lot of blood. What stopped it?"

"Not what, but who, and this is the part that gives me some real encouragement. A dozen or so of our own students saw the incident in the hall and tipped us off about the fight during last period. The group was white and black, mostly seniors. They were up front with it, even going across the street with us. They put the family first: good Generals."

"What now?"

Pete rubbed his chin and stepped into the faculty. "Specifically, we make sure we're in the halls between passing periods. If students want to talk with you after class, steer them into the halls so you can be a presence there. Otherwise, just continue with our high expectations. If they want to talk about it in class, it's okay to spend a few minutes, but stress that Andrew Jackson is a special place, and it's our place."

"Can we expect this sort of thing to become more prevalent next year?"

"No! I won't allow our discipline to slip. These were five of our youngest students who haven't yet become Generals. I'll guarantee you these boys will behave themselves when they return. Even more than that, I'll see to it they help us to keep others from fighting." Pete's words were exactly what his faculty wanted to hear, and they left in an optimistic mood.

Chapter 24

Unlike the math and social studies departments, science had no turnovers over the summer, so Elyse had the same set of classes for her second year—all sophomores again. She spent less time lesson planning than Jonas did, and her classroom management improved. Cirillo did not assign her lunch duty, or any duty, in order to best utilize her time for the district's integration committee. The new Spanish teacher spoke Spanish as her native language, was in her late-thirties, and kept her previous circle of friends from Skinner Junior High in north Denver. Elyse missed Laura more than she thought she would, and the new teacher did not fill that void. Jonas filled several needs, but it was with Laura that Elyse could unburden her problems, both personal and professional. Jonas kept so many of his feelings hidden; he kept secrets and didn't frequently ask about Elyse's feelings.

It seemed to Elyse that less was expected of her this second year. When she spent evenings at Jonas' apartment, she had time to read or nap on the couch while he and Dave worked. A rash appeared on her neck that wouldn't go away. Dave's salve, his mother's home ointment, did not alleviate the itch, so it was red most of the time. When the three teachers talked, her students were not the focus since neither Jonas nor Dave knew many of them. Without Laura, the atmosphere changed.

While the two boys worked, Elyse had time to review handouts from the integration committee about the changing demographics of Denver. She learned that the suburban school population outnumbered Denver proper, and they were "whiter and wealthier." She met a neighbor of her parents from Greenwood Village who warned the committee that Denver's days of annexing nearby counties was over. Mrs. Freda Poundstone was pushing an amendment to the Colorado constitution that would keep Denver students out of suburban schools. A Denver University professor presented a paper on the easy movement of professionals into work sites in Denver because of the improved transportation system which allowed them to raise their families in the suburbs. "I-70 and I-25 are your enemies." By "your enemies," he meant the Denver public schools' enemies.

"Doesn't that seem a little paranoid?" asked Dave.

"It did to me when I first heard about it, but there are so many examples where our tax dollars seem to benefit one class over the other that I'm beginning to wonder," said Elyse.

"Be careful, Elyse. You're starting to sound like another girl I once knew," said Jonas. His remark ended the conversation, and Elyse shortly returned to her own apartment to watch TV and grade lab reports.

§

"Mr. Cullen, let's talk about Watergate today." Messi was the class expert on the subject; his family was long-time Denver Democrats.

"Well, Messi, if you can tie it in with the powers delegated to Congress in the Constitution, run with it."

"Mr. C," Rainer broke in, "while Messi's trying to remember anything that didn't happen in his lifetime, let me rescue him. I don't think the Framers ever thought the executive branch would get so powerful, and they weren't planning for political parties, if I remember our reading assignment correctly, so today's Congress has to create itself anew."

Messi turned slightly to respond. "Rainer, the Framers still wrote in provisions for checks and balances. They feared a President who might get too kingly, so they gave the Congress the power to impeach a President, which is what they ought to do with Nixon." He sat down and waited for the class Republicans to come to their man's defense. Mr. Cullen strolled to the radiator at the side of the room and leaned against it. So much for the three hours he spent lesson planning the previous night. He would pick up the creation of political parties tomorrow; Hamilton and Jefferson would have to argue behind closed doors for another day. Both Framers would have loved the argument that ensued for the remainder of the period.

§

While Annette Long and Archie King had separated, they remained friendly. Annette simply didn't want to be shared any longer. Archie was no longer welcome at her home. Maybe Archie was ready to settle into one girlfriend since he didn't try to talk Annette out of her decision to end the relationship. Neither one looked back.

"Annette, would you get your pad and come into my office." It was November 1, and Pete was wearing a black shirt, something he always did the day after Halloween, his way of signifying the end of good weather. In Denver there were often warm days after the first, but for Pete, November 1 marked the end of fall.

Annette, what's your opinion about Elyse's attitude this year? She seems dissatisfied or something."

Annette jotted her interpretation of her boss' words down on her pad. The teachers' union was getting more belligerent about defending its members in light of a handful of firings of experienced teachers over the summer. Now the District needed "documentation."

"Have you considered it might just be the sophomore slump? To answer your question, yeah, I've noticed a change, but I can't say why. She hasn't told me anything."

"Did I put too much on her plate with the district committee?"

"Pete, you always put too much on your teachers' plates. You have such high expectations, and they don't all have your abilities or stamina." Annette continued before Pete spoke again. "You also protect your science and math teachers. You give them lighter duties and don't require them to do extracurricular work. It's just your bias. You might have over-extended Elyse with the segregation assignment, though."

Pete pondered this; it was good to be reminded about it every other month or so. "She did some work over the summer for a research corporation. I'd hate to lose her to the private sector. Will you keep your antennae up?"

"Yeah. I'll see if I can get Dave or Jonas to say something." She wrote down a few more notes. "The guy I'm worried about is Dave."

§

Ben Lucas sat in a student desk to address Elyse's concerns. "This isn't just your concern; it's all of our concern. As more and more minorities attend Andrew Jackson, how we teach, how these new kids learn, will change. While we need to keep our expectations high, we also have to be realistic in what can be done upon their immediate arrival. Your teacher training assumed that sophomores had a certain level of abilities and skills. My training back in Ohio assumed the same thing. It's a challenge to see how adding a new ingredient into our stew, so to speak, will alter the flavor. As scientists, we explore this concept all the time." He smiled. "Integration, science, and cooking all in the same explanation: how about that?"

Elyse smiled back. "Hardly seems fair to inject such a complex mix on the new teacher in the department. Shouldn't I have four or five years to prepare for this? Maybe I could tell the committee to put this plan on hold while I catch up."

Ben knew Elyse was evolving. "Into the fire, Elyse, and you know how important fire is to our experiments in the lab. It changes everything. My advice to you? Grow! Allow all of this to let you grow into this profession. It's hard on a daily basis, but it's necessary." He looked to his young colleague for acceptance.

"Okay, but don't be surprised if I show up here every afternoon to get new words of wisdom after a difficult day."

§

Despite his teaching schedule, Jonas continued with his part time job at The Tattered Cover bookstore, although he had cut his hours when pre-season basketball practices began. He enjoyed the atmosphere, which was different from a high school classroom. Books and quiet introspection versus books and noisy discussions: each valuable in their own setting. He also enjoyed the owner and the quiet elegance of the owner's mother, who also worked at the store. The owner was a CU grad too, but Jonas had not known him then. About the same age as Jonas, he held strong opinions on the topics of the period and was forceful in delivering them. But mostly, it was the pleasant, friendly, and calm atmosphere--and the four dollars per hour that he earned--that kept Jonas there. The extra thirty dollars each week made a difference.

Trying to spend as much time with her boyfriend as she could, Elyse would often spend Saturday afternoons curled up with a book in the store's front bay window just so she could be with Jonas. If Jonas could have seen inside Elyse, he would have been aware of the great tension she carried. But he assumed all was right between them.

November 10 was one of those Saturdays. Jonas went directly from basketball tryouts to the bookstore and was working behind the counter when Elyse arrived around 1:00. She brought lunch for both of them. The owner's mother, always in a dress, took over at the counter, while Elyse and Jonas sat just outside the front of the store to enjoy the sunshine.

"Thanks, Elyse." He kissed her on the check and opened his lunch sack. "Did you see where Judge Sirica sentenced the Watergate defendants yesterday? Liddy continues to stonewall it. Mr. Macho!" He didn't notice Elyse's impatience.

"No, I didn't read the paper this morning. I'm trying to have a real life. Care to join me?"

Jonas looked directly at her and paused. "I guess I've been going at it pretty hard, huh. Sorry, I just don't want to fail."

"Oh, for crying out loud, Jonas, you won't." Her anger expressed itself in tears.

Jonas placed his right hand on Elyse's thigh and waited. He didn't know how to console her; he didn't have the words or the experience to make this uncomfortable feeling go away. When she looked up, he saw how desperate she was, but all he could utter was, "Elyse, I'm sorry."

Elyse didn't accept his apology. Instead, she quickly stood and left the bookstore. From The Tattered Cover, Elyse drove to the Hungarian Freedom Park on Speer Boulevard, where she parked and found a bench. What was wrong with this year? Did teaching demand such a time commitment that two people had no time for one another? What was wrong with Jonas that he couldn't see what she wanted to give him? Elyse blinked away her tears and wondered more about what teaching required than how Jonas was ignoring her. Did she really want to continue along this path? This second year was proving more stressful than her first due to her own expectations—and a lack of support from her peers. Jonas assumed her teaching was going fine. Laura's calls and letters were all about her resurrected teaching career, and Elyse's father's attitude never changed; teaching was a stepping-stone job into a real profession. Elyse didn't know how to ask for help, but she feared being overwhelmed like Laura had been. Unlike the rash on her neck, this was an itch she found impossible to scratch. This rash went deep into her soul.

After a short time, she calmed, and her thoughts returned to Jonas. Elyse knew of his desire to succeed as a teacher, made stronger by Pete's and Archie's praises. He was a solitary man by nature, and she wondered if she could penetrate the space where he went to protect himself. He hadn't opened up about the problems he was having with two of his classes, the non-AP courses. Elyse didn't know if she had the energy, but if he would let her, she would try. She knew Jonas would not ask for it.

She also knew it would be a long time before she made love to Jonas again—if ever—and both her heart and body ached.

§

Jonas left work early and returned to school. He entered the building through the gym, where he exchanged small talk with Coach Ragni. Jonas then went to his classroom on the second floor. From his closet, he took a spray bottle of ammonia and a rag and began scrubbing the marks from the student desks—a mindless chore. Six rows—each with six desks. A rectangular room. His desk sat near the windows so that the front of the room was open, allowing him to pace from side-to-side as he taught. Students entered at the room's front; tardies couldn't sneak in. The green chalkboards were his history canvas, covered with graphs, drawings, and vocabulary words by the end of each period. Elyse would often leave notes on the board behind his desk and sign them with her initials in lower case cursive.

He finished cleaning, put the bottle back in the closet, and hung the rag on a hook outside the closet to dry. He walked to the back of his room and sat on the worktable. He hadn't done much to earn Elyse; she was the driving force in their relationship. Every part of his experience at Andrew Jackson was connected to Elyse, from her kiss in the office on his first day to yesterday's teasing hump behind his desk at lunch. And everything in between, both serious and not so serious. She was his foundation here. He thought about her every day, but he had taken her for granted—and hurt her.

§

That evening, after eating a dinner of Ramon noodles and hamburger, Jonas received a call from Paul Garrity. "Hey, Paul, how are you doing?"

"Hey, HoJo. Good. You?" Jonas laughed. Paul had given him that nickname at CU after a night of protesting on The Hill in Boulder. Neither could remember exactly why, something about Ho Chi Minh, but it stuck. They talked about Paul's health, Abby in prison, and teaching, although Jonas did not mention Elyse.

Jonas sat by the phone after he hung up, but his thoughts were of Elyse. This would be the first night since they got together that they wouldn't communicate in some way. He wondered if he would become what he was raised to be, his father's son, a man whose women just up and left.

CHAPTER 25

Laur,

Well, Jonas and I are done. He's a shit! No, not really. It's just he's so busy, so wrapped up in being Mr. Teacher-of-the-Year. He has those two AP history classes he prepares for every night, even on the weekends. He tweaks his other three courses too. Now, basketball has started, so he has practice every night and on Saturday mornings. Then he goes to work after practice. We didn't have a date last week at all. I went to my apartment, and he went to his each evening. And night! Dave says all he does is read, read, read. Maybe a break will help him get his head on straight and see what a good thing I am. It's more than time, Laur, it's, and don't laugh at me from fifty miles away, it's his heart—and my heart—, our bodies, his focus, his involvement. Pieces are missing, and they don't have to be. I know there are great demands on both of us as second year teachers, but, crap, we can work this out. I just think we're so good for each other. He's just being a toad right now.

Mr. Cirillo called me in last week to ask how I was doing. I just started crying, so he called in Annette and left. I'll bet if he called in Jonas, he wouldn't cry. She knew right away it was Jonas. We talked for over two hours—told each other things about our love lives. It really surprised me she would do that, but then I realized she probably hasn't talked with anyone since ending it with Archie, so it was good for her, I think. She's never been married. She said she was pretty serious a couple of times when she was young, but she was lucky she didn't hook up with either guy. When she started seeing Archie, he was already in a relationship with another woman. Did you know he's pretty rich? At first, it was secretive, but then they just decided he would have two women. That's icky to me. I told her I could never do that.

Then she told me about Mr. King. His real name isn't Archie King. He comes from a prominent South Carolina family named Archibald, but I guess he had some kind of big fight with his father and left. He changed his name to King in honor of Martin Luther King, but kept his nickname, which was Archie. He had it legally changed and has never spoken with his father since. Annette said the fight was over the Vietnam War. How many families have been split up over the war?

Then she told me about Mr. Cirillo. He married his high school sweetheart and has three kids, which I knew.

Did I tell you that Jonas is a shit!

My dad called earlier tonight to tell me a representative from that engineering company I worked for this summer called. I guess they want to talk to me about working there full time. I'll call next week.

So, how did your long weekend with Tippy turn out? You're lucky to have a boyfriend who isn't indifferent to your needs.

Oh yeah, Mr. Cirillo said I didn't have to be the school's liaison to the desegregation committee any longer if I didn't want to. I told him I was just so busy, and it might be a good idea to find someone else. He got Ben Lucas to do it for a while. I'm planning on helping him later this year. He'll be better than me anyway because he supports the idea. I'm not sure I do. Busing is just going to screw things up, I think.

It was a two-beer afternoon. I need to spend some time with you. Take care, honey-pooh. I'll call.

Elyse

§

El,

Jonas is a shit! I'll come down and kick his ass! Hang in there, he'll see what a mistake he's making. By the way, I haven't needed two beers

*any day this semester (but it's still early). Care to join me up here? I
know a couple of teachers who I could set you up with.*

    Love ya,
    Laur

§

Laur,

    *I might be ready to leave Andrew Jackson, and yeah, set me up. It
might be refreshing to have someone actually pay attention to me.*

Elyse

§

Jonas spoke only with the personnel secretary and filled out a
single form. "This just tells us of your interest; it's exploratory only,
and you'll need to come in again if you want to pursue this." It was a
spontaneous action on Jonas' part, in case he decided the move was
necessary or really a part of his long-term teaching goals. It wasn't
as if he was dissatisfied with Andrew Jackson, and it was a topic
he'd discussed with Pete and Archie several times. Afterwards, he
thought it was a sorry-ass response to his breakup with Elyse and
didn't give it further thought.

CHAPTER 26

"Come on, Mr. C, don't give us any homework over Thanksgiving."

§

The only students left in the building when Annette said good-bye to her boss at 5:00 o'clock on Wednesday afternoon were practicing basketball or wrestling in the gym. Pete Cirillo opened his bottom desk drawer and lifted a bottle of bourbon onto his desk. *Jefferson Reserve*. Ninety proof, aged fifteen years. He had seen it at the liquor store and bought it as his silent protest to Andrew Jackson, the man. His only protest. In all other ways, Pete loved his high school.

He poured a half-glass and leaned back in his chair, sipping gently. "Well, Pete," he said aloud to himself, "we're about a third of the way through, and everything's going pretty good." Andrew Jackson High School was his school, from its bells to its smells. When he was appointed as the principal, he had the bell sound changed from a loud beep to the traditional bell of his childhood. His first hire was the head janitor, Carlos Herrera. Stole him from West High School, where Carlos was the night custodian. In many ways, a principal and his chief custodian are the joint caretakers of a school, and Pete was proud of his partner. No school in Denver was cleaner, healthier, or better cared for. If anyone spent more hours at Jackson than Pete, it was Carlos. Pete instructed Carlos to use wood products containing an Old English smell to maintain a traditional odor to the forty-year-old school. For Pete tradition was foundational in maintaining the learning environment.

Support the tradition with solid attendance policies, tight discipline in the classrooms and in the halls, good teachers, and high expectations. Pete knew a school was more than reading, writing, and arithmetic. It was a culture. It was the social center of the neighborhoods which fed their children into the maw. The common experience of America. The generational tie to the great American experiment. Pete raised his eyes to read the quote over his door, a quote he tried to read every day before he left for home: "And we shall be as a city upon a hill."

The various uncertainties of possible court-ordered busing forced him out of his comfort zone. He witnessed it wearing on both his students and teachers—what did each day hold in meaning and consequence? It also wore on Pete. He couldn't control his school's environment to the extent he had in the past, so he was unable to reassure his teachers with confidence about their futures, and he saw himself as their chief support. He believed this would all be fine in the coming years, but he knew that he wanted to believe it to be so, to hold on to a belief that had guided him in the past. His doctor slapped him on the back after his most recent physical, telling him that he was still in great shape except for a mild spike in his blood pressure and cholesterol. "It comes with the territory," answered Pete.

§

Even when the top students are skimmed from the general population and placed into advanced or accelerated classes, a new hierarchy develops. In Jonas Cullen's AP history classes, the cream of the crop had clearly shown itself by Thanksgiving. In second hour it was Rainer, Betty, Rick, Erin, and Junior. In sixth period it was Messi, Liz, Sandy, and Stacey. All the students in the two advanced placement history classes were juniors, with one exception in sixth period. Jonas' other three classes were made up of sophomores, just like the previous year. At least he had a year of preparation for those sections.

Mrs. Froman called on the Thanksgiving Friday to check in on Jonas, to see if he was on schedule to complete the Civil War by Christmas. Falling behind first semester would mean the classes would either not finish the course curriculum in time for the AP exam in early May, or they would have to rush through some very important material. "Regardless, your students won't be prepared adequately. You must follow my outlines. How far are you behind?" Mrs. Froman was adamant.

"The hard part is limiting the discussion on current events. So much is going on in the world: Watergate, the end of Vietnam, the Yom Kippur War. Am I just supposed to ignore it?" Current events were Jonas' forte, his passion, and it was difficult not beginning each class with an update, plus his students were interested.

"Yes, Jonas, I'm afraid that's exactly what you need to do. If you finish a lesson early some days, then you can discuss current events. By moving those discussions to the end of the period, it limits the time you waste on them." Mrs. Froman was not anti-news; it was simply a matter of preparing the students for their year-end exam in a difficult course, one that could earn them college credit. In the sophomore classes, "You can discuss the Arabs and Israelis or Watergate all you want."

Jonas had other questions for the previous AP teacher. "A two-page vocabulary sheet for every chapter really wears them down. Should I be grading them? Could they maybe use them on their chapter quizzes? What about allowing them to work with a partner? Most of these kids are taking a pretty hard schedule, plus they're involved in so many other things here at school."

"Jonas, my dear boy, they can do it all," she paused, "if you make it the expectation. These students are the leaders of our society in the next generation. We don't want them to be soft and undisciplined. We have enough hippies and ne'er-do-wells just now, so keep them busy. They'll thank you for it later on." Mrs. Froman had a way of not answering his questions directly, leaving it to him to search for the details of her directives. "Oh, and Jonas, so can you."

§

Jane Walburg asked Jonas out for dinner during the Thanksgiving break. He hesitated before accepting. He knew Elyse was dating, but he didn't think there was one particular guy, and he hadn't thought about seeing any other women. Jane was older than Jonas and quite attractive, and they knew one another through team teaching their AP History and English classes on a research paper. She was as good a teacher who worked at Andrew Jackson, but beyond the classroom Jonas knew little about Jane's private life. Since Jane asked Jonas out, she drove and picked the restaurant, which was a fancy Italian ristorante south of Denver University.

"I'm more of a fish person," said Jane, "and the scampi here is divine. Will a rosso Montepulciano be acceptable?"

"You know I'm from Montana, and you ask me about wine?" Jonas replied. He sensed she was teasing and accepted it in good humor. "How's the spaghetti?"

"Wonderful."

"You've been here before."

Jane nodded. "It's been a few years, but this place was always special."

The food and wine were excellent, and the couple talked mostly about their classes and teaching in general. Over an after-dinner coffee, Jane reached across the table and touched Jonas' hand, which startled him. She paused, withdrew her hand, and smiled. "Jonas, I have a devious streak in me that I hope, after tonight, you'll both appreciate and forgive."

"I'm not following you," said Jonas.

"Let me continue. I asked you here to tell you this because I liked what I saw in you and Elyse. I was married once. We had to get past some things, and we didn't. We didn't talk out our problems. He wasn't perfect, but he was perfect for me, and as I step back from our time together, I know he loved me to his core, to my core. And as flawed as I am, I was perfect for him." Jane went into her past for a moment and then returned. "When we were together, we could solve anything, but when we were apart, we let a day go by, and one day apart led to another day apart, and another."

"I suspect he let you get away too."

Jane's expression agreed with Jonas' assessment, but she let it go. "He lacked a certain confidence in himself about me because, I think, he had never loved a woman as he did me and didn't believe he deserved me. I pushed him away and never told him why. I shouldn't have been so stubborn, so . . ."

"Where is he now?"

Jane pursed her lips and swallowed. "Let's just say he's gone and leave it at that. Jonas, I asked you out tonight to tell you this. Don't screw it up with Elyse. She is a unique girl, and you are a unique, young man. You'll regret it forever. Whatever happened, patch it up, and do it now."

"It's teaching, the amount of time I'm spending on teaching," said Jonas. "I don't deserve her; she's right to go."

"This profession can do that. It makes you think it's the most important thing, but you can't put it in front of the one you love. Don't ever do that, ever. And don't sell yourself short when it comes to love. It's an equalizer."

When the bill arrived, each insisted on paying, but Jane won the argument. "Maybe you can buy me dinner down the road," said Jane.

"Count on it." Jonas had an uneasy feeling and took a chance. "Jane, are you happy?"

She brushed aside the question. "Let's keep this date a secret—our secret. You know, if there was no Elyse . . ." Jane smiled that devious smile. "Just kidding, I'm too old for you."

§

Freda Poundstone paced between the yellow notepad on her kitchen counter and the front window. It had to be attacked on several fronts; first and foremost, that Denver's history of annexing surrounding districts was arrogant and abusive. Local citizens should have a voice on whether they wanted to be a part of the core city. There were reasons why she and her neighbors lived in a rural environment. It would require a constitutional amendment, not an easy task, but then her reputation was built on taking on the difficult tasks and winning. People paid her well for that outcome.

Freda was no ideologue, but she had basic beliefs, and court-ordered busing went against these. If the Supreme Court ruled that Denver must desegregate, and from all indications that would be the verdict, then she would be ready. An amendment to prevent the court from imposing forced busing on Greenwood Village and the southern counties, all the surrounding counties for that matter, would be necessary, and she was the one person tough enough to defy the order.

She jotted down several areas of attack. She would be prepared and organized—and she was confident she could win.

§

Jonas ate dinner with Elyse at her parents' home on the first of December, just a few days after Jonas' date with Jane. Mr. and Mrs. Cottage were unaware their daughter and her boyfriend were struggling since Elyse had kept her problems secret. The young couple did nothing to let them know during the day; in fact, Elyse thought Jonas was behaving more like his old self, especially with his eyes. Over the past few months, Jonas did not allow his eyes to maintain contact with Elyse, but on this day, he held his gaze, and it seemed to say he was ready to call time-in.

"Elyse tells us you've been very busy, Jonas." Mr. Cottage was loading his plate with a little bit of everything Mrs. Cottage had prepared. Just then, he was ladling gravy onto his mashed potatoes and peas. "When you wear yourself out and get tired of teaching, let me know, and I'll make some contacts for you in the business world. I think I've got a promising one for Elyse that could pan out if she'd pursue it more actively." He glanced over at his daughter and winked.

Jonas was used to this line and let it slide, but internally, he burned. His old anger was held in check—barely. Instead, he commented on the food. "Don't hog all the gravy; I'll need some for my second helping." Teaching, to Elyse's dad, was not a profession for a competent man, or for that matter, as a career for a competent woman. Low pay and anyone could do it. Part of the reason Jonas did not respond was because his own father had similar feelings. The difference between the two fathers was that one was college educated and the other was a high school dropout.

After dinner Elyse and Jonas went to a movie at Villa Italia mall. A date! At a south Denver IHOP afterwards, they drank coffee and talked about their relationship for the first time since they had stepped back from each other.

Jonas apologized. "I'm sorry for my lack of attention this fall. I kind of got wrapped up in school a bit too much, huh."

"Was that all it was?" asked Elyse.

"I know you've been out on a few dates recently. I was jealous, am jealous, but I understand. Are you thinking my feelings for you had changed?"

Elyse paused. "Either that or Abby." She looked down into her coffee when she mentioned Abby's name.

Jonas let go of his coffee cup and reached across the table for Elyse's hand. "Do you remember when we held hands for the first time—in the restaurant when the Israeli athletes were murdered?" asked Jonas. Elyse smiled because she fondly did. "That had such an impact on me, and it still does. We hold hands well."

Elyse nodded. "Yes, we do. It led to your hug by our cars and our first real kiss."

Many thoughts and feelings passed between them before Jonas spoke again. "Hey, how many times do I have to tell you I don't have those kinds of feelings for Abby?" Phrased as a question, Jonas was telling Elyse his real feelings about his old girlfriend. It was awkward, but it was true. Any thoughts Jonas had about Abby Archer would go away if she were released from prison. She would then become a memory, different in some ways from other college romances, but a memory just the same.

"You'll probably have to tell me often, especially since we've had our first breakup." Elyse had a way of hiding difficult feelings, but now her eyes welled up. "Last year was hard, but, in its own way, I don't know, perfect. The four of us were always happy and . . ."

"Naive?"

"Yeah, but in our ignorance, we were happy. Now everything's changed. School is such a strain on everyone, and with you so preoccupied, I'm just lost."

Jonas slid out of his side of the booth and slid in next to Elyse. He put his arm around her and held her. He said nothing.

Finally, Elyse wiped her nose with her paper napkin and regained her composure. "Sorry, I guess I've been holding it in for quite a while." She decided to stop her words and see if Jonas could start his. There were things she needed to hear.

Jonas sensed her need. "One night, after we had gone to bed and you were sleeping, I told you I loved you." He shook his head. "Pretty brave of me to say it to you while you were asleep. Anyway, I do love you, Elyse, and I've missed you. I carry on this running conversation with you all day long. I ask you how my lesson plans are, whether my tie matches my shirt, if you've noticed anything weird about any of our students. I've had girlfriends before, but I've never had one that I let get into my head and heart. I've never been in a place to consider the future. I am now; we are now. That's a little scary for a hick from Montana. I don't open up well, and when I do, I stumble over words. But know, Elyse, I think you are magnificent." Jonas had never told another girlfriend that he loved her, not even Abby.

They finished their coffees and drove around south Denver while they continued their make-up talk. They stopped at a Safeway for ice cream before ending up at Elyse's apartment for the night. They talked until about two, when they fell asleep in each other's arms on the couch. Elyse vowed there would be no sex for a time if they made up, and Jonas did not initiate it. He seemed intent on talking and getting their conflict worked out. Most of their conversation dealt with students, stories they had denied one another during their split. Elyse called Laura in the morning. "Hey, Laur, Jonas isn't a shit anymore."

§

The custodian stood alongside the bleachers watching the lone athlete practice fifteen-foot jump shots near the free-throw line. Over and over after taking two quick dribbles. Form and technique.

The athlete was talking to himself, coaching himself in the otherwise empty gym. "Don't drift, Junior! Straight up. Hold the release. Don't follow your shot; you've got to get back. You're the point guard, Warren, not the rebounder."

Carlos Herrera walked onto the court. "How about you let me rebound? The reason you keep stepping in after the shot is because you eventually have to get the ball to do it again. Understandable, but it builds a habit. Remember, son, you're always practicing habits—either good ones or bad ones." Carlos nodded to Junior. "Shoot, land, get back. I'll retrieve the ball." For the next ten minutes, the only sounds were basketball sounds that echoed throughout the cavernous gym and the gentle encouraging word "Good" from the custodian after each shot.

Finally, Junior stopped and addressed Carlos. "You've played before. Every pass was perfect."

"A long time ago, son. I was never at your level though."

"Thanks. I have to get better to be accepted over here."

The custodian put his hand on Junior's shoulder. "Let's sit for a moment. You wore this old man out." While Junior toweled away his sweat, Carlos continued. "I've watched you play. Aside from your obvious abilities, you have grit. Courage. You play with no fear. I admire that."

"There's fear, sir, I just disguise it well."

"I understand that, son."

"Out here, I can immediately show my abilities."

"It's not that easy in the other world, is it," said Carlos.

"No. I need to prove everything. In a strange way, it motivates me, but it's still hard. I hate to say 'white people' because it's not all of them, but sometimes it seems like most of them have this philosophy that says I'm unqualified for this—and undeserving."

"Because you're black?"

"Yeah."

"You came over to this school to challenge that philosophy. Do you have the courage to go forward and do this?"

The two men thought about their brief conversation for a

moment before the younger one spoke. "During games I get held on screens, and the refs don't call it. Any suggestions?"

"Anticipate them a second earlier, then fight through them more aggressively. Get your elbows involved. Knock someone down occasionally."

CHAPTER 27

"It's a wash, Annette. Seven transfers in at the semester and seven out." Pete rubbed his head with his left hand wondering what the trend would be. He thought he knew, and it troubled him.

"We're losing seven pretty good kids, Pete. Can we afford this?"

"We'll have to, but I'll need to talk with Ben to see if we can meet with our PTA. We need convince them nothing will change regarding our standards. If we can just maintain our base heading into next year, then I think we can prove to them they don't have anything to fear. Gawd, it's the rumors that are going to kill this whole process. If it were up to me, I'd start busing in January and not allow the summer to take its toll."

Annette smirked. "Just keep your finger in the dike, Hans."

§

Archie, Ben, and Pete attended every school board meeting together from the spring of 1972 through 1974. Ben took copious notes. Pete jotted down thoughts that were inspired by the things said at the podium. Archie reacted to statements with audible grunts. More than once, Pete placed a hand on Archie's shoulder to calm him down. The board meetings were held in the South High School auditorium because attendance had grown so large. Archie believed that holding these meetings at South was a deliberate, provocative move against the black community. Confederate flags hung in the halls and on the auditorium stage, although the stage flag was removed after the first few meetings. Archie threatened to take it down himself and would have if Pete and Ben would have let him. Archie saw racism in every action and conspiracy behind every closed-door school board meeting. South High was Andrew Jackson's closest neighbor and had similar demographics, but Jackson did not display overt Confederate symbols like its rival.

The December school board meeting was contentious, but it was clear the city had accepted the fact there was no retreat from the Supreme Court rulings. Busing, in some form, was coming. Even the anti-busing Citizens Association for Neighborhood Schools seemed to be falling in line, albeit reluctantly, and was losing its clout. Members of this group, however, were putting their Denver homes up for sale. The board extended its directives for teacher training before desegregation began. What the board labeled as training, Archie saw as a violation of academic freedom. Before Pete could restrain him, he bolted out of his seat and yelled, "What about our First Amendment right of free speech!" The board ignored him and shortly adjourned. They were waiting for Judge Doyle's addendum to the *Keyes'* Case. He would present his findings on December 17, 1973.

At the back of the room, Freda Poundstone sat quietly, but wrote furiously. So, the School Board would acquiesce despite the citizens' obvious opposition to busing, despite their voting record to keep this from happening. She observed the audience, looking for allies and adversaries. They were mostly allies, and those who weren't were too emotional to see the big picture. *Go ahead, Supreme Court, order Denver to desegregate. What else can you do in today's political atmosphere? Just know that even you have limitations if the people are determined—and if they have strong leadership. There are other ways to do this.*

§

Instead of a study hall in the library, Junior Warren asked Mr. Cullen if he could be his student aide: grade papers, tutor sophomores, do his homework in a classroom. Jonas eagerly accepted. Junior also wanted to sit in on Mr. Cullen's current events discussions, which were a big part of Mr. C's lesson plans for sophomore American Government. Watergate was discussed nearly every day, and Junior participated in those talks. Also, there were three other black students in the class, all of whom were transfers from schools north of Colfax Avenue.

In October, Junior wrote a telegram to the White House protesting the "Saturday Night Massacre" and convinced the entire government class to sign it. Mr. Cullen said it was telegrams like this that forced the President to turn over the disputed tapes to Judge Sirica. In November Junior portrayed the role of Judge Sirica for the class as it argued what penalty should be administered to the break-in defendants. "Judge" Junior Warren finally came down hard on all of them, but especially so on Gordon Liddy. "Stay in prison until America restores its constitutional mess." In December, the class wondered how the new vice-president Gerald Ford would be accepted by the old White House staff.

Throughout the fall Junior rode city buses to Andrew Jackson rather than drive his car. The Arab oil embargo forced his family to make some concessions, and one of those was to limit car use for a while. Junior's mother thought that might bring him back to East High School, but he was determined to desegregate on his terms. While the morning bus ride was simple, the evening commute after basketball practice was testy. Standing at night in the cold in a white neighborhood was scary.

§

Junior Warren's transition to Andrew Jackson was going well; he was making straight As in his classes; he was the point guard on a winning team, although it had been soundly defeated by his old school, East, during which he was roundly booed by his old classmates; and he had made some good friends, especially among the accelerated classes. Rick and Rainer took him under their wings early on, and because of a common interest in politics, he and Messi were now good buddies. There were problems, though, including the slurs made toward him in the hallways, but he had anticipated these.

The biggest disappointment for Junior, however, was that his grand plan in transferring to Jackson had not occurred. Junior hoped and planned for dozens of other black kids from East and Manual to follow him to Jackson, making busing unnecessary for at least one Denver school. He wrote letters, made phone calls, lobbied at athletic contests, and enlisted the support of prominent black professionals in his drive to get scores of black students to transfer to Jackson. Seven other black students came to Jackson at the beginning of the first semester followed by just three others under the open enrollment option available in Denver.

Junior did not think court-ordered desegregation using a forced busing plan would effectively improve either education or race relations. It was the subject he most wanted to discuss in his social studies class, but the rest of the class seemed more interested in Watergate, or as he referred to it, "a Washington white man's problem." It was as if white kids and teachers wanted to talk about problems far away, problems that did not directly impact them, but maybe upper middle-class kids didn't have real problems in the early Seventies. Junior was finally able to turn a class discussion held during the first week back from the holiday break about Reconstruction politics into a debate over current issues.

"Mr. C," asked Messi, who was now in the second period AP history class due to a scheduling need, "what right did the federal government have to take over schools in the South, even if the short-term changes were necessary?"

"Explain further. What I mean is, Messi, who was running the Southern state legislatures?"

"Well, it was Republicans. Lots of carpetbaggers."

"Were these men federal politicians?"

Betty "Friedan" Norton jumped in. "The educational reforms were made by the state legislatures, but they might as well have been from Washington, so isn't it the same thing? After all, Confederate states had to ratify Congressional legislation in order to be readmitted into the Union: things like the constitutional amendments, the Freedman's Bureau, and the Civil Rights Act."

Jonas kept pushing for precision. "Does that distinction make a difference?"

Junior didn't start out to tackle the *Keyes* decision. "Mr. Cullen, when the legislatures in the southern states first reconvened, they passed Black Codes and re-elected Confederate officers. Only then did the federal Congress step in, almost like they had no choice if the Civil War was to have any meaning."

"What were the social conditions after the war?"

Rainer stood to answer. "Most of the schools were closed. Those operating were for white students only. Millions of blacks had been given freedom, but what's freedom without an education?"

Now, Junior saw a connection and a chance. "Whoa! What did our class's smartest student just say? 'What's freedom without an education?' And what was the economic situation like? I'm not sure but weren't there just a few 'neeegroes' out of work. Let's see, unemployment for young blacks in Denver right now is about fifty percent. And some of you in here wonder why the federal government has injected itself into the educational controversy in Denver."

Sandy Morgan, who believed every situation could be solved if people would just take responsibility for their own actions, stood. "Before Christmas you said you opposed the court's decision; that it was wrong. I need an explanation."

Junior responded. "Yeah, I did. The court is saying that the only way a black student can learn is by sitting next to a white student. I said the decision was wrong. I didn't say it didn't have the authority. What happened in the South, though, when Reconstruction ended? Blacks went back to their former conditions. Schools were segregated and inferior. Tell the class about *Plessey v. Ferguson*, Mr. Cullen."

"Separate but equal schools were legalized by the Supreme Court. What are you getting at, Junior?"

"I live in two worlds, Mr. Cullen. I live in black Denver, but I go to school in a nearly all-white neighborhood. By choice, I admit, but there's a reason for it." The class was tuned in. "My family is part of the new black professional class, the 'black bourgeoisie.' Both of my parents support some kind of forced busing plan for Denver, but at the same time, they think they can manipulate the system to keep me at East. Most of you guys think black kids like me are okay, you know, rich black kids. But you never see the other kind. Most black students are poor, and the current recession is making it much worse. These are the kids you'll get next year. They won't be in this class. You'll be segregated from them every time you close the classroom door." Junior turned to Sandy Morgan. "You say welfare for blacks is wrong, but what's the answer? Your answer is to tell them to get a job. Jobs, not welfare, but black males can't always get a job. For most blacks in Denver, life is brutal. It denies young males a sense of self-worth." He turned to Rick Parris. "You tease me that if I wasn't a basketball player, I'd be a Black Panther, a radical. Maybe, but I don't think so. I sort of believe what Sandy says, that blacks have to accept what is and go out a get a job. Capitalism. But it has to be a different kind of capitalism; it can't be the white capitalism you guys have because blacks don't have the same chance. Inferior education, fewer contacts to the successful business class, and even fewer black role models." He paused to collect himself.

Rainer asked gently. "But then, wouldn't you support the *Keyes* decision?"

"I don't because I think it will be just like the situation in the South when the federal troops and Radical Republicans left. We'll be left out again. You can't force the schools to change society. Watch what will happen, what already is happening. Whites are leaving! *Keyes* will send us out to your schools away from Colfax Avenue, and then whites will move. I hate it's taking so long to change, but if the courts force you guys to accept us in your schools, the whites will leave. It's already happening."

"So, what do we do, Junior?" asked Rainer.

"I don't have the answers. Encourage transfers in both directions, hire more black teachers, and wait for capitalism to do its thing. It has its inequities, but I don't know what else to do. One body at a time."

§

Jonas went looking for Archie after school let out.

"Jonas, if that's what Junior believes, he's wrong," said Archie emphatically.

§

Rainer met with Junior after school in the cafeteria. He could only talk for ten minutes, since he had to be at basketball practice by 3:30. When her mother arrived home from her job as a clerk at Joslin's, Rainer had chips and sodas already sitting on the table.

"Mom, should I stay, or should I go?"

§

The overwhelming majority of Andrew Jackson's staff opposed the court's ruling ordering mandatory busing in some form. Archie constantly complained to Pete that regardless of their political affiliation, teachers were conservatives in the manner in which they led their lives. The staff at Andrew Jackson believed they were effective, that their graduates were well prepared for college or adult responsibilities. Test scores were high. The school served its neighborhoods with distinction.

"Damn it, Pete, isn't that enough?" was the common sentiment from the staff.

The principal held strong feelings on all the impending issues, but he was a good soldier too. "In this era, probably not. We have," and here he paused, "larger responsibilities." He laughed ironically. "The Civil War proved we were national before we were statists. Is that a word? Well, you know what I mean. We can't bury our heads in the sand to the events occurring all around us. The Civil Rights Movement has reached another stage—we here at Jackson High School. Many of us applauded the Supreme Court when it told the South to desegregate. Now, for the same reasons, it's telling us. I know there are differences, but they're subtle. If it was up to me, I'd do it differently, but it's not. Judge Doyle didn't say exactly how this will be done in his statements from Monday, but it will be worked out over the next three months. Then, I think, we'll know. All I can tell you as we head out for Christmas break is to forget about it during the holiday season and concentrate on your families. I know it weighs heavily on us all, but we can't do anything about it, so let's do what we do best, and that's teach."

After words about schedules and events that would occur when they returned in January, the staff filed out for Christmas break.

CHAPTER 28

Laura Sanders came down to stay with Elyse for the weekend, so the gang met together at her apartment for dinner on Friday. Elyse hoped they could put the desegregation cloud behind them for the holiday break. Laura didn't bring Tippy and Dave had broken up with his partner in the fall, so it would be like old times. Dave and Laura were as close as ever.

Dave started drinking as soon as he arrived. He didn't come with Jonas for several reasons. Jonas was at basketball practice; the team still had one more game on Saturday, a non-league affair against Aurora Central. Jonas was also planning on spending the night with Elyse as he had been for the past few weeks. Most importantly, he was anxious to see Laura. Dave was the odd man out when she left, the one whom Laura had rarely corresponded with since their rookie year ended and she left for Erie, Colorado.

Jonas arrived showered and shaven around seven. Laura hugged him before Elyse.

"It's a good thing you're back together with Elyse, or else I'd have to punch you."

"Nice to see you too, Laura." As he spoke, Elyse slid her arm around his waist and kissed him. She whispered something in his ear which caused him to look over at Dave. "Hey, roomie, slow down a bit and let me catch up."

Both the girls were worried he was drinking too much too fast, something Jonas had mentioned to Elyse earlier in the year. Because he didn't have an afterschool extracurricular duty, Dave came back

187

to the apartment around four and didn't go out after that. His math classes were good, but since his breakup, he had put on weight. Probably of greater concern was that his vision was rapidly declining in the eye that had been struck by the baseball. Doctors seemed unable to do anything about it. What Elyse had felt about Jonas' inattention was multiplied for Dave Fallon. No one realized how much he was dependent on Jonas, Elyse, and Laura.

Jonas took Dave's can from. "No more of this until after dinner."

For the next two hours, life was once again in sync for the gang of four. Their students were comical rather than problems; their principals were always on their side; parent calls didn't seem as threatening. They told stories and laughed. Laura had become more confident in her new school, an equal among her friends.

"Jonas, tell Laura about what Rainer did last week. Laura, she hasn't stopped being everyone's favorite, but Jonas is obviously her most favorite. I think she even has a crush on him," said Elyse. Jonas rolled his eyes at her.

Laura was sitting on Dave's lap, partly to keep him from getting up to get a beer and partly in friendship. "We don't have anyone quite like her in my school, at least as far as I know."

Jonas wiped a crumb from the corner of his mouth and smiled. "We were studying the Civil War a couple of weeks ago, and she asked me if she could memorize Lincoln's Gettysburg Address and present it to the class. Of course, I said yes, so the next day she comes in with a stove pipe hat on and gives a stirring rendition of the speech. The class gives her a standing O, and the one black student, a new kid named Junior Warren, starts calling her the Great Emancipatress. He's a pretty special kid too. Anyway, after class she asks if she could present the speech to the teachers at the next faculty meeting, and again, I say yes. Seemed like a great idea. So last week on Tuesday morning, she comes in again wearing her hat and a long black coat, and I introduce her, even though everyone at school already knows her."

"Jonas is all pumped up taking credit for this wonderful student," added Dave.

"Anyway, she's substituted parts of the Address with her own creations, making it relevant to the current desegregation situation here in Denver. Parts of it are funny, but it had meaning. She's not sure where she stands on the busing issue either, but I think Junior's having an impact on her. She dedicated the issue to the students who 'hopefully have not studied in vain.'" Dave laughed at Jonas' attempt to mimic Rainer's voice. "When she finished, out pops about ten of her classmates who wanted to see how she would pull it off."

Dave spoke again. "I don't know about Jonas, but she has Cirillo wrapped around her finger. If I was in high school, I'd ask her out."

"What happened then?" asked Laura.

Elyse got up and took a picture from her refrigerator door. "She passed out these autographed photos of Abraham Lincoln, bowed, and ran out with her gang of friends.

Jonas simply said, "It was really cool!"

§

No one left Elyse's that Friday night. Sometime after midnight, after Jonas had embarrassed Elyse by telling stories of their awkward moments in her parents' house, they turned in. Dave got the couch, Laura the guest bedroom, and Jonas was back in Elyse's bed. Dave didn't drink any more after Jonas had taken his beer at seven, which limited what the other three consumed. Elyse and Jonas quietly made love, comfortable again in their relationship.

"When will you leave for Montana?"

"They're predicting a few nice days starting Monday, so I think I'll leave then to avoid any bad weather on the roads. Hopefully, I can make it in one day. Depends on the roads."

"When will you come home?"

"Home. I guess this is my home now, isn't it. I'll stay until at least next weekend. Then I'll look for a break in the weather again and come home to you." Jonas smiled.

"You really had me scared this fall, you know."

"I was lucky you'd have me back."

For a moment they were quiet. Then Elyse spoke again. "Do you ever wonder about your mom? I mean, especially at Christmas."

"Wonder's the right word. I'm not sure how else to describe it. I think it's more brain than heart. I wonder why she left, where she went, what she's doing; those kinds of things."

"Do you miss her?"

"Can't miss what I never had."

"Tough guy, huh?"

Quiet again.

"I'm worried about Dave."

Jonas leaned up on his left elbow to indicate he was ready to listen more closely. "What are you really worried about, Elyse?"

Without looking at her boyfriend, she spoke. "That everything happening at school and in Denver will change." She paused and Jonas waited. "Including us. I worry I won't survive the stress. I don't handle it well. I worry it will consume you. I worry you'll go to a downtown school, like Manual. You'll thrive in this chaos; a little bit of idealism and a lot of love for kids like you. You see it as a beautiful mess."

When Elyse stopped, Jonas stayed quiet, not knowing quite how to respond. It allowed her to continue. "You're not like us, my love. Laura left, Dave won't stay here forever, and I could leave and go into the business sector. This isn't what I bargained for when I was taking education classes. It isn't like that fantasy called Kent Girls School. It's harder than hell and wears me down. I think I'll make it, but some days . . . I just don't know. But it's exactly what you wanted when you were preparing for this. I see it in you at faculty meetings when everyone is scared. You're not." She finally had said enough.

Jonas moved his right hand from Elyse's arm to her face. Gently tracing her features with his index finger, he spoke. "Mr. Cirillo called me in the other day to talk about all this. Dave's leaving at the end of the semester. He got another job in Alamosa. He asked me if I knew what you were going to do. He asked if I would stay with him if you left. I didn't know how to answer because it never really occurred to me you might go. I told him I would, that I was in this for the long haul. I've got to see how this all turns out. Stubborn and bull-headed."

"Does that mean the end of us if I don't stay?"

"No," he said. "It just means we can't share a hump at lunch every day."

"Seriously?"

"Seriously. As long as we can stay in Denver, we can be a couple--if you can stand me. But you know what, Elyse? I don't think you'll leave Andrew Jackson. What I know about you that you won't admit to yourself is you're every bit as tough as me, in some ways tougher, and you've been bitten too. Cirillo told me how you handled that fight in the hall a couple of weeks ago. And he said you haven't needed any reassurance about your class discipline either. Cirillo gives me the easy kids, the top classes. You're still in the trenches where the real teaching is. Shit, Elyse, I'm in awe of you as a teacher. And more importantly, I believe in you."

She rolled on top of him. "Oh, Jonas."

§

Elyse allowed Jonas to sleep in on Saturday morning. When he finally did roll out of bed around nine, he found his three friends eating waffles and laughing, just like old times. He walked over to Elyse and gave her a kiss, then kissed both Laura and Dave on the top of their heads.

"Just don't want to show any favoritism." He walked to the frig and pulled out the pitcher of orange juice as if it were his apartment. "How do I order breakfast?"

Laura got up. "Your kiss is payment. One or two waffles?"

"Just one."

"You're spoiled, you know," said Dave.

"I know, and I don't know what I did to deserve it either."

Elyse suggested they go Christmas shopping all day and then take in a movie in the evening.

"The shopping's good, but I've got a basketball game tonight. My C-team doesn't play, just the varsity and JV, but I've got to be there." After some moaning, Jonas convinced them to go with him. "Besides, Laura, some of the faculty would love to see you."

The conversation was about nothing in particular, while Jonas ate his breakfast. Everyone seemed to be relaxed and ready for the two-week Christmas break. Jonas, however, was looking for an opportunity to ask Dave about his decision to leave Denver and relocate in Alamosa.

"Did we ever crash so early last year?" asked Laura.

"I think everyone has just been going ninety miles per hour for the past few weeks," said Elyse.

Dave opened the door for Jonas. "And some of us have a lot on our minds." He looked at Jonas. "You know, don't you?"

"Yeah. Cirillo told me last week. Can I talk you out of it?"

Laura was lost. "What am I missing?"

"I'm leaving at the semester. Going back to rural America. The high school there will give me a job next year. I just got lost in all the excitement and realized I'm not a city-boy. I'll be happier in a small town. We all have our own niche, and Andrew Jackson isn't mine."

Elyse reached across the table and took Dave's hand as Jonas spoke. "I should have been less self-centered this fall. Sorry, buddy."

"Hell, it's not your fault. This will be better. I'm sorry about not telling you guys sooner. Guess you'll have to find a new roomie."

"No sweat. I've got an idea about one anyway."

§

Either Laura or Elyse walked arm-in-arm with Dave while they shopped, except when he was with Jonas. At the Cherry Creek mall, the women spent quite a bit of time in stores created to make men uncomfortable. Dave and Jonas spent those times sitting on the benches in the walkways.

"I'll miss you, dumbass," said Dave.

"I heard Laura tell you we'll keep in touch, but I doubt if we will much. This fall was a good example. But you've been a good friend for this first year and a half. I'll miss your ass too," said Jonas.

§

The crowd at the basketball game was sparse, but there were a dozen or so Jackson teachers in attendance, all of whom were happy to see Laura. The faculty section was six rows up from the team bench, so Jonas was able to stare and smile at Elyse during timeouts and between quarters. Both the varsity and JVs won handily. Junior Warren was all that his reputation indicated he would be. Playing every minute of the first three quarters, he led the varsity to a twenty-two-point lead before sitting out the fourth with the other starters. Junior ended up with eleven points and ten assists and a handful of steals. Junior had beaten out Jack Winge for the starting spot, but Jack's outside shot was improving, so he was getting some varsity minutes. Rick Parris was the team's leading scorer, and Junior's competitiveness made Rick pay attention; otherwise, he became the focus of the point guard's wrath. On this night Rick scored nineteen, and he, too, sat the bench in the last quarter.

Coach Ragni kept his post-game comments short, so Jonas was able to join the gang quickly. They went first to McDonald's for burgers to go before heading to Jonas' and Dave's apartment.

"If you're not going to finish those fries, don't throw them away."

"I'll take your pickles."

"Cheeseburgers and beer. Are we back in college?"

"Hey, Jonas, does it bother you Jack Winge isn't starting?" asked Dave.

"No, Junior is clearly better. Even Jack sees it. Besides, I'm getting pretty close to Junior in class and with him being my aide. Great kid."

"Does he say anything about the black kids we're going to get next year?"

"Yeah. He tells me things will be different, that not all the new black students will be AP."

"What else?"

"He said a lot of the kids will want it to work, but a lot of them won't stand for any 'white shit.'"

§

Jonas thought it would be good for Laura to have Elyse for herself for the night, but Elyse vetoed that action. "Sit on the couch and watch TV while we talk, but when I go to bed, I'll expect you to be there."

"Oooh," said Dave.

Saturday night turned out the same way Friday had. Dave came back over to Elyse's apartment and slept on the couch. He and Jonas did watch a movie, while the women talked in the kitchen.

"Remember when we first started last year, and we all thought we'd be together for our whole careers? Now only you and Jonas will be left, and we're just in our second year," said Laura.

Elyse had already played this scenario. What she had begun to understand was how hard teaching really was. She believed her principal when he said she was doing a good job. What he meant was she was doing a good job for a young teacher. There was a universe between her abilities, any of the gang's abilities for that matter, and an experienced teacher. Despite Jonas' confidence in her, Elyse didn't know if she had the stuff to make it, especially in a large high school.

"You know who I feel sorry for, Laur?" Elyse didn't wait for Laura to answer. "Dave. He'll leave here and think he's failed."

"How is he different from me? That's how I felt last year."

"It's different. You made a decision to go, and you aren't back in your old hometown. Dave's just, I don't know, lost it. Jonas isn't even sure Dave will teach when he goes home."

Laura stretched her head from side to side. "Ever wonder how many new teachers just give it up? I mean, we go to college for four years or more, do our student teaching, and everything's all roses. Then we get out into the real world and find it's not for us and go do something else."

"I thought the second year would be easier, but in some ways, it's harder. Each of us is our own worst enemy." Elyse looked from the kitchen into the living room where the boys were sprawled out on the couch. She leaned closer to Laura. "Don't you dare give up, girl. I'm going to make it, and so are you. We're going to get better every year, and young teachers will use us for examples of tough women who they look up to."

"So, you're going to be the new Mrs. Bentert, huh?" Elyse

pounded Laura in the arm for her comment but reflected on it later. Elyse vowed never to be like Susan Bentert! She wondered too, if teaching could really be her life's path or whether her words were meant just to boost Laura's confidence.

§

Saturday night. Christmas break. At Andrew Jackson High School, the principal and his secretary evaluated resumes that were nearly a year old. Math teachers were hard to replace.

"Are we pathetic or what?" Annette laughed. "Shouldn't I have a date tonight?"

"You do. With Andy. General Jackson. Besides, we're professionals. At least it's what I tell my wife."

"Your wife is a saint, Pete."

"No kidding!" Pete slapped down another folder containing the resume of a candidate for Dave Fallon's job. "Are there any in-district candidates with less than three years of experience?"

Annette leaned over to grab a second pile. "We went through it last week and didn't find anyone. Are we desperate yet?"

"Yes, maybe we're missing something."

"Pete, it's eight-thirty. I'm tired. You're tired. We both have headaches. Trust your ability to train someone to do the job. This Torrez guy is young, hasn't been in jail like Jonas, and can coach. You liked him in the interview last year, except he took seven years to get his degree. Maybe we ought to see it as a positive, that he was prolonging a fun time in his life." Annette smiled.

"Okay. Call him after Christmas and schedule an appointment." Pete laughed. "The way Jonas is progressing, maybe we ought to seek more candidates from the federal lockup."

§

Laura understood this might be the last time she would ever see Dave, so she brought out the comforter from the guest room and curled up at the end of the couch where his feet were and started reminiscing.

"Remember when" became the recurrent theme. They tried to be quiet so as not to disturb Jonas and Elyse, but it just couldn't be done. Realizing that, Laura finally got up, went to Elyse's door, and knocked.

"When you guys are done, come out and join us. You know, one last night and all."

CHAPTER 29

"May the souls of the departed, through the mercy of God, rest in peace."

Barbara Deaver promised God on Sunday, December 23, that she would move forward with her life in the next year. No more looking back. She had applied for and was hired as the building secretary for the new Bryson City High School, which was scheduled to open in early January. The town's children would once again be completing their schooling at home. Ms. Deaver asked for His guidance in finding her other son. So many years had passed; should she try to communicate with him? Would it be going against her vow of moving forward? To find him, she would need to communicate with her former husband. Could she do that? Would her living son even want to meet her?

§

In December of 1973, Paul Garrity sent a letter to the U.S. Department of Corrections asking to be placed on the approved list for written communications for Abby Archer. He also received his honorable discharge from the U.S. Army. He had regained his weight back, traveled to California to meet with his best friend from college, and talked with Jonas about teaching, but had mostly decided not to pursue that occupation.

In January, he wrote his first letter to Abby.

Dear Abby,

Jonas told me about your predicament and mentioned that you had asked about me and my health. I can finally say I have physically recovered, although there are still heavy scars on my emotions. He also said you weren't speaking with anyone connected to the prison system. Because of my experience with this, I fully understand why you might choose this path. Anger, fear, and lack of trust were my daily partners. The other daily partner was the physical abuse. I can only hope you don't experience any of this.

My goal while I was a prisoner became to stay alive and get back home. I clung to my family and friends. I tried not to cooperate with my captors as best I could. But to tell the truth, daily existence was easier when I did cooperate just a little. I didn't tell them anything or make statements against the United States, but I began to acknowledge them to an extent, and it helped. I would ask you to think about it.

Jonas told me about his classes. He seems like the type of teacher I would work hard for. He talked about his students; I guess he writes about them to you too. Jonas has bags under his eyes like he's not sleeping enough. I'll bet we could both tell him something about not sleeping. He credits you with encouraging him about teaching. If you'd like for me to continue writing to you, I will. I know the prison system will read everything we write but exchanging experiences about confinement might help the both of us. I never got to know you well at CU, but if I can help, I will.

Paul Garrity

Chapter 30

Steve Torrez was hired as Andrew Jackson's new math teacher. Twenty-eight years old, he was teaching at Cole Junior High, a predominantly black school in the Five Points area with a reputation for "teacher busting." Torrez was a second-generation citizen whose parents immigrated to the United States during World War II under the Bracero Program and then migrated from southern California to northern Colorado to thin sugar beets on Weld County farms. He was the first in his family to graduate from high school, took seven years to get his degree in mathematics, and accepted the only offer he received to teach. Dave Fallon's two junior trig sections were transferred to a more experienced math teacher, and Torrez began his high school career with five sophomore algebra classes.

Jonas met Steve at Archie's Groundhog Day party on February 2. Archie introduced them. "Steve, this is Jonas. Jonas, Steve here is a radical revolutionary too. Brown Beret. Chicano Movement. UMAS at CU." All this was tongue-in-cheek by Archie, but, except for the United Mexican American Students, it was true. "Steve, Jonas had a girlfriend who blew up buildings and robbed banks to protest the war. You two will have a lot to talk about." With that, Archie walked away.

Jonas started first. "The part about robbing banks is true, but the bombings aren't. How have your first few weeks gone?"

"Really well. This has been a piece of cake so far, a lot different from my last assignment in the junior high."

"UMAS, huh. So, you went to CU too?"

"No, Metro State actually, but I have been active in the Chicano protests. Were you a war protester?"

Jonas smiled. He was an observer, one of those college students who watched and then discussed the merits of the protest without standing in the streets with a placard. The two men talked at length about their recent pasts, and each found the other interesting and compatible. Neither was with a date, but like Jonas, Steve had a serious girlfriend. One difference, however, was Steve was an unwed father.

"It's put a damper on my revolutionary involvement. My lady keeps a tight rein on me. It's good for me, though. I was pretty wild most of the time."

"Are you going to marry her?"

"Probably. No hurry. She has to grow up some. We live together in Edgewater with her parents. When I get a house, we'll tie the knot. As I said, no hurry."

Elyse arrived around nine with news about her mother. "Just as I thought, severe heartburn. We really didn't need to take her to the hospital though. She said to say hi."

"You took her to the hospital? Why didn't you call?"

"I did, but you must have already left. I couldn't reach you. It turned out to be no big deal," said Elyse.

Jonas accepted that. "Elyse, this is Steve Torrez, the guy who's taking Dave's position."

Steve bowed slightly. "I guess you guys were pretty close. What really happened to make him leave?"

"What did you hear?"

"That he got a higher paying job in Alamosa. I know that's not true. Those small towns pay next to nothing, and a small college town can get new teachers whenever the need arises. No need to pay well."

Jonas felt comfortable telling him. "He was a lonely guy who didn't really fit in the big city. With Elyse and me spending so much time together, we kind of ignored him. Sort of let him slowly die on the vine, so he went home." It was an honest statement made with real remorse. Elyse squeezed his upper arm and leaned in and gave him a kiss on the cheek.

Steve realized the moment. "It'll probably be a better fit. The city's a hard-ass place. It can beat a guy down. Don't blame yourself." There was a moment of silence, and then Steve excused himself. "Well, I better wander and correct the lies Archie's spreading about me to the rest of the staff. See you guys around." They all shook hands, and Steve walked away.

The silence remained for a few seconds. Then Elyse turned to face her boyfriend. "Are you all right?"

Jonas smiled. "Yeah, I guess I needed to get it out, but Steve's right. Dave will be happier." He paused. "So, are your parents going to be okay with us living together?"

§

On Wednesday, February 6, Jonas wheeled a television into his classroom so the students could watch the House of Representatives discuss whether there was enough evidence to impeach President Nixon. An unrelated story dealt with the kidnapping of Patricia Hearst by a group calling itself the Symbionese Liberation Army. Hearst was just nineteen years old and the heir to a fortune made by her grandfather in the newspaper business.

"Let's ignore the kidnapping story for now and focus on the House Judiciary Committee's debates. We won't know the outcome until later tonight, but this will give you a chance to see if the Constitution works." Jonas was more interested than his students. This wasn't simply a blow-off day of television, but real drama directly impacting the nation.

As the class watched, Pete entered the room to speak with Jonas. He rubbed his chin and smiled before he spoke. "Well, Jonas, it appears as if it's happened again. The pickup truck that scrapes the snow off our sidewalks slid into your car. It's not drivable."

Jonas slumped onto the heat register and slapped his forehead. "What is it with me and cars?" It was a rhetorical question.

Pete reached into his pocket and pulled out his ring of keys. Sorting through them quickly, he found the dirty gold one for his old Chevy, the one Jonas borrowed after his car burned up at the beginning of his first year. "I'll have my wife drive it over and leave it for you. You better go and check it out. I'll stay here until Archie comes down."

By the end of the day, the House of Representatives had voted overwhelmingly to proceed with the impeachment process.

§

Coach Cullen's sophomore team defeated the Kennedy Commanders 47-41 on Saturday morning, raising their record to 9-4 with five games to go. Jonas was excited because he felt as if his coaching skills were improving, at least in the practice sessions. "I get too wrapped up in the action during games to help the kids much," he told Steve Torrez.

"You'd never know it. You just sit on the bench and clap."

"That's what I mean. I freeze. Coaching isn't like teaching in a classroom."

Elyse walked up to congratulate her new roommate with a kiss as he stood by the bench. Unlike varsity games where the players shook hands and then went into the locker room to shower and dress, sophomores usually wore their uniforms to the games and stood around afterward talking with their friends and parents. Parents liked Coach Cullen because he played every kid at least six minutes. Rainer sat with him on the bench and kept track of every kid's minutes as well as shots, assists, and turnovers.

Jonas called her over after she added up her numbers. "Hey, Rainer, I want you to meet someone. Rainer, this is Mr. Torrez, our new math teacher. Steve, this is our school's most unique young lady, also, one you need to watch out for."

The two shook hands and waited for either Jonas or Elyse to add to the introduction. Rainer was used to Mr. Cullen fawning over her to his colleagues. "Rainer is our school's student liaison to the district's committee on school desegregation. Evidently, she's stirred things up pretty good last week by challenging the school board to come up with a real plan or get out of the way. By the way, did you talk to Junior about that yet?"

Rainer shook her head and then turned to Mr. Torrez. "How's this busing thing going to impact the Chicano population? Are they going to be included in the desegregation plan?"

Mr. Torrez didn't flinch. "Right now, they'd like to avoid it if they could for a while. They're satisfied with their neighborhood schools just now, but I'm not sure the court will allow it. If they don't, we'll just riot." He raised his eyebrows and smiled.

Rainer smiled back. "Invite him to class next time Junior goes off. It could be interesting." With that, she handed Jonas her statistics and strolled over to take Rick Parris' hand and lead him out of the gym. Jonas was surprised.

"They've been a thing for a few months now. Pull your head out, dear. They have lives outside of your classroom, you know." Elyse put her arm around Jonas' waist and led him out of the gym. Title IX.

§

Tension within the faculty erupted on Friday in the teachers' lounge. Archie was lecturing the faculty about institutional racism, when Gary Dessins told him to "Shut the fuck up, King, and let us eat our lunch." Dessins often used the f-word, but normally it was interpreted simply as his way of saying "damn." Not this day. He and several of his colleagues chaffed at the district's mandatory meetings about desegregation and the perceived accusation teachers were racists.

"We were hired by Denver, not Andrew Jackson. Most of us were simply placed here. We could've been sent to any secondary school, but we ended up here. You think you're the damn expert because you lived in the South when the Court decided on *Brown*. If that makes you the expert, then we're all the new experts because we teach when the Court decided *Keyes*. Quit your preaching. We've had enough of it!" Dessins stared at Archie for five seconds after he quit talking, then turned back to his bologna sandwich.

Instead of letting it go and responding later, Archie, who was standing against the back wall eating a Snickers bar, laughed. "I said 'institutional racism,' not 'personal racism.' A little touchy aren't you, Gary?"

Before anyone could stop him, Dessins was out of his chair, which went sprawling, and had Archie pinned against the wall. Dessins had his left forearm in Archie's neck with his right hand squeezing his cheeks. Dessins had leverage and was looking up at Archie. "You never know when to shutup, do you, asshole! You didn't like the South, so you left."

Archie was able to push Dessins' hand off his face but could do no more. Dessins now held Archie's left wrist.

"You went to Vietnam and then came back and bad-mouthed the government. If you can't support us here at Jackson, then get the hell out. It's your nature, asshole!" Three male teachers tried to restrain Dessins, but the woodworking teacher was too incensed and too strong. Archie turned red in the face before Dessins finally released him, but he let Archie have one more shove against the wall and issued a threat. "If you lecture me one more time in front of this staff, I'll catch you in the parking lot and kick your ass. If you ever want to say anything to me again, you see me alone and talk man-to-man." With that, he pulled back. The three teachers patted Dessins on the back and walked him to his chair.

The last seven minutes of the twenty-five-minute lunch period passed in silence.

News of the lunch-time fight spread rapidly among the faculty. Rumors seemed to fly as easily as if it had been a sophomore girl fight over a junior boy. Pete Cirillo called a hasty teachers' meeting for 3:30.

As the teachers filed into the library, an air of solemnity accompanied them. Just as teachers stand outside their doors during passing periods, Pete stood at the library door. He wasn't smiling. This was not an optional meeting, and Pete did a silent count as each teacher walked past him. At precisely 3:30, he closed the door with all teachers, except for three head coaches, present.

"As you know, Gary and Archie got into a shoving match at lunch today. I blame Archie. Let me state unequivocally, neither

Gary Dessins nor anyone on this staff is a racist. If I'm wrong about any one of you, stop by my office so I can have you transferred." Pete was angry. "People, we're going to have enough crap to deal with in the coming months, so please don't turn on each other. I intend for Andrew Jackson to be Fortress Jackson. We will teach every student who comes through our doors next year with the same skill and concern and discipline we teach this year's kids. We're going to gain some good kids, but we're going to lose some good kids. Regardless of what plan the school board or the court gives us, we'll implement it and do what we do best. If you support desegregation in theory, that's the best we can do. *The Coleman Report* said black kids learn better in integrated classes. We're going to find out, but no one will be able to say the plan failed because we here at Jackson didn't give it our best efforts." He stopped and collected himself. Then he turned to his right where Archie sat. "You got anything you want to say, Arch?"

Archie stood and faced his colleagues. "I'm sorry. It's not the first time I haven't been able to shut up. Despite Gary's offer, I'm not leaving." He sought out Dessins with his eyes. "Sorry, man, I was out of line. It won't happen again." He nodded at Gary and sat down.

Gary stood up and caught Pete's attention. "I'm sorry, too. We tell our kids to handle themselves when they're called names. Pretty sorry example I set. Archie and I have gone at it before and then shared a beer. We'll do it again over this . . . if he buys." Some members of the faculty laughed cautiously. "It just shows how much stress can build over this issue, stress we all have to be aware of." He sat down.

Pete blew out a deep breath. "If any student asks you what happened, tell them truthfully what you know. Don't embellish the story. If you're uncomfortable answering their questions, send them to me or Gary or Archie. Maybe we can show them how much this issue matters to us too." He bobbed his head and then asked for questions.

Ben Lucas raised his hand. "Where should we go so Archie can buy us all that beer?"

As it turned out, it was Jonny's Tavern.

As the teachers filed out, Pete took Jonas' arm and pulled him aside, holding him until the room emptied. Then he asked, "If you want to transfer to Manual next year, I understand, but why do I have to hear about it from Chartwell?"

CHAPTER 31

Elyse interrupted Jonas' reading around 11:00. Since moving in together, her worries about his obsessive lesson planning and preparation had dissipated; she could sit with him or easily divert his attention. Not only were they lovers, but they were also good roommates. "Watcha doin'?" she asked as she wrapped her arms around his shoulders from behind where he sat at the dining room table, pressing her breasts against his back.

He held up a slim paperback called *The Other America*. "Did you ever read this?" Elyse said she hadn't. "I had to read it for one of my college classes, and I really liked it. I thought Harrington was right on. I thought it might remind me of some of the problems Denver will be confronted with next year. Reading it now, I have more questions."

"Like what?"

Jonas repositioned himself and let Elyse sit facing him on his lap, a little too intimate for an intellectual conversation, but he tried. "When he wrote this, the American economic engine was going full steam; it seemed as if that alone could solve many of the country's problems. There was a lot of good will towards the poor, a lot of good intentions to make a difference. Now all that capital has been used up."

"What do you mean 'capital'?"

"Sort of like stockpiling energy and good intentions during good times, so if a problem develops, people mobilize to solve it. Does that make sense?" Elyse nodded. "Well, Vietnam and the recession have used up all of that capital."

"And where is all of this going?" She knew Jonas' thoughts always led somewhere.

"An extension of Harrington's thesis would be that with awareness, an end to the public's indifference, and enlightened governmental policies, the crisis in black education could be solved." If Jonas had been sexually aroused, his hands would be moving on Elyse's body, but his remained on her thighs. "Busing being enlightened governmental policy."

"Second thoughts?"

"Yeah. The attitude of our staff is we'll do what we have to, but only because we're good soldiers. We respect Pete, so we'll do what he wants. Color aside, Elyse, we're going to exchange a lot of good students for students with some pretty poor educational habits. When Harrington talked about a culture of poverty, he seemed to suggest there wouldn't be any resistance from the poor themselves. We know now that many did. It seems the *Keyes* decision takes the same stand Harrington did. Just bring black students into white schools and everything will work itself out." Jonas was looking to Elyse for help.

"But there's no capital for busing, is there?"

"No. Even in good times, there would be resistance. But now, I think the school system could come apart."

"Kind of up to us to see that it doesn't, you know."

Jonas semi-smiled. "Front line soldiers." He removed his hands from her thighs and clasped them behind his head for a moment and looked into Elyse's eyes.

She knew her soldier was seldom tortured or paralyzed by his thoughts. Instead, he would redouble his efforts and take it upon himself to do what he could. It was one of his most endearing qualities, one part of his character she loved. She blinked, smiled back, and then moved her forehead to his. "What else?"

"Nothing else, except I wonder if I'm up to this. I wonder if any of us are."

Elyse stood, took Jonas' hand and led him to the couch, where she sat him down. She returned to the kitchen for two beers. She took two frozen mugs out of the freezer, poured each one full, and returned to Jonas. "I was wondering about myself earlier this year, but then I said, 'Screw it!' I can do this, and you're more committed than me." She handed Jonas a mug, sat down at the opposite end of the couch, and chugged a third of her beer. "That's good."

Jonas smiled. "I don't know about being stronger, but I do know I've got an easier schedule."

"Which of your students are you worried about? Every time you have a crisis of confidence, it's because one of your AP kids is having a problem you can't immediately fix." She took another drink and waited for Jonas to answer.

"It's not the kids this time, Elyse. I'm hardly an inner-city guy. All white Jonas in all ways moves to Denver, and the resident Denver whites begin to move out. Ironic, huh. I came here with unrealistic dreams about race relations and inner-city schools, but I find myself wanting to stay at Jackson and teach accelerated classes, especially if our school loses its AP kids or the program," Jonas was interrupted.

"Don't be silly, the district won't do that. It's a show piece for minority participation."

"Yeah, but my point is I want to work with college level students. I'm fooling myself to say I only want to teach in the inner-city. Rainer, Junior, Betty, Rick, Messi—those are the students I want to work with."

"Then go start an AP program up north. You'd be inner city and working with the AP kids." Elyse played Jonas' game when he was full of doubts. She hoped he would stay at Andrew Jackson.

Jonas smiled. "Rainer asked me today what they could do to have me for a teacher next year. I told her I'd create an alternative American history class that focused on the evils of Manifest Destiny. An elective. She seemed to think that would work."

"Lover, it's a remarkable class. I don't have the experience to know, but all the teachers say so. Once every ten years." Elyse put her bare feet in Jonas' lap, a signal for him to rub them. He put his beer on the end table and did as directed. "That feels so good. Where did you learn to do that?"

"You won't believe this, but my dad used to do this for me when I was a kid. It was the only physical part of his nature. No hugs, no kissing, but I did get my feet rubbed, all the way up through high school." Jonas stopped for a moment for a drink of beer and then continued. "I'll bet your parents were affectionate with you."

"They still are. You've seen that."

"My students are teaching me I have to be. We've talked about this before, haven't we?" said Jonas.

"Yeah, but I still like to hear about your growth as a sensitive male. Your basketball practices are unlike any I ever saw."

"How many have you seen?"

"In high school we practiced our cheerleader routines at the same time the varsity practiced basketball. The coach swore all the time; his favorite words were ass and pussy. He had a free throw drill involving girls' pink underwear. We all knew how it came out, but we never got to actually watch."

"I thought you went to an all-girl school," asked Jonas.

"The boys used our gym to practice," answered Elyse.

"Loser had to wear the pink panties for the rest of practice, huh. We had a similar drill in high school. I've got to tell you, I hated it. Really demeaning. I never planned to coach as a teacher; didn't want to be that kind of an adult, but it's been good. Coaches see students in a different way." Jonas paused. "It was funny though when someone else had to wear the panties."

"And students see teachers in a different way, too." Elyse smiled and removed her feet from Jonas' lap. She finished her beer and repositioned herself so that her head was in his lap. Jonas pushed his fingers into her scalp.

"You know, I think I'm finished with book learnin' for tonight. How about we get naked and forget school even exists."

"Oh, Jonas, that's the best idea you've had in weeks."

§

Archie asked Annette if she wanted to join him and Pete in Pete's office for a Friday afternoon drink on the last Friday in February, but she declined. She had moved on. Archie had been subdued since his tussle with Gary Dessins, both in his classroom and in his personal life. Archie knew he was an asshole, always had been, and probably always would be, but there were times when he didn't like himself. He understood that much of his effectiveness as the self-proclaimed conscience of the staff had been diminished by his recent actions.

More than anyone else, Pete understood Archie. They came to this juncture of their careers by different paths, but they put the education of all students at the center of their philosophies. Pete graduated from college in 1952 and then served three years in the Army, one of which was in Korea. He began teaching in the fall of '55 in the west Denver suburb of Lakewood. He taught PE, coached football, basketball, and baseball, sponsored student council and Latin Club, and served as the building union chief for two schools. His father had been a union boss in the Pueblo steel mills. After eight years, he turned to administration, the "dark side," and never looked back. He rose rapidly, getting his own building at the age of thirty-eight. Andrew Jackson had a sterling reputation, much of it the result of Pete's efforts.

Archie was a late comer into education. He neither understood the bureaucratic process nor accepted it. When he came to Andrew Jackson, he believed schools should lead society to a higher plane, and he had never come off that position. Pete found himself protecting Archie behind the scenes while supporting his optimistic position. On this Friday Pete realized Archie needed his support.

"Scotch or whiskey?"

"Double shot of both, Pete."

"Everything okay at home?" asked Pete.

"That part is good. It's just my artist girlfriend isn't fully cognizant of what really goes on here, so there's some loneliness there."

"You're not the only one who feels like that, Arch. Not many people out there truly understand what goes on in here." Pete took a sip from his scotch. "I think all teachers are a bit lonely."

"Desperate?"

"No, Archie, just lonely from all the time they're locked up in their own classrooms. Most of the time, you guys are on your own with thirty kids whose brains and emotions haven't come in sync yet. It's like Jonas. One incident interrupts his routine, and his world gets tossed upside-down. When Elyse broke up with him, he went down to the personnel office and filled out a transfer form. He thought it was just a preliminary form—which it was—but that dick Chartwell got a hold of it and saw it as a way to get back at me. Charles assigned him to Manual for next year. Luckily, I have friends above Chartwell who were able to stop that action, but it shows the stress my teachers are working under."

"In five years, we won't be able to differentiate Andrew Jackson from Manual or Lincoln or West. Not a bad thing," said Archie.

"If you mean those other schools rise to our standards, then you're right. It won't be a bad thing."

§

By the end of March, Jonas was spent. He had been teaching or taking classes for twenty straight months, and he was exhausted. His preparation suffered, and it was noticeable in his advanced placement courses. Spring Break did not help much. Instead of going south for a true vacation as Elyse urged, he believed he needed to stay in Denver and plan for the final push. However, most of his time was spent sleeping, but at least he was rested for the final push after spring break.

<h1>CHAPTER 32</h1>

Jonas couldn't remember who came to his classroom door to give him the news. It probably was Pete, but it might have been Archie or even Ben. All he could remember was the feeling of being punched in the stomach harder than any blow he had ever suffered. Rainer was involved in a serious car accident on Broadway near the State Capitol. A drunk driver blew through a red light at eight in the morning, broad-siding Rainer's car directly where she sat. She was scheduled to give a special presentation to the full Colorado legislature on the impact of court ordered busing on high school students. Thursday, April 18, 1974. Being a teacher changed for Jonas Cullen that day.

Ironically, Jonas and his second period AP students were discussing Rainer's recent rant at the Denver school board meeting the previous week. She challenged the two most pro-busing members on their failure to differentiate between elementary students, who were just entering into the system, and high school students, whose ties to their high schools constituted the largest part of their young lives. Certainly, she was speaking about herself, but the implication impacted over ninety percent of Denver's high school students. Because she felt she had not influenced the Board's policies, she maneuvered an appointment to speak to the legislature within a week. The class laughed. "If it could be done, it would be done by Rainer!"

Details of the crash were still sketchy, but Rainer was transported to Denver General Hospital in critical condition. With as much composure as he could muster, Jonas stepped back into his classroom.

"I don't know quite how to tell you this," he swallowed hard and bit his lower lip. "Rainer's been in a car accident. I don't know how badly she's hurt, but she's been taken to the hospital." His eyes filled with tears. "Someone's going to come down to watch the class for the rest of the period. I need to go." He started to leave and then turned back to his class. "Say a prayer." He walked back into the hall where Coach Ragni was just coming up.

"I'll take care of them, son. You hurry down to the hospital."

Jonas nodded in appreciation.

"Don't come back today. You'll have coverage for all your classes. Don't worry about anything here. Understand?" Ragni put his hands on Jonas' shoulders. "She'll be okay. She's the toughest kid we got."

The drive from Andrew Jackson to Denver General took fifteen minutes. Jonas parked illegally in a doctor's space near the emergency room and ran into the hospital. An ambulance was parked near the emergency room entrance, and Jonas wondered if it was the one that transported Rainer. At the desk, he asked where Rainer was being treated. The nurse asked if he was a relative.

"No, I'm her teacher. I have to be with her. Just point me in the direction."

For some instinctive reason, the nurse understood, rose from her chair, and whispered to a colleague who took over the desk. The nurse then led Jonas through the metal doors separating the waiting room from the treatment rooms and walked him to a glass enclosed operating room where Rainer lay. Rainer's mother turned to see Jonas just as he was being fitted with a surgical mask. She moved to him and wrapped her arms around his waist. Her eyes told him it was bad. Jonas waited for her to speak, allowing her to hold on to someone who knew her daughter. She shook violently for several moments before she pulled back.

"She's not going to make it, Mr. Cullen. They're keeping her alive, so they can take some of her organs for others. I didn't even get to say goodbye." A look of pure anguish took over Rainer's mother.

Jonas firmly held her shoulder and guided her over to the bed. "Whisper into her ear that you love her. Tell her everything you want her to know. She'll hear you."

The two physicians and four nurses made no attempt to prevent them from getting close to the red-haired girl whose life was being preserved in order to save others. The left side of Rainer's skull had taken the brunt of the crash and was purple and red. Rainer's mother bent into the right ear of her daughter and began to speak softly. A nurse slid a chair under her seat. Jonas stepped gently to the head of the bed and placed his left hand on Rainer's scalp and his right hand on her right shoulder. His eyes were red, but he held the tears, as he stood at the head of his first favorite student, protecting for one last time the girl who would shape his feelings for every student he would teach for the next thirty-three years.

Jonas heard snippets of the mother's last words to her dying daughter, but tried to tune them out, allowing them a last private moment. He listened to the medical talk going on among the hospital staff, talk that seemed to have been muted when the mother began whispering to her daughter. Jonas' own thoughts were all over the place. He remembered Rainer's unique way of getting her friends to come around to her point of view without denigrating their ideas. He remembered the day she won Pete Cirillo over to her side forever during a class evaluation. He couldn't remember if she was dating Rick Parris at the moment; it was such an on-again, off-again affair. It was Rainer who didn't want to get serious, and Jonas knew Rick would be crushed. Jonas seemed to recall it was the eyes of Junior Warren that held his just before he left his classroom to rush to the hospital. Rainer and Junior were now best friends; she had been his early protector, even though he hadn't needed it, but Junior remembered.

Jonas' final recollection before leaving the emergency operating room was of Rainer taking his arm and putting it around her shoulder a few months earlier. "Mr. C, are you afraid of girls or just cold? You need to learn how to hug us high school girls without making us feel uncomfortable and without making us think you have a crush on us. Enough of us already have enormous crushes on you, so your hug can't encourage us. There, we remain side-by-side, and you just use the one arm. Squeeze and then relax, like you're hugging a little kid. Maybe that's what you need to remember; we're still little kids for another year or two. But the touching tells us you love us in a teacher-sort-of-way." Every day after, when Rainer walked into his classroom, she would say, "Practice," and give him a hug, a hug that was always exactly as she had taught him. Finally, a tear fell onto his surgical mask.

The female doctor in the room, Dr. Huang, touched him on the shoulder. Somehow, she had learned his name. "Jonas, we're going to take Rainer upstairs. Could you help Mrs. Brecht? You can follow us and stay with Rainer when we get there, but we can't stay here any longer."

§

Shortly after getting Rainer's mother comfortable next to her daughter, which took about an hour, Jonas leaned into Rainer's right ear and whispered the words he needed to say. "Rainer, it's Mr. Cullen. I'm sorry I didn't drive you to the legislature this morning, but I'm so proud of you for going. You know, don't you, you've been my teacher more than I've been yours. Thank you for my growth, for showing me how to hug students, for keeping me on my toes, for challenging me to be my best every day, for making me laugh at myself. Thank you for sharing your poetry with me, and for trying to help me understand it. I never knew a person could control his anger by writing out his thoughts. My poetry isn't very good yet, but I'll keep at it. Look over my shoulder and read them, okay. I'll never forget you, and I won't let you down. Goodbye, my beautiful girl. Keep in touch, okay." He kissed the top of Rainer's head, brushed her red bangs from her forehead, touched Mrs. Brecht on the shoulder, and then left to return to the visitors' room to call the school and let them know about Rainer's condition. He tried to think how he would phrase his response, but he couldn't come up with anything satisfactory.

The elevator door opened directly into the visitors' room, and to his surprise the room was packed with every AP history student from both of his sections. Each kid held a yellow carnation, Rainer's favorite color. "I've got too much red in my life already," she would have said. Pete, Elyse, and Jane Walburg were standing in the back, also holding carnations.

The students stood as one and moved close to touch Mr. Cullen. They already knew Rainer's condition was grave, so their action was to support Jonas and to fill an emptiness that existed in the waiting room. Junior spoke so gently.

"Mr. C, are you okay?"

Jonas shook his head no but maintained his composure. He pulled Junior and Friedan into his body as he addressed the twenty-seven students. "The question is how are you guys?" Their red eyes gave him his answer. "We're going to have a long day and night ahead of us, but we'll hold on to one another and get through this. Rainer's extended family will be coming in to say goodbye during the night, and I don't know what the hospital's policy is on us staying all night." He looked at Pete to see if he had any information. The principal nodded and walked over to the reception desk.

Elyse, who was hugging Julia and Martha in the back of the room, finally caught Jonas' eyes and moved to his side, putting both arms around his waist and allowing him to bury his head into her shoulder. Quietly, she asked, "Are you okay?"

Jonas swallowed hard and whispered, "I didn't see the cat." Elyse understood, and she gently kissed him next to his ear. "How did all my kids get here so quickly?

"Pete got a bus; drove it here himself."

Walburg, who was holding onto Stacey and Rick, spoke only loud enough to be heard over the quiet crying of the students. "Some of the faculty will be bringing some food over for dinner, and they'll drive any of you home or to wherever you need to be this evening." She looked at Jonas with the deepest sense of kindness. "Mr. Cirillo cancelled school for tomorrow. That will give us all a chance to deal with this." Jonas nodded and blinked back tears.

He blinked again, cleared his throat, and spoke, "Why don't we take over the area farthest from these doors. Use the floor, too, but let's leave some room for others who may need to visit other patients and for Rainer's family." Pete got Jonas' attention behind the students, and silently affirmed that the kids could stay as long as they wanted. "Some of you will need to use the pay phone to call your parents. I know some of you will need to leave at some point. Don't think you have to stay all night and don't feel bad about leaving. That you're here now is what matters." Jonas finished speaking and breathed out deeply.

"So, no homework tonight then, Mr. C," said Ian in an attempt to remove the somber atmosphere. There was a bit of nervous, relieved laughter.

"No, Ian," Jonas said with a subdued smile. "No homework."

§

Rainer was allowed to die the following afternoon.

CHAPTER 33

Jonas believed the primary reason Rainer was so well adjusted was that her mother understood her, accepted her, and encouraged her to explore life. From the very first parent-teacher conference back in September of Rainer's sophomore year, Jonas marveled at this mother-daughter relationship. Rainer always accompanied her mother to these meetings, making sure she met all her teachers and asked the relevant questions. Rainer would go on to tell her mother of the goings-on in the classes, of how "Mr. C" handled his students, and of how, in reality, she was instructing him how to teach. Jonas knew that while Rainer was teasing him in front of her mother, she was partly accurate. Such a perceptive student. Jonas also knew he was one of Rainer's favorites.

Rainer's mother called Jonas on Saturday afternoon after her daughter's passing for advice. "Mr. Cullen, my daughter didn't want to be buried, but instead wanted to be cremated. We talked about everything, including death. Rainer was always so curious. You know she was sampling other religions right now, and currently, it's Buddhism mixed with a bit of Hinduism."

Jonas knew of Rainer's search for a comfortable faith; they had talked at length about it after school several times, and she had shared her poems with him. She was further along the path of self-exploration regarding the spiritual world than Jonas, but he hung on her words more out of fascination with this unique student than out of respect for the teacher-student relationship, which was important to him.

"What I need your help on, Mr. Cullen, is how to handle the expectations of everyone who loved Rainer, especially those at your school." She paused, and Jonas could hear her breathing change from the control she exhibited at the start of the call to breaths mixed with sniffles. "My family wants a Christian burial, and I don't know." She could not proceed.

A few moments of silence passed while the two people who had suddenly become closely tied to one another collected their emotions. Finally, when Jonas believed Rainer's mother was breathing more gently again, he began to answer her dilemma.

"Sometimes when Rainer and I talked, she referred to you by your first name, and I thought it was cute, but now I know it was an indication of her love, and so much of that love was based on trust. So, would you mind if I call you Kate?

"I'd like that, Mr. Cullen."

"Jonas." He spoke so gently now, knowing he was about to reveal private conversations to a grieving mother. "Sometimes she called you Mama Kate, especially if she was telling me about some personal incident." On his end Jonas smiled. "There was one morning when she came in a little angry that Mama Kate wouldn't let her stay out late with Rick on a school night. Evidently, you had raised the possibility she was getting a little too physical with him, and late hours sometimes lead a girl to make bad decisions. She assured me sex with Rick was not a part of the equation, but I told her it wasn't me she needed to reassure. Another time, she was upset that Mama Kate thought hanging out with Junior and some of his East High friends might not be such a good idea." Jonas hesitated for just a moment before going on. "I don't remember her exact words, but the gist of it was she felt like a red-headed girl with fat cheeks ought to be allowed to go cruising with a black kid just to be with someone who understood her minority status." Jonas paused. "You know your daughter and Junior are close, probably closer than she is with either Erin or Betty. Rainer and Junior are two sensitive, gifted kids, and she did protect him early on here." Jonas did not realize he was referring to Rainer in the present tense.

"I hope you know on both of those occasions we talked it out," said Mrs. Brecht. "I enjoy her friends. Rick is such a nice boy and always treated Rainer so well, and when Junior came over, he was so polite. I just worried because Rainer was so physical with her friends, and it made me uncomfortable at times."

"Kate, it was just her nature. She wouldn't have been that special girl without the physical part. Do you remember your first parent-teacher conference? The two of you came into my room holding hands. Kate, Rainer adored you. You were her best friend, and when she referred to you as Mama Kate or Katie-Kate, it was a term of endearment. She trusted you completely." Jonas allowed his words to sink in. "Whatever you need to do to satisfy the hundreds of people who will attend her funeral, she will understand. I would suggest somewhere in the service, you include a small Buddhist rite, maybe not so noticeable that most see it, but there nevertheless."

Katherine Brecht spoke through the sniffles. "Jonas, will you help me with this?"

§

A traditional Catholic service was held at the south Denver Annunciation Church near Washington Park. A celebration of Rainer's life was held two days later in the Andrew Jackson High School auditorium for those students who wanted to attend. Two large white candles burned on either side of the stage. Rubber Soul, Sgt. Pepper, and The Magical Mystery Tour played in the background, and the smell of incense was heavy. As Pete Cirillo took his place at the podium, twenty-seven Advanced Placement students walked in together, all wearing yellow tee-shirts. Rick Parris led the group carrying a pole with a pure white banner attached. Each student carried a bowl with multi-colored flower petals in it. Jonas escorted Rainer's mother to a seat in the front row to the left of the stage. Both were also wearing yellow tee-shirts. He kissed her on the cheek, slipped on a navy sports-jacket over his tee-shirt, and then climbed the seven steps to the stage to join Pete and Jane Walburg. After exchanging a few words with his two colleagues, Jonas stepped to the microphone and pulled a folded paper out of his coat pocket. He smiled courageously, swallowed, and nodded his head to the AP students who sat in the front rows.

"I speak not only for myself, but for the entire student body and faculty of Andrew Jackson High School, especially for the Advanced Placement classes. I hope my words adequately reflect the feelings we all have for Rainer." He turned his head and cleared his throat. "Rainer was a remarkable young lady, and we will miss her tremendously. While you all know how she died, what you may not know is what she was going to say to the legislature. Rainer was going to tell them how Andrew Jackson is a special place, a family place, and how busing could damage its soul. She was going to propose that no current student from here be bused. We would be excited to take in next year's sophomore class and begin to bring about an end to the terrible injustice of segregation. She believed adding students from throughout Denver, one class at a time, was the right thing to do. Adding sophomores into our family would be healthy for both of us, those already here and for the 'newbies,' as she called them, to see what a special place this is."

Jonas was interrupted by the gentle applause of the students. Then he lost his composure, his ability to speak further. He gripped the podium with both hands and dropped his head. When the applause died down, Pete walked over to Jonas and led him to a seat next to his. Pete handed the prepared speech to Jane Walburg who read its contents. In it, Jonas told of the four organs being donated to others so they might live. He told stories from Rainer's life, especially from high school that involved fellow students, of her friendship with Rick, Junior, and Betty, of her love for "all things Andrew Jackson." He closed with a poem Rainer had given to him about her mother several months earlier. Its last line said, "and her greatest gift to me is my happiness."

Walburg looked up and smiled. "We will not be sad after this day. We will celebrate Rainer's life, and we will thank God that we were fortunate to share a part of our lives with her. Our teams will not wear a black band on their uniforms; instead, we will wear a plain yellow patch." She waited for the applause to stop and then continued. "We invite you all to share lunch with us. The cooks have made Rainer's favorite meal—chili and cinnamon rolls. And by the way, a small portion of Rainer's ashes will be spread on the front steps of our school to welcome everyone. Thank you for coming. Now, please join me in saying the Lord's Prayer."

§

Dear Ruth,

Rainer died last week. So sad. She was one of our best students, but you know that from some of our earlier talks.

This is not about Rainer, though. This is about the people I work with: my teachers and my principal, my cooks and my custodians. I am so honored to be a part of this staff. In the midst of this terrible tragedy, their first concern was for our students. Oh, Ruth, this desegregation crisis has us all under a great deal of stress. We are not in agreement about how to proceed, whether it's right or wrong, who's staying and who's going. We bicker among ourselves, but, as you always tell me, "Good from bad."

This week, my people were one. They had one concern only--to care for our students here at Andrew Jackson. From the moment I received the call Rainer had been in the accident until today when I sent her file downtown to the Ad Building for permanent storage—nine days—the adults in this building held every student in the palms of their hands. Even our most hardened veterans were lenient with homework assignments and testing dates. Carlos set up over a hundred extra chairs in the auditorium so it could accommodate everyone at the service. He did this after 9:00 o'clock the night before. The building was spotless too.

Pete was, well, Pete. He is a rock. He was here earlier than normal, which means around 5:30, and he stayed late into each night. Elyse has been caring for Jonas, who is under tremendous strain. She came in yesterday to see Pete, just to get a little more strength. Do you know what he told her? He said, "A principal's job is to demand high performance from his teachers, and when he gets it, to support them. Elyse, this week, I have gotten the highest performance from my entire staff. All I have done is support you all." Then he walked around the desk and hugged Elyse and said, "And you have supported Jonas in his hour of greatest need. You have shown strength and compassion, and I know you have been hurting over Rainer too."

We will get through this and press on, and the busing issue will remain, but I am convinced we will do our best under any condition and succeed. Thanks for watching over us, Ruth.

Annette Long tucked the letter into a manila folder containing several other letters to Ruth and returned the folder to her lower desk drawer.

CHAPTER 34

Jack Stark, a minister from Bismarck, North Dakota, delivered a letter from Barbara Deaver to Jonas' dad in Clyde Park, Montana. The minister waited for a response. Mr. Cullen read the letter, pondered for a few moments, then handed the letter back to the minister with a scowl, and closed the door.

CHAPTER **35**

M r. Cirillo stared at the clock, waiting for the end of the day. He had not left his office since just after one when he received the call. He skipped hall duty, something he seldom missed. The dark oak memorial plaque lay on the corner of his desk. Andrew Thorson, 1971. Pete's jaw tightened. No longer Andrew Jackson's last.

At 3:15 Pete marched upstairs to Jonas' room where he found Jonas erasing his blackboards, removing all traces of the AP review timeline for the Civil Rights Movement. "Hey, Jonas, got a minute? I got the information." Jonas nodded. "The driver who hit Rainer was formally charged this morning—misdemeanor. He was drunk at 8:00 in the morning. Son-of-a-bitch!" Pete's words spewed through clenched teeth.

Neither man spoke for a moment. Jonas' breathing took on a frustrated cadence and his eyes narrowed; he seemed to want to respond but was unable to speak. Three students burst in without knocking, ready to serve their detention. "I'll come down after I get these guys settled in. Give me ten minutes."

While he stood by his desk waiting for Jonas, Cirillo tried to regain his composure. Annette had shielded him all afternoon from interruptions, knowing that his temper was volatile, knowing that this afternoon he was ready to explode. She had watched him manage Rainer's passing for two weeks, massaging teachers and students, holding his school together. When any of his students—or teachers—was placed in danger, he rose up. She had seen it before.

When Jonas arrived at the principal's office, Annette put her finger to her lips as a warning. "Let Mr. Cirillo vent," she seemed to be saying. Pete started talking as soon as Jonas walked in. "Rainer won't be your last one. I've lost seven, now eight, for no reason at all. Six car accidents, one shooting, and one suicide—the last four to drunk drivers. None of these bastards ever spent a day in jail for killing my kids." Jonas listened to his boss and knew he must remain quiet. If he allowed his own anger to surface, if he joined in Pete's rant, it would only intensify Mr. Cirillo's. For Rainer's sake, in her memory, Jonas would remain calm. Pete slammed his fist into his desk. He stopped and breathed in heavily before continuing. "I took the plaque down to get Rainer's name put on, but I'm not going to do it. Maybe this summer." Jonas nodded and stayed silent.

Jonas' control transferred across the room and Pete's rage seemed to subside. Pete took a photo from his desk drawer and studied it before speaking. "In a while you might need to . . . I don't know, for lack of a better phrase, scream at the sky. I've sensed your anger too." He handed the photo to Jonas.

"What's this?" asked Jonas. "It looks like a rock in a river."

"It's my spot. Up Clear Creek Canyon. It was taken in the fall a few years back. The yellow colors reminded me of Rainer." Pete's eyes went away from Jonas for a moment, and then he returned. "How are your kids?" For Pete, it always came back to the students and their well-being. He knew each one was important; each one was a part of something larger. Each one was a part of that heartbeat he knew as Andrew Jackson High School.

Jonas had left the door ajar. Hearing her boss' voice lowering, Annette entered with her legal notepad and sat down. "I called to cancel the engraving; I'll take the plaque out with me when I go. You have four phone calls to return, but all of them can wait until tomorrow. Jonas, Elyse came in. She said she'll wait for you in her room." She checked off two items on her pad, reached over for the plaque, and stood to go. "Oh, and Mr. Cirillo, you wanted me to remind you about Jonas' new student.

Pete nodded thanks to Annette, and she left. "You're getting a new student in your AP History class."

"Isn't it a little late to be adding a student now? The exam is in just a few weeks." Jonas was hoping his principal would explain his action.

"You know the young man. It's Murray Oyler, your basketball manager, and since he's only a sophomore, he can take the full course next year. His father came in to see if there was a way to transfer Murray into your class. I explained the situation, but Mr. Oyler was adamant his boy could do the work. My compromise was to have him tested. It all sort of got lost in the events of the past few weeks until I got the counselor's evaluation. We were all stunned. Murray has an IQ off the charts."

Jonas' blink indicated some new understanding. "Murray's so quiet, but, you know, there were times during the season when we would talk, always about the team, but his insights were revealing." Jonas shook his head. "Still, will he gain anything by being in my class just as we begin our review?"

"Jonas, I'd never spoken with Murray or his father before this. They seemed to think Murray would benefit from being in your AP class this last month and then be more prepared when he took the class next year. I had the feeling all of this was Murray's idea, but it was his dad who was talking. Mr. Oyler is a mechanic, and I doubt if he ever finished high school."

"Well, Pete, maybe Murray is another Junior Warren story, a kid who tells his parents what he has decided and then acts on it. I'm excited to have him."

§

Murray Oyler stood four feet eight. He was standing outside Jonas' door waiting for him. Murray smiled broadly when he saw Jonas arrive, but he did not speak.

"Good morning, Murray. Mr. Cirillo told me you were going to be in my class for the rest of the semester. I hope you weren't waiting long." Jonas tousled the little guy's curly brown hair.

"Just a little while, Coach."

Inside the room Jonas hung up his jacket, turned on his coffee pot, and tightened his tie. Turning back to Murray, he nodded. "The first thing you need is a textbook." Jonas walked over to the below-window bookshelf and took one of the three remaining AP history texts. "This is a college level book, Murray. From what I've heard, you can read at this level." He looked into Murray's eyes for affirmation. When he got it, he continued. "The next thing you'll need is a seat. I have a vacant one right up front."

Murray turned to locate it.

"Yep, this one right here." Jonas placed his hand gently on the top of the desk. "It was Rainer's, and I think she would be happy to see you sitting here. You have to know, Murray, anyone who sits in this desk has to be pretty special, and I'll expect you to work very hard."

Neither spoke for a moment. Then Murray walked two steps to his new assigned seat and sat down. Looking up, he spoke very gently, "I will, Coach, but you have to promise me something."

"What's that, Murray?"

"Promise me you won't look past me, you know, ignore me like some people do." The little guy stared straight into Jonas' eyes.

"I won't, Murray, I won't."

§

For the Advanced Placement students at Andrew Jackson and across the country, the last week in April and the first week in May were days of feverish review for their exams. Long hours looking over notes, skimming chapters, completing labs, and taking practice tests in preparation for the grueling AP exams that were administered nationwide created a stressful environment for both the students and AP teachers. For Mr. Cullen's AP students, Murray devised a strategy to help his classmates review. Since joining the AP history class, he had attacked the reading, often reading two chapters a day. Then, during class, before school, at lunch, and after school, he would sit with small groups of his fellow classmates and discuss the material. Junior Warren realized Murray was learning more than the students in his groups, so he began doing the same thing. Two other students quickly began the mentoring process, so each day, there were at least four study groups reviewing specific sections of history. Mr. Cullen used the last twenty minutes of each class to work on the essay practices.

§

On the Tuesday evening before the AP exam, Elyse took Jonas out for dinner at a fancy French restaurant in downtown Denver.

"They don't have these kinds of restaurants in Montana, you know."

Elyse reached across the small table and took Jonas' hand. "They don't have me in Montana either, Jonas, and you're sampling me." Her eyes bore in on her boyfriend. She understood Jonas' lingering hurts, felt his fatigue, and held him together. "This dinner is just a diversion. Your real surprise comes later this evening." Jonas smiled at this suggestive remark.

Elyse pulled her car into the driveway. The slight bump of the sidewalk curb awakened Jonas, who had fallen asleep almost immediately upon getting in the car after dinner.

"I'm sorry. I hope this won't affect your surprise for me?"

Elyse smiled warmly. "No, dear, it won't, and it's not my surprise. As I said, I'm just the diversion. Let's go inside."

Jonas didn't know what was to come, and it showed on his face. As the couple walked to the porch, he noticed the light wasn't on, and the apartment was dark. He unlocked the door and held it open for Elyse, then reached in to switch on a light.

"SURPRISE!"

Twenty-eight students screamed in unison, all dressed in pajamas and party-hats. A four foot, brightly painted banner pinned to the living room wall read simply, "THANK YOU, MR. C" and was signed by each student in both AP History sections. The apartment floor was covered with sleeping bags and pillows, the tables with pizza boxes and pop cans, and a wrapped present lay on the coffee table.

Betty "Friedan" hugged Mr. Cullen and handed him a card. "You have house guests tonight, Mr. C."

Rick Parris put party hats on both Jonas and Elyse. "After cake

I have a few questions about the free-response part of tomorrow's test."

Ian handed Mr. Cullen another card. "This one's from our parents, but you can open it tomorrow."

Junior and Lauren picked up the wrapped gift and presented it to their teacher. "Open it, Mr. C."

Jonas pushed a sleeping bag off the couch, sat down with Lauren and Erin on either side, and slowly unwrapped the gift, a picture frame with two photos. The larger photo was a recent one of the entire AP history class in front of Andrew Jackson High School, taken only a few days earlier. All the students were in formal attire. The smaller inset photo was of Jonas standing with Rainer at the Masonic Lodge when she received the outstanding junior of the year award from that service group. An absolute silence came over the room.

Finally, David Vasone, probably the group's most active student at school spoke. "At different times during the year, different teachers were Rainer's favorite. It just so happened because of the busing thing, you were her favorite at the end. She always told us since you were so naïve and inexperienced, she could get anything she wanted from you. Mostly, you gave us your time. We decided that she should be included too." He paused briefly to lighten the load. "I'm not sure who all of those nice-looking students are, though." At that, the students laughed, surged forward, and dog-piled Mr. Cullen.

§

Most of the students were asleep by one. Jonas and Elyse were admonished to "behave themselves" by one of the boys who had a crush on Miss Cottage, and to that end Jonas took a couple of blankets and lay down next to Murray in the kitchen. Since Murray was not taking the test in the morning, the two talked in hushed tones much of the night.

"This was pretty cool, Coach. It started out as Betty's idea, but David organized most of it."

"I suspect you played your part too, Murray."

The conversation hit many topics, some serious, some not.

Murray was constantly giggling, holding his hands over his mouth in a feeble attempt not to waken his classmates. Around two, Jonas asked Murray what he wanted to be in life.

"Short term, Coach, I want to make the basketball team, but if I'm too small, I'll be your manager again. Long term, I want to go to college and become an astronaut. I know I'm too short for the military requirements to go into space, but maybe I can become so smart they'll have to include me as an engineer. Someday, space flights will be all about experiments, about getting information from space, about doing those experiments under near-zero gravitation. Physics. Also, I want to go because I think it would be so much fun."

"What do you think about busing, Murray?"

"Sometimes you have to step back to see, Coach. This is not going to work. Schools work because parents care, because schools are the center of the neighborhood. My dad falsified our address so I could come here, but we had always moved around a lot. I won't be attending Andrew Jackson next year, unless I'm bused in. Otherwise, I'll be at North. For one year, I wanted to attend the best high school in Denver." Murray locked his eyes on his teacher.

"Somehow, Murray, you'll be in my class next year. Count on it." Jonas knew this was a promise he had to keep.

Both young men fell asleep around three.

§

Loud knocks on the door at seven woke the students. It was the parents bringing breakfast: scrambled eggs, pop tarts, bacon, cereal, fresh fruit, doughnuts, toast and jelly, orange juice, apple juice, coffee. Each student was given a good-luck card and a pencil inscribed with Mr. Cullen's favorite, if overused, slogan, "Do your best, and that will be good enough." Rainer's mother gave a card to Murray that read, "Next year."

§

On the same night, a thousand miles away, Abby Archer re-read Jonas' letter about Rainer and cried. Then she stood at her cell door and waited for one of the guards to pass by. When one did, she cleared her throat to get the guard's attention. "I just want to apologize for being a bitch all the time. I'll try to change." Abby stared straight ahead.

Chapter 36

Mr. Cullen collected the textbooks at the beginning of the period, carefully checking for pencil marks in the margin or underlining in the body of the text. None of those marks would have been malicious. AP students simply used college skills to help them with the difficult reading. Only Murray kept his text, and even though he had been in the class for less than a month, he had read or skimmed all thirty-six chapters. As Mr. Cullen did this, the students talked excitedly among themselves. Most of them had taken three AP courses, and all the tests were over. When all the books were checked in and stacked on the front table, Mr. Cullen handed out a debriefing sheet on which the students were to comment on the class, the AP exam, and make suggestions for Mr. Cullen as he prepared for the next school year. "Be brutally honest with your evaluations. You've earned the right, and I certainly need some help if I'm to improve as I move forward with this class."

He was sure that his students' scores on the AP exam would only be average, certainly not at Mrs. Froman's level. Officially, the scores wouldn't come in until mid-summer, but Jonas knew from the discussion he conducted on the day after the test. Yeah, he thought to himself, *be brutally honest.*

The students grew quiet as they wrote out their comments. Mr. Cullen sat pensively at his desk and surveyed his students. He thought about moving around the room to touch each kid on the shoulder but decided against it this day. He didn't want them to feel ill-at-ease as they filled in their comments. *Next week*, he thought.

When the last of these sheets was turned in, Mr. Cullen folded them together and bound them with a rubber band. He slipped them into his briefcase and moved around to the front of his desk. He smiled and shook his head up and down.

"Well, our work here is done," and with that, the class broke out into a spontaneous outburst of applause and cheering. Tears came to Mr. Cullen's eyes.

Betty Friedan Norton raised her hand. "Mr. Cullen, what does it really matter, this whole busing crap? It's really just us, isn't it? You and us in this room. And next year, we'll do it again. We're kids, and we'll be fine. The new kids will be fine too. You'll see."

Perfect timing: it was Friday and the bell rang, excusing the students to their next class. One more week of classes and then summer break. Jonas knew Betty was wrong. Schools would change and students would be damaged. He wondered how he could protect his.

§

On this same Friday, Miss Cottage's classes were conducting their last lab experiment, a modified exam on their techniques. It meant Elyse was scrambling to get one class completed and the equipment ready for the next class. There was no time for sentiment or reflection just yet. She borrowed students from AP courses to help her with the sophomores, since these upper-class AP students were done with meaningful work. Sadie washed test tubes and tongs as fast as her little hands allowed her. Elyse's students would complete the lab on Friday, have the weekend to write it up, and then turn it in for a grade on Monday. She would be busy right up to the end of the semester. Mr. Cirillo delayed her second-year evaluation until the Thursday before school let out to give her time to complete her tasks. It would be a formality, since she was rapidly becoming one of Andrew Jackson's finest teachers, the teacher Pete believed she would be when he hired her. She had shed her debutante aura and was a tough, demanding science teacher. "There's quite a bit of Miss Walburg in her," Pete said to Annette.

§

Pete used Jonas' evaluation to let him know money was available for summer tuition if he wanted to continue with his graduate classes at Northern Colorado. He was also welcome to stay at the Greeley principal's house again.

"Thanks, Pete, but I'm going to sit this summer out. I need a break."

Pete leaned back in his chair, clasped his hands behind his head, and stretched out his shoulders. "I know it's been tough on you, but I don't want you to lose your momentum."

Jonas shook his head and let out a breath. "I'm running on empty. I just may sleep for a week when this is all over, but more than that, I want to get in my car and get away, do some thinking."

"I understand your desire to get off by yourself, to be alone for a while," said Pete.

Jonas laughed slightly. "Not completely alone, Pete. There's a young lady I want to be alone with. I'd like to give her my complete attention and see if she likes me that way. We've always had diversions in our relationship. She's a very remarkable woman, and she's given more than she's taken. I need to reciprocate before she finds someone else."

"I don't think that's going to happen, Jonas. She's pretty smitten with you."

§

Archie King sat with Gary Dessins in his woodshop after school. They were waiting for Ben Lucas and Steve Torrez to join them, and then they were heading to the Denver Public Library to hear a presentation on the impact court-ordered busing would have on the housing patterns of Denver neighborhoods. Gary was not one to sit still in his shop, so he was cleaning the band saw and changing the blade. One of his students had used a wood blade to cut a metal rod, and the result was predictable.

"I work with the kid all semester, and he forgets to check the blade. He could have maimed himself."

Archie laughed. "It's a good thing it wasn't me who did it, or you would have killed me." Since their altercation, the two men had talked it out, and, in fact, spent considerable time together trying to get a handle on the effects busing would have on their school. Both men loved Andrew Jackson, but they showed it in entirely different ways. Gary built all the sets for the plays, repaired any wooden structures around school that could be done over a weekend, and generally spent his summers coming into the school on his own time to sand banisters or re-stain desks and bookshelves. He and Carlos spent many hours together repairing needed items. Ever the union man, Archie had tried to get the district to pay Gary for his work, but Gary refused to pursue it, saying it was his hobby.

Steve and Ben arrived together at the shop, which was a building separate from the main structure. Ben volunteered to drive. The talk on the short drive was about how the courts were not the friends of the schools.

"How in the hell can the judge send Marvin back to us. He's been in at least a half-dozen fights I know of on school grounds, and that's not enough to get him expelled?" Ben was asking a rhetorical question.

"He's not the only one, Ben. The court thinks wood shop is the cure-all for juvenile delinquency. 'Let him work with his hands.' To hell with that! Sometimes we're just the dumping grounds for those kids, and they take away from the time serious students should be getting," said Gary.

Steve smiled. "Careful guys, I was one of those juvenile delinquents, and I suspect Archie was too. Wood shop saved my life, so to speak."

"So, should they always be sent back to the schools?" asked Ben.

"What I think should happen is the school principal should decide, not some judge who doesn't know the kid. Let the Pete Cirillos of the world make the decision. I'd trust him," answered Steve.

"Not every principal is like Pete, though," said Archie.

"No," said Steve, "but you need a guideline, and it can't be a judge who just wants to free up space in juvie. There are good principals and bad, just like there are good teachers and bad. We just have to run with what we have."

"We got a good one," said Gary.

Archie laughed out loud. "Shit, we got a pussy!"

§

Murray was well received by the AP students, but he knew there were limitations this year. He was a year or two younger than they were, and they were all physically bigger than he was. "Even the girls, Dad." Most of Murray's friends were sophomores from his regular classes. Among these students Murray was comfortable, and even felt a little superior. He was explaining to his girlfriend Sadie about how rockets were able to break through the Earth's lower levels to get into an orbit from a hundred to several thousand miles above the Earth's surface when Mr. Cullen walked past them.

"Hi, Coach, you look a little dazed." Murray's other friends thought it odd a fellow student could be so casual with a teacher, but not Sadie, who had a similar relationship with Miss Cottage. Jonas stopped and gently punched Murray in the arm. "You're pretty perceptive, my man. I've just been informed by Miss Lane that my car got hit by one of the seniors racing out of the parking lot."

"Seniors aren't supposed to be in the teachers' parking lot," said Sadie.

"I guess that's why this young girl was racing. She and her friends were spraying good-bye messages on all the teachers' cars, and I guess she lost control and hit mine. Hers is intertwined with mine. I'm on my way to see Miss Cottage to get a ride home."

Sadie's raised eyebrows registered some concern. She was protective of Miss Cottage, although if anyone was good enough for her, maybe it was Mr. Cullen.

§

In Bryson City, North Dakota, the principal of the high school, Mr. Andersen, who had hired Barbara Deaver to be his secretary, asked her to adopt the students of the new BC High as her own, and he gave her a six-by-eight dark oak frame with Jason's picture in it for her desk.

§

The phone rang around seven while Elyse and Jonas were having a romantic dinner. Jonas wanted to let it ring, but Elyse had a feeling.

"Hello. Oh, hi, Mr. Cullen. I'm fine; how are you? Yes, he's right here." Elyse handed Jonas the phone, lifting the cord over the table, so it wouldn't knock over the wine.

"Hi, Dad, what's up?"

"Patty left this past weekend. I sort of thought she might come home, but she called from Seattle and said it was permanent."

"How come?" asked Jonas.

"I have no idea."

Jonas shook his head before responding to his dad, "Who can understand women? I've never been able to." Then, he hung up.

Elyse burst out laughing at Jonas' matter-of-fact statement. "Oh Jonas, the more I'm with you, the more I believe that. You just don't get us."

They went back to their dinner, but it had lost a bit of the romanticism for the moment and became more of a reflection on the past school year. When they cleared the dishes and retired to the couch, Elyse said, "I told my dad last night to stop trying to get me a job outside of teaching. I told him that he was simply going to have to get used to this, that I was coming back here next year and for as long as Pete will have me." She paused. "He's good with it now." She paused again. "I'm scared, Jonas. This busing is too much about the community and not enough about the class-room. We'll do our part, but I just fear it won't be enough, and it will tear our soul apart."

Jonas locked his eyes to Elyse's. "Regardless, you and I will do this together, and we'll get through it. I'll hang on to you, and you'll hang on me . . ."

Elyse finished his sentence. ". . . for as long as it takes."

"Yeah. For as long as it takes, and through all obstacles."

"Yeah. This is where we belong."
Lean on Me.

§

Pete Cirillo stood outside the counseling office watching his students pass through the halls of Andrew Jackson High School on the morning of the last day of school, May 31, 1974. Except for the one terrible day, it had been a wonderful year, a year he and his staff could be proud of. There was laughter and excitement from all corners of his building, and the pace of each student was quickened. There were no seniors in the building, as they had been excused a week earlier, a new idea for the Denver schools. Graduation would be tomorrow, Saturday, June 1, and then summer vacation would officially begin—for the students, for his teachers, but not for himself. When you're a principal, there is no vacation. Pete would have it no other way; it was why he became a principal. This was his building, these were his teachers, the students in every class were his kids, and he was responsible. He was responsible.

On this day in this school, there was little apprehension about the imminent decisions to be made about integrating Denver's schools. Pete sensed his faculty had come to grips with school busing. Not all of them accepted its premise, there was nervousness for the unknown, but the doors would open in the fall to a new set of students, and Andrew Jackson would do what it always had. Archie summed up the faculty's feelings at the morning breakfast, when he said they were anxious to see who came through the front doors in September, just as they always were. What concerned them the most was losing some of their current crop of promising students, students with whom they had spent one- or two-years training in the "Andrew Jackson Way."

"At least," Pete told the faculty earlier, "we will be sending out fine ambassadors to the rest of Denver."

§

Freda Poundstone held meetings in her living room in a southern suburb and mapped out the strategy she would use to try to nullify any desegregation plan issued by the Supreme Court. She would not allow, without a battle, for Denver to simply annex more counties in order to implement a busing plan that she believed would damage already good schools.

"I know that there are dedicated educators in Denver," she told the gathered, "who will do their best to make this work, but all that aside, I don't believe the Court has the right to impose desegregation on us in this manner. God bless those teachers and principals, but it doesn't change the situation." She smiled and then added, "We have a busy five months ahead of us."

§

Graduation for the class of 1974 was held at 10:00 in the morning. For Jonas Cullen and Elyse Cottage, another year was in the books, and their futures seemed tied now to Andrew Jackson High School. Laura Sanders signed a contract extension in Erie, and Dave Fallon was offered a full-year contract in Alamosa. He also had successful eye surgery. Petey Cirillo smoked marijuana for the first time with a handful of his junior high buddies. Steve Torrez married his girlfriend. Abby Archer was transferred in with the general prison population and began seeing a counselor. In her final letter to Jonas, she thanked him for carrying her, but she was doing fine and would be corresponding with Paul Garrity as she moved forward. Richard Nixon resigned his presidency in the face of growing popular support for his impeachment and the loss of support from his own party. Jonas' brother Jake was forced to give up football when he was caught under a load of logs that had not been securely fastened to a truck at the pulp mill in Montana where Jonas' father worked. Steve Cogil sold The Tattered Cover to Joyce Meskis who would eventually make it one of the nation's most exciting independent bookstores. Carlos Herrera's oldest daughter, Carmen, graduated from West High School with honors and earned a scholarship to Colorado State University. Mr. Elzey began walking on his own after a year of rehabilitation and told Mr. Zachariah to expect him back teaching in the fall. Jorgen Andersen gave up the assistant football coaching assignment so he could devote full time to being Bryson City's principal. Jonas took Elyse to Montana to meet his father and brother.

Denver opened two new private high schools, and counties to the west and south of Denver voted to build additional schools for the flood of families moving out of Denver. Andrew Jackson and the other Denver high schools were now placed in the front lines of the Civil Rights Movement, fighting battles whose outcomes would be determined not so much by their actions as by the decisions made in courtrooms and private homes.

IV

FALL 1974

CHAPTER **37**

The new FBI agent was accompanied by the suitman. Jonas just shook his head and followed Pete into his office, knowing there was little else to do. He couldn't punch either agent, and, in fact, he didn't have the urge. Pete reminded Jonas that the initial faculty meeting for the upcoming week started at 10:00, and that he expected him to be there. Before he left, Pete told the agent to make it quick.

The suitman remained quiet while the older man spoke. "We told you we'd keep looking, no matter how long it took. I'm new to your case, but Chaney here tells me you have quite a temper. I'd strongly recommend you keep it in check." He looked over Jonas as a warning. "Beginning of your third year, huh? Admirable," he said sarcastically. "Your girlfriend is back among the general population, acting as though she might be sorry for what she did. What do you think, Cullen, do you think she's sorry?" He waited for a response, but Jonas stayed silent.

The agent stood with his hands in his pockets slowly nodding his head and thrusting his jaw. He turned to the suitman, who now had a name, Chaney, and asked, "Didn't your friend here punch you once up in Montana? This guy doesn't have long hair, are you sure it's the same guy?" The agent turned back to Jonas. "Are you the same guy, Cullen?"

Jonas thought of all the philosophical answers he could respond with but decided to avoid a confrontation. "I'm the same guy. A little older, a little wiser, hopefully. Definitely a little more respectful."

"Humph. We'll see. Our bureau in California found your name in some papers they confiscated from the Weathermen in Los Angeles. 'J. Cullen, an associate of Abby Archer living in Boulder, Colorado.' Are you going to tell me all you did in Boulder was go to school and smoke dope, J. Cullen?"

"No dope. Mostly beer. Lots of beer, to be truthful."

"Miss Archer claims it was dope. Is she lying?"

"Mistaken most likely, if that's what she said."

"Are you curious about why your name would show up in Weathermen notes? We sure are. You want to comment on that?"

Jonas was curious, but he stayed silent for a moment to ponder his answer. "I talked with SDS members at CU a couple of times about the war, but I never knew any Weathermen. What else did their notes say about me?"

The agent ignored Jonas' question and forged ahead. "Did they try to recruit you, Cullen?"

"Who? SDS or the Weathermen?"

"Either one."

"Not exactly. Abby did, but I refused. It really pissed her off. That's why she left. I had used up all her patience . . . what little she had."

"So now you're a teacher." The agent allowed that sentence to hang in the air. "Your principal says you're a good one too. I think we've used up his patience on this matter." Jonas noticed a softening of the agent's tone. "A teacher. If I talked to your students, what would they tell me about you?" Jonas shook his head. "Well, Cullen, I did talk to a couple of them, and they think you're top-notch. One of them did say that you try too hard, but I guess I can excuse that." The agent walked to the window and looked out for several minutes, all the time nodding his head.

Jonas looked over to the suitman and studied him, trying to see him in a different light. "Chaney. I never knew your name. Maybe if I did, it would have changed the situation some. You just charged up like a tough guy assuming I was a radical and put your hands on me. Sorry about hitting you." The suitman nodded as if he accepted Jonas' apology. Jonas spoke again. "Is Chaney your first name or last?"

The suitman breathed heavily and seemed to relax. "It's Travis Chaney, and I'm from Montana too. Up near Bozeman." He stepped forward and offered his hand.

Jonas accepted it. "Maybe we'll have to share a beer someday under the big sky." He looked closely at the suitman. "You knew I wasn't guilty, didn't you?"

Before the suitman could respond, the older agent interrupted. "Cullen, everyone here seems to be in your corner, even Chaney. I'm going to close the books on you and let you concentrate on your teaching. You and your colleagues here in Denver are going to need all your energy to manage this year. Your comfortable teaching environment just took a major hit with this busing order. I don't envy you." The agent extended his hand to Jonas.

"While the two men shook hands, Jonas asked, "And what's your name, sir?"

"Travis Chaney. Travis Chaney, Senior." He smiled. "Your old girlfriend didn't rat on you. She's talking now; cooperating. She said to tell you hi. Everything you said today matches what she said."

"We're good then?" asked Jonas.

Both Chaneys nodded and the older agent spoke. "Nice to meet you, Cullen. You get out of here now and get to that meeting. Your boss isn't going to tolerate you being late to his show."

§

The faculty meeting started precisely on Cirillo Time, but Pete had a bandage on his forehead over his left eye. Blood seeped to the front. It was Archie who asked, "What happened, General Jackson, did we lose the battle before the war even started?' Several of the teachers laughed.

"Nothing so glorious. I missed that last step coming down from the second floor and took a tumble. Nothing serious, and this will be the last I hear about it." It was an order and Archie saluted. Pete returned the salute, signaling the meeting was to begin. He turned to Elyse and Ben to ask if they had anything new from the district's integration committee. Elyse shook her head no. Pete then stepped closer to the podium. "As you know, the first three days will be primarily for registration and will only be half-days with only one class. Next Thursday will be the real opening day with all our students in attendance. We will be getting 172 students from the north side of Colfax. More than half of them will be sophomores from Smiley Junior High, from the Park Hill neighborhood. You know what that means. Park Hill was the area that filed the lawsuit, so I expect the press to focus in on us for these first few weeks. The first yellow Blue Bird will arrive at 7:45 next Tuesday. I would like to have as many of you as are free to greet our new students as they step off the bus. Most of our new students will be scared to death, especially those new sophs. I want them to receive a warm welcome."

§

Jonas and Elyse spent no time together in the morning as both were in their classrooms preparing when Pete wasn't holding a meeting. Early in the afternoon, she went up to his room to check on his FBI meeting. Finding out that it went well and that he would give her the details when they got home, she told him about another meeting.

"My mom called this morning and wants me to come to a block party she's holding. I told her I'd come if I could bring you. I'll know most of the people there." Elyse smiled to herself, knowing Jonas would refuse, but she really hadn't set the hook yet.

"Your parents don't need me there unless I'll work in the kitchen or serve coffee. You go, so I don't piss them off. By the way, when is it?"

"Next Thursday." Elyse walked around Jonas, brushing his back. She leaned in and kissed his neck. "Pretty please. I'd be bored without you, and it would be fun to see you trying to hold your tongue for two hours while my neighbors decry the collapse of civilization due to busing. We could giggle and make fun of the fears of old people."

"That's not fair, you know." Jonas turned around. "Just your neighbors?"

"As far as I know. Mom said it would be informal, just a

fundraiser to keep the poor, black, and brown out of the suburbs. We'd be like spies in the enemy camp."

Jonas succumbed. "You'll owe me big time, you know. Have you met any of the new teachers yet?"

§

Three teachers opted to leave Andrew Jackson voluntarily and seek employment outside of Denver. All three secured jobs easily as Pete kept his promise to write honest evaluations with no mention of their attitudes about busing. Each teacher was a star in the classroom and a valuable member of the Generals' staff, and they would be missed. Pete replaced them with three experienced black teachers recruited from inside Denver.

After their new teacher orientation with Mr. Cirillo, Annette took them aside to warn them that they would be called upon to sing the school's fight song. "Are you serious?" asked the new science teacher. Annette assured them they would be treated no differently than any other new teacher. Ben and Elyse, who were in the office to greet them and give them a building tour, nodded in agreement.

"Tradition," laughed Ben.

"I thought we were here in large part to break some traditions," said the new social studies teacher, a huge man who would also help coach.

"Get the song right on the first rendition, and that will break tradition," said Elyse. She swung her arm to indicate "Let's go," and they headed out towards the science area.

At that moment, Junior, Rick, and one of the new students bolted out of a classroom, nearly crashing into the five teachers in the hallway. "Oh, sorry, Miss Cottage, Mr. Lucas."

Elyse introduced them to the new teachers and asked why they were in the building before summer was officially over. "Murray's idea. The little guy thought maybe we could alleviate some of the tension if we hung some signs in the rooms," said Rick.

"Team building," said Junior with a grin.

"Are any of you new to Jackson?" asked the science teacher.

"Me," answered Marcus.

"What do you think about this whole thing?"

"Football's helped. That's where I got to know these guys. I'd rather be at my old school, but I'll give it a chance. So far, so good."

Elyse jumped in. "Where's Murray?"

"With Mr. C and Sadie and Friedan. They're making the signs. We just hang them," said Rick.

"How about this," said Ben. "Why don't the three of you escort our new teachers around? Elyse and I will help Jonas with the signs, and our new partners can ask you anything they want. I want you to answer honestly and candidly. Don't pull any punches." Ben then turned to the teachers. "When you're done, these guys will take you back to the office."

§

"She's a bigot!"

"You don't know that, Archie," said Pete. "She's on the wrong side of your issue, so you start name-calling?"

"Our issue, boss. She's not afraid to fan the fire to get her ballot initiative passed, I know that much. She uses forced busing to scare the crap out of the voters." Archie was reading the *News*, and then commenting on the articles about the upcoming school year. "If she's willing to use race to sell her position, to scare all of Colorado's white people, then she's a bigot."

Cirillo shook his head. "Politics. Poundstone comes across as angry and indignant, as the city's protector of the little guy against the big, bad Supreme Court, but I haven't seen evidence that she's a bigot. Maybe she is, but we have to fight her on her ideas."

"You do, Pete, because you're a man of integrity, but I don't because I'm an asshole. If her amendment passes, it'll draw a line around Denver and fence in the minorities. She can say all she wants about keeping the rural counties intact, but it's about keeping black kids out of her precious Greenwood Village."

Pete wondered. If Freda Poundstone's efforts were simply an attempt to prevent the poor and black from mixing in, then she was. He would give her the benefit of the doubt . . . for now. If the ballot initiative passed, white flight would accelerate. The *Keyes* decision would be effectively nullified, and integration would not occur in Denver. The Court's decision to desegregate the schools would end at the city's limits, and the line Archie talked about would become permanent.

"Arch, I've got to run. Ben wants me to sit in on the science department's meeting this morning. The new guy doesn't like his schedule. I need to get it straightened out before classes start next weekend. Instead of stewing, why don't you make a list of points to refute Ballot 1?" The principal laughed out loud. "If this was a game and you were a captain choosing sides, I'm pretty sure you'd pick Poundstone for your team. She seems to attack issues like you do. I may not agree with her, but I do like her sass."

§

Jonas did it on a whim. From all accounts Lylaus and Wilfred Keyes were generous, gracious, and decent, so Jonas called Rachel Noel, the only black school board member in Denver, and asked her if she would introduce him to the family who became the lead plaintiffs in Denver's desegregation case. Mrs. Noel did more than that. She arranged for him to meet them in their home in Park Hill for afternoon coffee and cookies. As he sat in his car outside their brick home waiting for his watch to read 3:00 o'clock straight up, he worried that he was intruding on a family that had put itself in such a dangerous and controversial position. Jonas adjusted his tie, left his car, and walked up the steps to the Keyes' front door, a door that had been firebombed just a few years back. He was greeted by a young black man at the front door.

"Dr. and Mrs. Keyes are expecting you, Mr. Cullen. Let me get the door for you."

Inside, Mrs. Keyes extended her hand. "Welcome, Jonas. It's so nice to have you in our home." Standing behind Mrs. Keyes was her husband, a tall, handsome doctor. "Welcome, son. Please, come in." Dr. Keyes placed his hand on Jonas' shoulder. This is Max. He sits on our porch and reads. He claims he's watching out for whatever, but I think he's just avoiding real work to read interesting books." Max shook Jonas' hand, nodded, and returned to the porch. Jonas was led into the kitchen where coffee cups adorned the table.

Jonas had memorized his opening lines. "Thank you for seeing me. I apologize for encroaching on your privacy, but I'm such an admirer of what you have done."

Wilfred Keyes responded quickly, "No, no. There are so many who have contributed to this effort to improve our schools, to right a serious wrong. Lylaus and I are just two, and while our name adorns the court decision, we are not special. Warriors such as Rachel Noel and Fred Thomas deserve much more credit."

Mrs. Keyes handed the plate of cookies to Jonas. "So, you teach at Andrew Jackson in the southern part of Denver. You have an important job. Rachel gave us a rundown on you. She discovered that you once taught at Emma Goldman. Wil and I visited that school before it closed and thought it was such a grand idea. We were sad when it closed. What did you do after that?"

"I went to jail." As soon as he said it, Jonas wanted to retract his words.

Dr. Keyes turned to his wife. "Did we allow a felon to enter our house?"

He was joking, and his wife laid her hand on Jonas' arm. "Please excuse my husband; he thinks he's a comedian. Why were you in jail, Jonas?"

"A friend of mine robbed a bank in California and then hid out in my apartment. The FBI thought I was harboring a fugitive, and I guess technically I was, but I didn't know she had robbed the bank. She was my ex-girlfriend, so the FBI assumed I was a part of her radical group and arrested me. They let me out though."

The Keyes laughed. "And what do owe your visit to, Jonas?" ask Wilfred Keyes.

"I have a thousand questions, but that would be rude. I got into teaching to do something positive for my community, which at the time was Boulder. That ex-girlfriend got me the job at Goldman, and it made me want to teach in the inner-city. I think

I was comfortable there. All of us knew about the events going on in Denver. Mrs. Noel doesn't remember me, but I met her at that school and was so impressed by her courage. She seemed to want to avoid the violence of other cities, but at the same time, effect change. That non-violent approach seems to be your philosophy too."

Dr. Keyes bit into his cookie. "Lylaus and I left Kansas City because we thought we could give our children a solid education here in Denver without regard to race. Oh, don't get me wrong, son, we are well aware of our color, but we hoped our children's schools were colorblind. The teachers certainly were, which is why we have such a high regard for the work you do, and my wife has worked as a special education teacher, but the Denver School Board kept redrawing those darn boundary lines to segregate our schools. It was clear there was a well-conceived plan to keep black and white children separated. Eventually, we had enough of those moveable boundary lines, so we joined with some others to seek a way to prevent the school board from discriminating."

"And you know the rest. Would you like a warm-up?" asked Mrs. Keyes. Jonas shook his head. "So, tell me, Jonas, are you ready for all those black students to show up at your school next Tuesday?"

"I think so, Mrs. Keyes. I certainly hope so." And then Jonas added, "I would be honored, and I think my school would be to, if you would visit our school in the near future."

"It's a small world, Jonas," said Dr. Keyes. "When Rachel told me that you wanted to meet us, I asked a neighbor of ours if he knew you. As it turns out, he knows you very well. We have known Junior Warren since he was a small boy. He and I talked at length about his transfer from East to Jackson, and it seems the action that Lylaus and I took played a part in his decision to go. It was a brave decision that turned out well. He enjoyed his first year very much, and he speaks highly of you. Thank you for your invitation, and we will be pleased to come visit your school at some point. And would you tell Archie King we send our regards."

Jonas stayed for another ten minutes, and the Keyes spoke mostly about their own two children. They asked about Jonas' students and about Ballot 1, and then invited him to come back later in the school year. "Maybe our children will be home next time. We'd like for you to meet them."

§

The school year for Denver's secondary students began with a staggered schedule. Only seniors reported to their assigned schools on Friday, August 30. After Labor Day, on Tuesday, September 3, juniors showed up, and on Wednesday the new sophomores attended. On each day, the students registered for classes and received an orientation. Attendance was only slightly down for those first three days, half-days, which Denver's school superintendent, Kishkunis, attributed to parent anxiety. He was quoted in the papers as saying that the process was "peaceful and uneventful, that school was opening as normal." The first full day with all three grades would be Thursday.

At sunrise on Thursday, Pete and Carlos walked the perimeter of their school looking for anything suspicious. Pete had received a hate call on Labor Day, a school holiday, threatening his building for this day. He believed it to be a cowardly hoax, but he took no chances. A police crew scoured the halls and classrooms of the school the night before, but Pete and Carlos did a final walk-around. Others began to arrive before 7:00. "Others" included the Denver and national media, setting up their cameras on large tripods, positioning their personnel in the most advantageous locations to record comments from anyone with anything to say. District personnel, including the assistant superintendent, were out to monitor their schools. Charles Chartwell strode among the protestors listening to their complaints and nodding his head, all the while saying, "I hear ya." A small group representing La Raza Unida and wearing brown berets observed the circus from a short distance. As the time neared 7:45, most of Andrew Jackson's teachers filed out of the building to welcome their new students.

The Revolution arrived on September 5, 1974, in yellow chariots carrying warriors disguised as anxious students. The protestors moved closer to the school's circle drive and became more vocal, more vile. They carried signs decrying court-ordered busing. The buses would become one of the two lasting images of Denver's first day of busing, three yellow school buses creeping through those protestors with the Front Range in the background. The second image would be of fourteen-year-old Lyncoya Jackson as she stepped off that first bus with her oversized book bag over her shoulder, her head held high, a big smile, but her eyes fixed straight ahead. It was no accident; she had been coached for this moment.

Ironically, but appropriately named, Lyncoya walked half-way to the front doors of her new school before she was met by Betty Freidan Norton and two other students who shook her hand, handed her a symbolic yellow carnation, and escorted her into the building. Lyncoya spoke to no one and disappeared as soon as the large doors closed behind her. Next off the bus was Eddie Butler. Unlike Lyncoya, Eddie waited on the sidewalk for three friends, and when they were all gathered, they strolled toward the entrance like a victorious team, capturing the cameras and crowd.

"Do you think the two motorcycle cops are necessary, Mr. Cirillo?" asked Junior, who found himself standing next to his principal.

"Probably. At least for today and tomorrow. Look at those people across the street. They've been here every morning so far. I don't know if you remember the pictures of the people in Boston when it started busing. It can turn violent in a second."

"Are you worried that it will happen here?"

"Not so much worried as concerned. Having you and so many of our students supporting these new kids helps. The press helps keep the violence down, but cameras can also encourage poor behavior too." Pete put his hand on Junior's shoulder. "Thousands of students are being bused to new schools this morning, and at each school there is a demonstration against this action. Lines of buses are clogging Denver's streets taking kids out of familiar neighborhoods into hostile neighborhoods. Protestors have been whipped to frenzy by firebrands who hate this action. Junior, I'll be surprised if there aren't some violent acts this morning somewhere in Denver."

"Do you ever get to voice your opinion on this, Mr. Cirillo, or do you always have to play the role of good soldier?"

"I have my opinions, Junior, but they stay in private. My wife knows. Mr. King thinks he knows. Sometimes it's frustrating, but what I most want is just to run my school with whatever students show up and educate them. This stuff… this is just crazy nonsense."

§

"I'm glad I'm standing with you this morning watching the students get off the buses. Our first two years have just been the prelude to this drama, a preparation for the big show." Elyse took hold of Jonas' hand and squeezed it. "I think I understand you just a little bit better today, understand a little bit about what you've been pushing for. We're their guardians for the next three years, aren't we?"

Jonas wanted to hug his girlfriend and kiss her, maybe swing her around. Yes, it was a victory today. Yes, it was all that he had hoped for. "That little girl who got off the bus first, with her Afro all poofed, she could be the black Sadie. I'll bet the counselors assigned her to your science section." Jonas took in everything. "Those crowds across the street will vote for Ballot 1 in two months. We have to stand up to them with what we do." Then he noticed something about Elyse. "You aren't nervous, are you?"

"Too late for that, don't you think? I'm just ready to set up a lab and see what we're in for."

§

Most of the noise in front of Andrew Jackson was yelling from the protestors. Cars along the roads honked, and people put their fists out of their windows and shook them. Each bus emptied its passengers, and they all walked into the school as if they belonged there, ignoring the protestors as much as possible, ready to move on to the next step. As the empty buses drove away and the students and faculty withdrew behind Andrew Jackson's front doors, the protestors focused more on attracting the attention of the media.

Archie King and Gary Dessins watched from a short distance away. The shop teacher spoke to the social studies teacher. "Looks like we may avoid any violence this morning. Mark that on your calendar of minor successes."

"The morning's not over yet, Gary. You and I could accidently get to close to one of those screamers and, you know, accidently bump into him, and, well, have him fall down. Look at them. Such jerks."

Dessins nudged his partner. "Look who's being interviewed by Channel 9. Your good buddy Charlie Chartwell. Maybe that's who we should accidently bump into."

Archie smiled. "Come on. Let's go stand behind him and get into the photo."

"Pete won't be happy."

The two men walked the thirty yards to where Chartwell stood and positioned themselves on either side of the administrator, who immediately felt uncomfortable. Nobody spoke to another, but Archie placed his hand on Chartwell's shoulder. It was the journalist who asked, "Are you also from the district office?"

Archie answered. "Oh, no. We're just the grunts here. Chuck's the officer. We just came over to offer him our unconditional support. He's got a tough job fending off all these protestors."

Gary patted Chartwell on the back in a condescending way. "Keep up the good work, Chuck. Make sure you show up for these photo ops and tell the good people of Denver that we're behind the efforts to educate all their children."

"I think we're done here, Gary. We better get back to class." The journalist tried to ask Archie and Gary to comment further, but the two men refused and returned to their school. The episode was broadcast on the 5:00 o'clock news, and Pete pretended to be upset the next day.

§

The tardy bell rang and the students in Miss Cottage's science class found seats. Thirty-one sophomores. It looked to Elyse like there were eighteen whites, ten blacks, and three Chicanos. She smiled and addressed the day head on. "So, how was the bus ride?" Several of the students laughed. "My drive here in the morning is about ten to twelve minutes, depending on the lights. I guess some of you spent over 45 minutes on the bus plus the time you stood at the pickup sites. That can't be too much fun. All of you in here are new to Andrew Jackson, so all of you probably have a little apprehension about high school, but I won't ignore the fact that many of you have extra stress. Whatever I can do to help alleviate that, I will. I think you will find that each teacher here will do the same thing." She waited a moment. "This is my third year. My first year scared the living daylights out of me, but over time, I got over it. I hope that you all will give this school time, give yourself time. Here at Jackson, we take pride in our school, in being a family. I know you don't feel that today, but if you try, I think you will. We call ourselves Generals. The man who roams the halls wearing a short-sleeved white shirt and a narrow black tie is Mr. Cirillo. He's the principal, and you won't find a fairer man anywhere, so get to know him."

Elyse walked to the side of her classroom. "In a few days, maybe next week, I'll assign you to a specific seat, but for today and the rest of this week, I think you might be more comfortable sitting near someone you know." She smiled. "Okay, this is a science lab class, and as such, there are specific rules you must follow for your safety." She passed out a handout to each student and began her first class under Judge Doyle's rule.

Upstairs, Mr. Cullen looked over his advanced placement class. Eighteen students, all juniors, only two black kids and no Hispanics. "The first Northern Europeans to settle along the upper East Coast arrived in 1607. Why did they come? Why does anyone go where they aren't wanted? One of the themes of our early chapters addresses this question. As I pass out your textbooks, I want you to peruse the first four chapters. Look at the pictures, maps, and graphs and see what comes to mind. When everyone has a book, we'll begin."

§

No one knew quite what to expect that first week, but when Pete met with his staff on Friday afternoon to debrief, he was mostly pleased. He thanked the staff for their extra efforts, and he asked for any anecdotes.

Dessins rose first. "One of my juniors said he thought black kids only knew how to fix cars. It was funny because he said it as a compliment for a coffee table the other kid was working on, but then realized what he had said and began apologizing. The half-dozen black students laughed pretty hard."

Elyse went next. "My sophomores from Five Points were amazed at all the stuff we have in the science lab. They had never looked through a microscope before. I have to tell you that I was a little ashamed about the disparity, but it's been good."

Several other teachers stood to give their accounts. Pete made a comment after the last anecdote about the bus schedule. "I don't know how to fix that, so I'm open to suggestions. Some of these kids are spending over an hour each way on that damn yellow monster. Several of our boys have said they'd like to play football, but they wouldn't have a ride home after practice. You know how important I think sports and after school activities are for a good education."

Martin Williams, the black social studies teacher from North High School, stood. "How about an activities bus? Maybe it can leave after practice ends and have drop-off points around town where our kids can be picked up by family or someone they know to get them back to their own neighborhood."

Pete cocked his head. "That's a great idea. I'll get the money for it, and we'll work on the second part of your idea over the weekend." He turned to Jonas. "Do you think Junior might want to help with this?"

"I think so, but he'll have a comment first. He'll ask what the big deal is in all this. Open the schools to whoever lives in the neighborhood and run them. Leave all the stupid prejudices at the doorstep and leave the kids alone. Then he'll say he'll do what he can."

CHAPTER 38

"Remember, Jonas, we have my mom's little party at the Cottage cottage tonight. She'll have plenty to eat," said Elyse as she brushed her hair one last time before heading off to school. "Are you ready?"

"She always does. Your mom is a generous person." Jonas was fond of Elyse's mother, even while he remained suspicious of her father. His redeeming feature, however, was his devotion to his daughter. "Did you forget? I have a quick meeting with Romero after school, so I'll take my own car and just meet you at your parents.'"

§

Nat Romero taught social studies at Lincoln High School. He and Jonas met at one of the district's training sessions for integration and were now planning some kind of activity involving a student swap for a day or longer, an activity where Jonas would teach Nat's students and Nat would teach Jonas'.

"You know the hang-up for this, Jonas? Our kids will have to be bused both ways, and they hate those rides. Remember when this would have just been a field trip and they would be excited. Now, everything is colored by the term. 'Busing!' Damn!"

"It's so politically charged," said Jonas. "Your community is gearing up for inclusion, isn't it?"

"Even though there was a Chicano family included in the lawsuit, nobody gave a rat's ass about us during this whole process.

Even our leaders were reluctant because they thought we might lose our cultural heritage. I have to laugh, not because I want to lose that heritage, but because we've had such an influx of Asians at Lincoln recently, and they say the same thing. Where will it end?"

Jonas nodded. "That's the great question, isn't it? Where will this end?"

Nat shook his head. "What's it like being an outsider to all this, Jonas? What's it like being a Montana rancher, a white Montana rancher teaching in Denver?"

Jonas laughed aloud. "Shit, Nat. All Montana ranchers are white. Let's see how we can make this student exchange work."

§

The house of Elyse's high school years was a sprawling ranch-style with acreage in the heart of Greenwood Village. Two dozen or more cars were already parked on the grass lawn just to the south of the house when Jonas arrived. Unlike the guests, Jonas entered through the kitchen door and quickly found Elyse and Mrs. Cottage fixing plates of hors d'oeuvres on silver platters for their friends. Jonas hugged them both, but kissed Elyse on the cheek before hanging his baseball cap on the key hook.

"How did the meeting with Romero go?" asked Elyse.

"Good. He suggested that he and I travel to the other school rather than have the students go, and that's probably what we'll do. He is one funny guy." Jonas reached for a piece of salami wrapped in cheese and got his hand playfully slapped by Mrs. Cottage.

"Not off the platter! Take some from the counter."

"I didn't bring my apron, Mrs. Cottage. Do you have one I can borrow?"

"Hush, Jonas. Take this one platter out, and then I don't want to see you in the kitchen again all night. Go out there and meet some of my friends. They're older, but nice. If you're going to marry my daughter, you have to learn to socialize with these sorts of people." She smiled excessively at Jonas. "Didn't you know? Elyse and I have it all worked out."

Jonas did as he was ordered. Later, as the evening progressed, he was aware that the party was moving toward a meaning, that it was to be political at its heart. Large pickle jars where strategically placed for donations. Mr. Cottage captured Jonas around 6:30 and introduced him to many of the guests. His introduction included a line about Jonas being a colleague of his daughter, but the guests were made aware that his presence was more than that. Elyse's attention made that obvious.

"Jonas, I want you to meet our guest of honor tonight," said Mr. Cottage. "Jonas, this is Mrs. Freda Poundstone."

Word had gotten around, and more people came than were formally invited, but the Cottages were happy to entertain them. Jonas and Elyse set up additional folding chairs on the patio, all told, around 60 guests could sit, and the remaining would stand on the perimeter. Elyse's father introduced Mrs. Poundstone, and she began her talk with an anecdote.

"Two of my daughters received riding instructions from Elyse, who, as some of you know, is an excellent equestrian. Elyse is a good example of why we are here tonight. Like many of you, like many of us I should say, she lived somewhere else before finding this wonderful place called Greenwood Village. Park Hill was once a beautiful neighborhood, but the struggles that it has been through over the past two decades changed it. It's nobody's fault, just the changing patterns of neighborhoods after the war. These things have a way of working themselves out, gradually, and those of us who are able can make decisions about where we want to live." She stopped and smiled at Elyse. "My girls say hi." Poundstone turned back to her audience. "We also have the right to choose where we send our children to school. Recently, we have become alarmed at the judicial activism of the courts, which have once again decided on a case that shows an abuse of power. They have stepped into a controversy best decided by the people of the communities at question. Judge Doyle and the Supreme Court have decided that they know what's best for Denver and the suburbs, even though none of them have children in our public schools." There was a smattering of applause and hoisting of glasses.

"Their actions, in an attempt to desegregate Denver's schools and to increase test scores of the minority populations, will, in fact, do the opposite. We aren't dumb, you know. As I said before, Denver's neighborhoods will work out their own solutions, and there are plenty of educational reforms that can be applied to improve the educations of our black students."

Jonas nudged Elyse. "Didn't you say something about me holding my tongue when you invited me to this wing-ding? I've got my work cut out for me." Elyse patted his butt, difficult since they were standing in a crowd.

Mrs. Poundstone continued. "Even the black neighborhoods are not in favor of the *Keyes* ruling. Most people expect this busing to increase racial tensions in Denver and not to accomplish what the courts said it would. The devil is in the details, but for now, we need to oppose this action." The applause this time was much greater.

Elyse raised her hand, and when Mrs. Poundstone noticed, she pointed at her. "Yes, Elyse."

"I hear what you're saying, but won't the Devil gnaw at our soul until he gets what he wants?"

Poundstone smiled. "Are you suggesting that I'm in cahoots with the Devil, my dear?"

Elyse stepped forward, into a space of her own. "You seem to be offering an exciting choice, but at what price? Desegregation is the right course, but your ballot initiative, if it passes, will probably make Denver schools more segregated over time, and we here in the Village won't be involved. We can stay above the fray."

Poundstone stepped forward also, as if to engage in battle. "It seems to have worked out well for you, Elyse. Now that you avoided it in your education, you're going to save the rest?"

"Not save them," said Elyse, "just teach them using the same materials, giving Denver students the same opportunity that I had. Have you spent a full day in our schools? Come visit mine; spend a day talking with my principal; talk with our students. Over a week has passed and things are going well. No race riots. Just good classroom instruction."

Poundstone was enjoying the debate. "Are your new black

students getting any smarter now that they're sitting next to the white kids?"

"No, of course not, except they have better classroom environments like lab equipment, books, teachers, and higher expectations under which they can learn. Your plan siphons out the money too, and you know it."

"Elyse, I've met some of the faculty at your school. Like me, they hold some strong opinions—which I admire—but until this year, it's been mostly white. Overwhelmingly white. Would they be willing to give that up and relocate to one of Denver's poorer schools? Would you go back to your old neighborhood to teach? I'm being provocative, but the larger question remains, are your black students getting a better education sitting next to white kids? Will this plan bring down the educational achievements of the higher kids?"

"Isn't it sort of the promise of America that we will provide an equal education for all? Or is it just the rudiments of an education?" Before his daughter could go further, Mr. Cottage stepped in and proposed a toast. "To education everywhere. And to our schools."

§

Jonas and Elyse lay on their backs after making love, calming their breathing. They were sweating and they held hands gently at their waists. Jonas thought about the night's party, about Elyse's challenge to, at the moment, Denver's most powerful woman. "And how long will we fight this battle for, for lack of a better term, our soul?" He rolled onto his side and ran his finger across her face. She continued to look at the ceiling.

"We, and by that I mean Andrew Jackson, adopted these new students from north of Colfax, kids like Lyncoya Jackson and Eddie Butler. Every school in Denver did the same thing, over one hundred and ten schools. They are our adopted students, and we owe them our best, not just in the classroom, but in the preparation of our classrooms. That pre-preparation means non-educators, politicians, and the business community. Either we fight for them, or we give up on them." Elyse turned to her boyfriend. "Either Denver fights for them or Denver runs. How long? For as long as it takes, Jonas, for as long as it takes."

They stared into each other's eyes for a moment before Jonas broke the silence. "I was awfully proud of you tonight, you know." He kissed her tenderly. "By the way, when were you going to tell me that we were engaged?"

§

At the end of September, Andrew Jackson's problems were like any other year. Other schools in Denver reported minor racial incidents, but not Pete Cirillo's school. Faculty bus duty, extensive hall monitoring, teachers eating their lunches with the students in the cafeteria, and a well-prepared staff kept anxious situations at a minimum. Pete's three hires were hands-on teachers and proactive in their methods to achieve learning. They knew Denver's busing was a social experiment, but they understood the job at hand and why they had been hired. Teachers were there to teach, and students were there to learn. Distractions of any type made that task more difficult.

§

David Vasone stopped by Mr. Cullen's room on that last Friday of September to speak with his old AP teacher. David had been sent to North High School, and his presence was missed. He had served as the junior class president the year before and was a school favorite.

Jonas got up to hug him when he came in. "David! Good to see you! Have you taken charge of your new school? I've missed you."

"I've missed you too, Mr. C. It's a lot different over there. Being a senior kind of keeps me from winning any election or being appointed to lead a group. I really miss everyone."

Jonas could see that David had more to say. "Sit down, buddy. Tell me all about it." Jonas then sat down in a desk next to David.

"I'm really having a hard time fitting in. None of the guys from last year's AP class are at North, and I don't really know any of the other Jackson students who get bused over."

"Are you playing any basketball?"

"Nah. I'm thinking I won't go out maybe. They won't be any good anyway. I was thinking about getting a job. I might be able to graduate at the semester, and then I could start college."

Jonas reached over and put his hand on David's neck. "I wish the district would have followed Rainer's suggestion to integrate one class at a time. It's pretty hard to move from your own high school, especially for your senior year."

David didn't raise his head for a moment, and Jonas knew his former student was holding back tears. Then he lifted his head and made eye contact with Jonas. "Is there any way you could get me back here?

Everyone at Andrew Jackson, everyone at every high school in Denver, knew someone who cheated the busing edict. Sadie used a phony address, one of her father's co-workers. Murray Oyler was registered at Rainer's mother's address. The district officials had looked the other way all summer, but when the school year began, they put an end to all transfers and ordered every principal to deny new transfers. Principals, in no uncertain terms, made it clear to their teachers that no new requests would be honored.

David had never asked for a short-cut, never accepted preferential treatment, worked hard for every one of his accomplishments, and had supported the concept of court-ordered busing to achieve racial integration. He played by the rules; his family played by the rules. Now, this social experiment was damaging one of Jonas' favorite students. Jonas swallowed hard. "I can't, David. I wish I could, but I can't."

"I shouldn't have asked. I'm sorry, Mr. C."

"Don't apologize, David. Hey, look up. If you can graduate early, I'll help you get into any college you choose. If you can't graduate, I want you to try out for the team. You'll make them better, and you'd regret it if you didn't." Jonas talked, but what he mostly wanted to do was run down to the district offices and get David back at Jackson. They talked for several more minutes before David left.

Jonas sat at his desk and felt helpless. At 4:00, Elyse came in to get him and go home.

CHAPTER 39

Colorado's mid-term election contained plenty of drama: a senate seat was being contested, the governor's office was at stake, and the fallout from Watergate and President Ford's subsequent pardon of Nixon was playing out in the state legislative contests. Ballot Measure 1 added pure energy and raw emotions to these races. Citizens gathered at every imaginable venue to listen to the results on the three Denver TV channels. The "Poundstone Amendment" was highly contested, as two well-financed campaigns spent record amounts to insure its passage or defeat. On election day, Tuesday, November 5, supporters of the measure were confident of its passage; polls were predicting it would carry by a large margin in the suburban counties. Opponents were hopeful that Denver voters would see the detrimental impact of its passage and turn out in large enough numbers to offset the suburbs.

Jonas and Elyse grabbed take-out from KFC before returning to school to join several of the Andrew Jackson staff and watch the returns come in. Archie set up three televisions in the counseling office, one for each major Denver station, so that the teachers could hear different perspectives on the vote. It would be a political junkie's heaven, with Archie playing St. Peter.

The counseling office was already crowded by six. Many of the teachers had not gone home or out for dinner but chose to remain until the action started. Pete brought his wife and son; his daughters were attending the rally for Senate candidate Gary Hart downtown. Annette raced around making sure the food was available in sufficient amounts. Gary Dessins avoided Archie. While they had become closer, Dessins still could get angry at Archie when he took on his "conscience of the community" air, and tonight he had. Carlos stood with Steve Torrez and two of the new teachers. A dozen other teachers were in attendance. Elyse was captured by Jane Walburg when she walked in with Jonas, leaving him alone to observe the room alone early on. This was the culmination of hours of work to defeat Ballot 1 and either a beginning or a continuation.

Jonas ate a chip and poured himself a glass of cola. He had much on his mind these past days, and he felt that he had taken Elyse for granted again, but she had not indicated any resentment. She, too, was pre-occupied. On Monday, they had discussed another casualty. Rodney Petersen dropped out. He had been assigned to ride the bus to Manual for his senior year and refused. Jonas had nurtured Rodney his sophomore year and tutored him weekly during his junior year to move him towards graduation, but when Rodney was sent away from Andrew Jackson, he quit. Rodney's dad called Jonas to tell him that his son had joined the Army and to thank Jonas for his efforts. "He got farther than we expected, so that's good." Not good enough for Jonas.

Jonas watched his colleagues, but his mind was elsewhere. It had been a wild ride from Montana to Denver on this night. Why he thought about it tonight puzzled him but leaning against the wall by himself probably triggered it. CU, Abby, Goldman Experimental, jail, ranching, teaching one semester in Montana, and then Archie King showed up on his doorstep. Archie. Jonas' mentor in so many ways, yet so unlike him. Still, there was no denying his influence over the past two years. Jonas thought that in the years to come, he might tell stories about Archie to some young teacher just like Archie related stories to him about Gross!Man. That would be a few years in the future, however. Teaching was all that he expected it would be, and nothing at all what he imagined. He looked over at Elyse who stood talking with Walburg. He imagined that she would never have this thought, since she hadn't expected anything two years ago, except that she probably wouldn't have continued in this field longer than a year or two.

Jonas shifted his focus to Pete across the room. He was turned slightly in his chair talking with two men who, by their collars and dark suits, appeared to be Catholic or Episcopal priests. Because of Pete's rotation, Jonas could see Pete's face. He looked beat, in need of a vacation. No one had worked more hours in the trenches to ensure the success of the *Keyes* ruling. As Pete spoke with the ministers, he rubbed his upper arm. He turned back to his son, whispered something, and then pointed at Jonas. Petey rose and walked to Jonas.

"My dad wants you to meet the men he's talking to," said Petey.

"How come you got stuck here tonight, Petey?" asked Jonas pushing himself off the wall and moving toward his principal.

"It's okay. Everyone in town is caught up in the election, so I told my parents I'd come with them over here when they asked."

"Brownie points, Petey. Save them up," said Jonas as they got to Pete's table.

Pete stood. "Hi, Jonas. I'd like you to meet Fathers Grey and Merna. They work for Denver's Council of Churches. They're on our side." Both men extended their hand to shake, although Father Merna was missing his right arm, so Jonas shook his left hand. "We've been discussing ways to ensure the success of busing. They have some good insights into the problem that I think would interest you." Pete turned to the priests. "Jonas is in his third year with us, but he's bent on." Pete finished his sentence, but it made no sense to Jonas. Pete staggered between Jonas and the two men before collapsing to the floor.

Pete's noisy fall scattered two chairs and startled and then scared the faculty. Carol Cirillo called out to her husband. Jonas tried to catch Pete as he went down but missed. Carol kneeled beside him, as did Jonas and Father Merna. Pete rolled himself onto his back.

"Honey, talk to me," said Carol as she placed her hands on his cheeks.

Pete's eyes were open, but he looked confused. Jonas put his hand on Pete's chest, not to check his heartbeat, but more to calm Pete, to reassure him. "Where do you hurt, Pete?"

The commotion among the staff was understandable as they pressed forward. They stepped back to give Pete room when Father Grey raised his arms. Someone asked if an ambulance should be called. Another ordered someone to get a cold rag for Pete's forehead. Then a quiet ensued. Pete's eyes seemed to focus, and he found his wife.

"What just happened?" he asked.

"I don't know. You just fell over," she answered.

"Hmmm." A moment passed, and then he pushed himself up into a sitting position.

"Be careful, honey."

Pete swiveled his head to look at the people who stood staring down at him, saw his son, and then looked back to his wife. "Where are Petey's friends?" he asked.

"We're at school, Pete. We're here to watch the election returns," said Mrs. Cirillo.

Pete processed her words. "We can do that at home, can't we?" He reached back to feel the back of his head. "That's a bump."

Archie knelt and felt Pete's head. "Yep, you got yourself a lump there. How about I drive you home and put you to bed?" Jane Walburg leaned in and handed Archie a cold cloth which he put on the bump. Jane placed her hands on Mrs. Cirillo's shoulders.

"I'll be fine," said Pete. "Help me into my chair." The cloud over his eyes seemed to be dissipating; his awareness returning. Jonas, Archie, and Father Merna lifted Pete into his chair. Pete breathed deeply a few times, and then smiled at his wife. "I guess you were right, darling. I have been pushing a little too hard, haven't I?"

The staff laughed at that and began clapping.

"Come on, old man. I'll take you home," said Archie. "Ben, will you follow us and bring me back?" Archie paused for effect. "After I put him to bed!"

As he headed out the door into the hall, his arm around his wife's shoulder for support, Pete looked back to his staff. "You all voted, didn't you?"

§

No results were available when Pete left, as the polls didn't close until 7:00. The party was subdued and only the two priests left, but when Archie called around 8:00 to say that Pete seemed to be fine, the excitement began to build. Archie and Ben returned shortly before 9:00, this time with liquor bottles, and nearly everyone had at least one drink. The first one was in Pete's honor. The second toast was, as Archie put it, "the anti-toast," and it was directed at Freda Poundstone.

"To the little lady who wants the Civil Rights Movement to end at her front door. May her children all marry minorities."

"Wouldn't that be a reward?" asked Steve Torrez with humor.

"Why would you want to inflict more punishment on my people," added Martin Williams. The faculty applauded and raised their glasses.

Walburg stepped forward. "Please, a little decorum . . . and respect for our opponent." She smiled. "The Measure 1 people have been riding pretty high these past few weeks with the polls indicating their amendment will pass easily, but" she took a drink from her mug, "with all the work our students did passing out literature and making phone calls, I think they may be in for a surprise. I just feel it."

From one of the smaller rooms, Elyse motioned for Jonas while holding up a telephone. He came in and she covered the mouthpiece. "It's Freidan and Junior. They want to talk to you."

Jonas kissed Elyse on the lips and took the receiver. "What's up, gang? Are your vibes good?"

"Mr. Cullen, we heard Mr. Cirillo went to the hospital. Is that true?"

"No, Junior. He fainted a few hours ago. Probably stress and fatigue. When he left here, he was doing better, and Mr. King and Mr. Lucas were with him and said he was okay when they left him at his house."

"Just a sec, Mr. C." There was no sound from the phone, so Jonas assumed Junior had covered the mouthpiece. Jonas waited until Junior returned. "Mr. C, we knew that, but Rick's little sister is in Petey's class at school, and she said an ambulance just took him to the hospital."

Jonas' face registered concern, and Elyse silently asked him what was wrong. "Just a minute, Junior." Now it was Jonas' turn to cover the phone with his hand. "The kids are saying an ambulance just took Pete to the hospital. Don't say anything to anyone, but go get Annette for me, okay." Elyse left, and Jonas spoke again to Junior. "You have a different source than I do, so let me see what I can find out. I'll call you right back." Jonas took the number for Betty's house and promised again that he would call as soon as he had more information.

Annette came into the room alone. "Ellie said you needed to see me but wouldn't say why. What's the big secret, Jonas?"

"Junior Warren just called me about Pete. I want you to call Pete's house just to check on him. Seems like they have their info screwed up, but I want to check."

Annette had Pete's number memorized. She dialed and waited while it rang. "What did Junior say?"

Before Jonas could answer, Annette said, "Hello, this is Annette Lane, Mr. Cirillo's secretary here at school. Who is this?" She waited and listened. "So, an ambulance did take him to the hospital. Did they say why? What do they think is wrong with him?" She listened again. "Do you know which hospital?" She glanced up at Jonas. "Okay. Will you write this number down please?" She gave the counseling office number, thanked the person on the other end, and softly hung up the phone.

"Well?" asked Jonas just as Elyse came back into the room.

"Junior was right. Pete's in the hospital, but his daughter doesn't know which one yet. She just got a call from her mother telling her to come home to be with Petey, so both girls returned from their rally. Pete's had a stroke."

From the larger part of the counseling office came a groan. The initial results concerning Ballot Measure 1 indicated that it would pass overwhelmingly. A moat would be dug around Denver, not to keep people out, but to keep certain people in. Jonas called Betty's house.

§

"Jonas, I have to tell you something." Elyse had stopped just inside their apartment door and waited for Jonas to hang his jacket on the hook. The night's news was wearing on them, but Elyse could no longer keep this secret from him. It was to be her surprise on this night, on this night when the people of Colorado verified the *Keyes* court decision. She would hug Jonas; he would be so happy, and they would make love.

"Jonas, I've kept a secret from you for the past month. Only a few people know. My parents know. Pete knows." She paused. Her boyfriend was exhausted, but he had to know. She could no longer keep this news from her. "Jonas, I won't be teaching at Andrew Jackson next semester."

CHAPTER 40

"No visitors. Mr. Cirillo will be fine. It was a mild stroke. Mr. Cirillo said to tell you all that if there's any breakdown in discipline, he'll come back and kick some butt. I can't repeat the word he used about Ballot 1 passing, but he said that Andrew Jackson wasn't going to let that drag it down. What will you do while he's out? For crying out loud, you're teachers, so teach. That's what my dad said. He'll be back before the month is over. Hold the fort." Petey Cirillo took every phone call that night and gave this response as if he were a recorded answering machine. He would then hang up without asking who had called and worry that what he said about his dad's recovery was too optimistic.

§

Between the time Pete was admitted to the hospital and midnight, several things occurred. The district information line let every high school principal in Denver know that one of their colleagues was down. JFK's principal volunteered to step into Pete's position, since he had worked there a few years earlier, and turn his school's duties over to the assistant principal, which was approved by Superintendent Kishkunis. South's principal offered any of his assistants to help. Charles Chartwell also volunteered to fill in as needed, but that was determined not to be necessary. At her victory party, Freda Poundstone heard about the Andrew Jackson principal and, despite the late hour, placed calls to Mrs. Cirillo and Elyse Cottage. Neither was home to receive the call.

Several of the Andrew Jackson staff remained at school well beyond midnight. The immediacy of the moment, concern for Pete's health and how to proceed without Pete under the new restrictions, passed, and a melancholy mood set in. Annette made fresh coffee, and the teachers sat together as a team. Annette and Carlos were first teamers on the squad.

"Certainly not the night I anticipated," said Ben. He shook his head and looked at Gary Dessins. "Doesn't this just beat all hell?"

"We all suspected busing would screw up the system, but this vote pretty much seals the deal. And Pete going down. It'll make it that much harder around here until he gets back," said Gary.

Archie leaned forward in his chair, a chair that he had turned around so that he was looking over its back. "Maybe, but not if we look at it from another point of view."

Gary interrupted. "You have another point of view, Arch? This'll be a first." The team laughed.

"Will our school score as high as it did last year or in the past? Probably not. Will as many go off to college? No. But isn't this busing more about the entire city of Denver? Break it down. Blacks and Chicanos will probably get a better education now. Our pessimism is over the white kids. A lot of them will be scared off and leave, go to the suburbs or a private school. Their educations won't suffer, so the net result could be positive."

"Jeez," said Gary. "You damn liberals can rationalize it any way you choose, but I still say this busing plan will screw it all up. Look at us here. We're all going to do our damnest to make this work, but it just got a lot harder tonight."

Marsh Daniels, still a political fanatic despite being retired for a year, pointed at the new social studies teacher. "If this is what you came to Andrew Jackson for, Martin, you sure as hell have it as of now."

"It's a good thing you said something, Marsh. I thought we might have to break up a fight between Archie and Gary again," said Ben. The team laughed, remembering the teachers' lounge incident of last year.

Walburg held up her coffee cup to get the room's attention again.

"How about we not worry about the rest of Denver and concentrate on what we do best here. This is still a damn fine school. I for one don't care who sits in my classroom, and I'm not being naïve, but I won't lower my standards." She paused. "Many of the new students do have fewer skills, but we can move them up pretty well. They all seem willing, and we haven't had many discipline problems. I have to admit, though, it'll be tougher with Pete out."

"Let's just hope it won't be for too long," said Carlos. "He looked pretty bad when he left here."

"He's a tough bastard. He'll be okay," said Gary.

"Ah, he's a pu . . ." Archie caught himself. "No. Tonight, I won't joke. I love the man, and we are all indebted to his service. We got the best one."

They all concurred and agreed that it was too late to talk further. Martin Williams asked, "What do we tell our students about him tomorrow morning?"

"That he's ill and will be back soon," said Ben. "And let's hope the hell that's the truth."

§

Elyse put her arms around Jonas' neck and smiled. It had been a difficult night, but she had planned this from the moment she found out and decided that Pete's sudden illness and the passing of the Poundstone Amendment weren't going to delay her news. Jonas had thought about staying at school with some of the other teachers, but Elyse vetoed that. After all, there was nothing more to be accomplished by staying and this news couldn't wait any longer.

She kissed him tenderly. "I'm pregnant." She watched his eyes for his response. It was there where she always discerned his first emotions. He was a tough Montana laborer in many ways, but through his eyes he revealed a tenderness that tough men so often seek to conceal, whether it's fear or disapproval or not being in charge. Jonas' eyes stayed clear and focused; he didn't blink or look away. His eyes told her what she wanted to know. Then she felt a little guilty. "Remember all those times over the past few years when I complained that I didn't have any rhythm?" asked Elyse.

"I was hoping it was birth control and not luck." Jonas was only half kidding.

"Jonas, you've always been comfortable here, from the first day. When you had problems, you didn't question your role here, you just worked harder to fix them. When I had problems, I questioned my decision to be a teacher, questioned whether I had what it takes." Jonas started to interrupt, but Elyse put her finger on his lips. "You were rewarded immediately with two AP courses. This is my third year and I still have all sophs. My department is pretty stable. I'd have sophs for the foreseeable future." Elyse dipped her head slightly towards Jonas' head, but kept her eyes fixed on his. "I talked to Pete and he understands. He doesn't like it, but he understands." All of a sudden, her eyes filled tears. "I'm kidding about being pregnant. I'm transferring over to Manual at the semester." She bit her lower lip but didn't waiver. "This makes sense. I asked myself, 'Why not me?' You've been preaching this for two years, but I never understood it until this year. On that first day when the black kids got off the bus and showed such courage, and then they came into my classroom with all their fears and showed such curiosity. It just clicked, and I felt it." She stopped and waited for a response. Jonas didn't say anything, but in a moment, he pulled her closer and held her tightly.

Since she couldn't see his eyes, she wouldn't be able to see his tears. He hugged Elyse for a full three minutes, trying to blink the tears away. Finally, he spoke. "I would have been good with you being pregnant." She pulled back far enough to see that he was crying.

"Hell, Jonas, I wouldn't have had this hard of a time telling you that." She reached up and wiped the tears from his cheeks. "Cowboy baby. Why are you crying?'

"Because I'm going to miss you each day, and I'm so proud of you."

"We don't see each other much during the day anyway, so nothing's going to change. We come home, we tell each other about what happened in our classes, we have dinner, we do lesson plans, and we make love. Same old routine." She was playing with him now.

Jonas sniffled. I just noticed you don't have your neck rash anymore. How did you get rid of it?"

"I stopped scratching it, and it went away."

CHAPTER **41**

Pete's stroke was more serious than first diagnosed, but he returned to his position at Andrew Jackson for the last week of school before Christmas. The doctor allowed him to work half-time, but he could not stay past the lunch hour. A test. His speech, which had suffered slightly, was as good as ever, and he used that voice to inspire his staff and students at an assembly on the last Friday of school. He did, however, walk with a bit of a limp. "No big deal," he said at the assembly, "I just won't be able to break tackles like I once did."

When school resumed in January, he was back full-time, back where he belonged; back where he was needed. He worried about the loss of momentum while he was gone, but it seemed as though the staff had stepped up and kept the energy flowing. He was impressed with the energy and competence of the new science teacher, Mr. Elzey, who replaced Elyse. Pete was sad to see her go, but he was proud of her courage as a General. Either she would be a tremendous success at Manual High School, or he would get her back. He was pretty sure the latter wouldn't happen.

Only one of the four teachers he hired two-and-a-half years earlier still remained at Andrew Jackson. Jonas Cullen. What a journey it had been for him! In mid-January, Pete had to loan Jonas the old station wagon again after Jonas' car was hit in the school's parking lot by a senior who lost control of her car on the ice and slid into Jonas' car. What Pete was proud of was that all four of his '72 hires were still teaching, spread out, but still teaching, and he felt confident that all four would make lifetime careers of it.

§

"Why are you here at Manual, Miss Cottage? Did you get fired at your old school?" Elyse had asked her junior biology class what questions they had for her on that first day. She stood in front of her desk, promising herself that her style would be among the students, not in front of them. Open and enthusiastic.

She walked away from the very tall girl who asked the question but kept her head up and her eyes on the student. "No, I didn't get fired. In fact, I loved Jackson High, but my time there was over. I'll miss my colleagues there, especially a certain social studies teacher . . ." she allowed that to settle over the class, which then got her meaning, "but I left for this class and you students. What I mean is that I left to teach juniors and seniors who have a purpose, who have goals beyond high school. Students like you." Elyse paused only for a moment. "And I still teach three sophomore classes to see if I can jump start their creative juices." She moved her eyes to seek out other students, but she had captured them with her answer. "An opening showed up and I applied," she paused, "and it feels like this is already my school." She moved again, away from the front of the room. "Any more questions? No? Then from now on, this class is about you, not about me. Let's get to work. Biology is, quite simply, the study of life. What could be more exciting than that?"

§

Since the second semester began on Thursday, January 2, Elyse had only two days with her students at Manual before she got a break. Jonas rewarded her with dinner and a night's stay in Evergreen. Back at the motel after dinner, Jonas gave Elyse a box from Sadie. "She's really going to miss you, but I told her you'd take her to lunch on Sunday. She wanted you to have this." It was a cheap, goofy necklace, one that only a teacher like Elyse would wear.

"Can we make this a yearly tradition?" asked Elyse.

Jonas smiled. "Yes. Interesting, isn't it. I started out to teach in an inner-city school, and I get mostly white, high achieving juniors and seniors. You do this on a whim and end up in the trenches of a social experiment at the blackest school in Denver. Funny how life leads us in unique directions."

Jonas reached behind her back, unbuttoned her dress, and then unfastened her black bra. Elyse helped him remove her clothes and then began to undress him. "Do you ever wonder if students think their teachers act like this?" Elyse asked.

"Oh, yeah, I almost forgot. I have a present for you too." He left the bed and returned quickly with another small box. Instead of climbing back into bed, he kneeled beside it and opened the box to show Elyse another piece of jewelry, a not so goofy or cheap ring.

<h1>Chapter 42</h1>

Dr. Betty Norton wandered around the secretary's area looking at the photos and plaques that hung on the walls, while her daughter met with the principal in his office. President Bill Clinton smiled down on her. Betty was taking the day off to get her daughter enrolled in her new school. Dr. Norton had taken a job over the summer at Bismarck State College and would be heading up the new graduate program in environmental studies. Her daughter Freedom was not happy about moving from Boulder to the northern Great Plains, and Betty hoped the principal would be able to assuage her feelings. Betty had chosen to live in a small town a few miles outside of Bismarck quite simply because she liked its feel. Large yards, no stoplights, no locks on the doors, kids playing unsupervised. Bryson City High School was about a seventh the size of Boulder High School and seemed more personal than Freedom's previous school. While Betty read the certificates and plaques that adorned the walls in the main office, an old woman entered the room with a cup of coffee.

"Hi. Dr. Norton? I'm Ms. Deaver. We talked on the phone a few weeks ago when you set up the appointment for Freedom to speak with Mr. Andersen. She says she likes to be called Freeda, with two ees. Is that right?" Dr. Norton nodded. "He took her on a tour of the building when you dropped her off, and now, I think, they're just finishing up a bit of paperwork. Our counselor isn't in today. Freeda seems like a very nice young lady, so polite, and her transcripts indicate she's very, very bright. We're placing her in all our upper-level classes."

Betty thanked Ms. Deaver for her kind words, and then they chatted for a few minutes. Finally, Betty asked who the handsome soldier was in the picture frame on Ms. Deaver's desk.

"That's my son. He died in Vietnam a long time ago."

"I'm so sorry. Do you have any other children?"

"Yes, Jason has a twin brother."

"Oh, and where is he now?"

Barbara Deaver lowered her head for only a moment. "I'm not really sure. My husband and I divorced when the boys were just infants, and I lost touch with him. We've never reconnected. His name is Jonas."

Betty felt a little uneasy with where the conversation seemed to end, so she spoke. "When I was in high school in Denver, I had a wonderful history teacher. His first name is Jonas. We keep in touch on a regular basis. He's still there, still being an excellent teacher."

Ms. Deaver smiled brightly. "He sounds like a good man. Maybe I'll borrow him as my long-lost son, so when anyone asks about my other son, I'll just tell them he grew up to be a teacher, and that I'm so very proud of him."

The End

ADDENDUM:

Non-fictional characters in the book (in no particular order):

Politicians

Richard Nixon	Hubert Humphrey	George McGovern
Barry Goldwater	Robert Kennedy	Henry Kissinger
Lyndon Johnson	Gerald Ford	Gary Hart

Watergate figures

H.R, Haldeman	Ben Bradlee	Martha Graham
Carl Bernstein	Bob Woodward	Sam Ervin
Judge John Sirica	James McCord	Gordon Liddy
Alexander Butterfield		

Munich Massacre

Jim McKay	Yasser Arafat	Mark Spitz

U.S. Supreme Court, Keyes Case

Lylaus & Wilfred Keyes	Fred Thomas	Betty Germany
Judge Doyle	Rachel Noel	Robert Gilberts
Mayor McNichols	Supt. Johnson	Freda Poundstone
Perrill Southworth		

Writers, Bookstore owners, Activists, Musicians, Others

Louis L'Amour	Kurt Vonnegut	Carole King
Eddie Holman	Johnny Horton	Emma Goldman
Reies Tijerina	Corky Gonzales	Patty Hearst
Steve Cogil	Joyce Meskis	Mario Savio
Dr. Martin Luther King		